Where Jazz Plays Shadows Fall

by
Pam Kumpe

Cover Design by: Pam Kumpe

ISBN: 979-8-9921326-9-4

DEDICATION
For those who hold to the truth even when
it costs them everything.
And for the ones who listened and
refused to look away.

"A time to tear, and a time to sew; a time to keep
silence, and a time to speak."
Ecclesiastes 3:7 (ESV)

DISCLAIMER

1

Distracted by Pelicans

IN THE PAST YEAR, I'VE inherited plenty from my dad, mostly his secrets, and now I've purchased The Blue Door. That old, abandoned bar. Closed down. Waiting for me. In New Orleans.

I hoped my dad would be proud of me for trying to bring the place he once adored back to life. Confirming this is challenging because of his passing, and it's tough to accept that a year has gone by since his death, let alone that he used to sing at a bar and play the piano. And I never knew this part of his life.

So here I am, driving my Honda Civic from Wyoming to Louisiana in October, like this is normal behavior. However, what is normal? And who decides what that looks like? I need to find a way for my dad's shadow to live in the future and make sense of it.

Besides, I don't sit still or hit pause well, and I create lists that require checking off—so I can breathe.

Secrets are humming under the floorboards of a forgotten jazz building on Chartres Street, and my dad never got the chance to finish his song—at least with me.

He gave me my guitar when I was five. So many years ago. A Christmas I'll cherish. But oh, I wanted him—his presence more than an instrument. And I longed for him to swoop in and love me in person, not just with rare visits, at Uncle Harlan and Aunt Diane's house, where my relatives, who raised my brother, Calvin, and me, lived.

A heavy whoomph-whoomph swept over my roof, a wingbeat sound that makes you duck even though you're inside a car. "Phew! What flew over me?"

I yanked the wheel, peeking out the window, and my Honda spun toward the ditch in the next second. Tires screeched, horns blared behind me, and then I crashed through the bushes that clawed at the fender. The airbag exploded into my face, knocking the wind right out of me and filling my mouth with powder.

For a second, everything rang.

I shoved the deflated bag aside, forced the door open, and stumbled out, legs wobbling. I headed toward the front end to assess the damage—only to catch my tennis shoe on something soft, and I tumbled over it, face down, mud in my mouth, the rain pelting a welcome to my arrival.

I wallowed, turned over, and found myself next to a woman's body in the tall grassy area by the brush.

My breath froze in my throat. I scrambled backward, grass and dirt sliding under my palms as I made a shaky beeline for the car. I needed my phone. I needed help. I needed… steadiness.

I leaned inside the car—and stopped.

A great white pelican sat calmly in my backseat, framed by shattered glass, and its wings tucked as if it had been chauffeured here on purpose. The bird blinked at me, utterly unimpressed with my panic.

"Oh, perfect," I whispered. "A body outside and a pelican inside. Dad… whatever this is… I wish you were here."

My hands shook so badly I nearly dropped the phone twice. I punched in 911, sucking in thin, shaky breaths while glancing over at the woman in the weeds. The dispatcher's calm voice felt miles away as I explained everything—the ditch and the body … the swoosh of tires spinning. I left out the pelican. I wasn't ready to sound *that* unhinged.

I called Calvin to tell him, but the voicemail kicked in, and before I could dial again, Renee Baptiste's call came through. I hit the button. "Hello, Renee?"

"Yes, Girl. Just checking to see how close you are to New Orleans. Are you nearing downtown?"

"Um, well. Something's happened. I've had a wreck on the highway outside of the city. The police are coming."

"What? I can help. That's what I do. Tell me. Where are you?"

"I'll call you back," I said, and hung up.

The first patrol car pulled up, lights strobing through the trees, and my legs had gone from wobbly to full-on gelatin. An officer jogged toward me, hand resting near his holster, eyes sharp. "Ma'am, are you injured?" he asked.

I answered, but the pelican chose that exact moment to honk from the backseat. Loudly. And the officer froze. I froze. The pelican did not freeze.

My phone buzzed with a text. It was Renee who asked, "Are you safe? Hurt? Let me know what I can do."

I rolled my eyes, not ready for the in-your-face questions from someone I haven't even met in person yet.

Within seconds, two more officers arrived, and chaos blossomed as if someone had hit fast-forward. One went to check the woman, another circled my car, and the first guided me away from the road. I kept apologizing—even though I wasn't sure what I was apologizing for.

Existing? Driving? The pelican?

Then the paramedics arrived, kneeling beside the woman, murmuring medical things I couldn't process. I stood there with my arms wrapped around myself, shivering even though the Louisiana air felt warm, despite the rain clouds and drizzle that drenched my entire being with a fall rain.

Every time I blinked, my dad's face flashed behind my eyes—him singing, laughing, disappearing. Why did *catastrophe* seem to follow me like some cosmic prank?

I paced as rain now sheeted down the highway as if invited to the entire state, and the ditch turned into muddy soup as blue-and-red strobes washed over everything.

I shivered, my arms still wrapped tight around my body, taking deep breaths, convincing my lungs that breathing was something they should keep doing. I knelt by the side of my car, unable to find the strength to know what to do next. An officer hovered beside me, pen poised, waiting for answers I couldn't line up in my head, let alone tell him.

The paramedics continued working a few yards away. One of them checked the woman's pulse, paused, and then slowly shook his head. A sheet was pulled over her—rain-soaked, clinging to every contour—and my stomach twisted hard.

She'd been here before me. She'd been here alone. I hadn't hit her.

Lightning flashed, followed by a distant rumble. Another officer jogged toward my Honda. The driver's side door gaped open, the interior light flickering weakly. I rose and watched him stop short, tilt his head, then lean in slowly like he wasn't sure what he was seeing.

The pelican shifted in my backseat, lifting its wings just enough to display several impressive feet of feathers. He blinked once, serenely, utterly unfazed by the patrolman gawking at him.

The officer backed up a step. "Ma'am... is that... bird with you?"

"No," I croaked. "He's, um... an uninvited guest."

"Uninvited," he murmured. "Right."

If I hadn't been so shaken, I might've laughed—or cried—or both. Instead, I stared at the rain bouncing off my shoes while the world spun around me in lights and noise.

A paramedic approached, speaking gently. "Ma'am, were you injured when the airbag deployed?"

"I don't think so," I whispered. "It knocked the wind out of me, but I'm okay."

"We'll check to be sure. Shock can mask things." He flashed a light in my eyes and pointed to the burn on my cheek from the airbag. "Are you sure we don't need to check that out?"

"I'm sure," I said, swallowing hard.

"You could be in shock," he muttered.

Shock. Yes. That felt about right.

Radios crackled. Officers murmured into shoulder mics. A tow truck rumbled somewhere behind me. And the pelican—because of course he did—let out a low grunt of displeasure, as if we were inconveniencing him.

Through all of it, I felt my phone vibrate in my hand.

I looked down. Cal's name lit up the screen.

Of course. My brother is calling me back now—when my car was wrecked, a stranger lay dead a few yards away, and a pelican claimed squatter's rights in the backseat. And paramedics and police were swarming around me.

I gulped, thumb hovering over the answer button, and finally swiped to answer, lifting the phone to my ear with a hand that wouldn't stop trembling.

"Hey, Cal," I whispered, trying—and failing—to sound normal. "Listen, don't panic, but I, um… had a minor accident." A pelican honked behind me, and I winced. "A weird accident. And there's… well… a situation." My voice cracked on the last word.

There was a pause, thick sounds of him swallowing, before his voice came through, low, calm, and maddeningly focused. "Emory. Breathe. Start at the beginning. And don't you dare say you're fine."

"Okay," I whispered, tears forming.

I shut my eyes as Cal continued, gentler now. "What happened? Really happened."

I told him about the low swoop of giant birds over my car, the ditch, the tires skidding, the airbag, the woman lying in the grass, and the pelican who apparently wanted a ride into downtown New Orleans. My words tumbled out broken and messy, and when I finally stopped talking, a quiet beat followed, my heart thumping like a drum.

"Em," Cal said at last, his voice soft but firm. "So again, the woman wasn't crossing the highway, right?"

"Right, the pelicans spooked me, and I lost control of my car, and she was… she was already there."

"And you're okay, right?"

"Yes, I'm rattled. There's a dead woman on the road. What do I do now?"

"Sis, you didn't cause this and didn't hit that woman. You didn't invite the birds. And you didn't choose the storm."

Another officer waved me toward her, but I didn't move, not until Cal finished talking to me. I called to the suit. "I'll be right there."

Cal went on, calming me. "You did nothing wrong. You got caught in something bigger than yourself. So, listen to the police, and let them handle the rest. I'm not there, but I'm with you. You're not alone, okay? And keep me posted. Let me know, and I'll be on the next flight."

"Okay, I've got to go. The officer is motioning for me."

The world spun as I moved to the officer's car, but then I ran back to my Honda just before the tow truck left, just before the ambulance rolled away, and right after the pelican flew from the back seat of my car and retrieved my suitcase and tote bag.

The scene's chaos dimmed, and the officer spoke as I approached her. "Emory Vaughn? Right?"

"Yes, ma'am," I said, my words low.

"I want to reassure you; you're not under suspicion. I'm Sergeant Laveau. But you are a valuable witness. Trust your instincts. If you remember anything, you can always call me. Anytime. People like us need to look out for one another."

I noted her words: *people like us.* And I nodded, slipping her card into my bag. The sergeant's words grounded my anxiety, and I didn't feel so alone in the tangled journey of how my entrance to New Orleans announced my arrival.

I spouted off unquestioningly. "What did you mean, people like us? We just met."

The sergeant coughed. "We're people who like answers. And I can tell that about you."

With raindrops splashing on my shoulders like ping-pong balls, I paused before crawling into the patrol car and glanced across the highway where hundreds of pelicans drifted toward the lake, settling into the water and along the shore, as if they owned the spot.

A lone pelican flew low over me, honking at the backed-up traffic, and joined its family—something the woman in the ditch will never experience again.

2

The Station, the Stranger, and Windex

THE POLICE STATION SMELLED like old coffee, and a hint of someone's leftover gumbo that had died a slow, fragrant death in the microwave. I sat in a metal chair that had zero sympathy for my back, spine, or my day. My tennis shoes dripped rainwater onto the scuffed tile floor, leaving a tiny puddle that felt like a metaphor of me, melting into a mess.

The officer named Sergeant Laveau, a tall woman with a sharp bun and the patience of a kindergarten teacher, nudged a Styrofoam cup of water toward me. "Drink," she insisted.

I obeyed because I didn't have the energy to argue. My hands still trembled from the wreck, from the sight of the woman in the ditch, from the realization that my Honda might never forgive me.

"We're waiting on a few confirmations from other drivers about what happened," Laveau said, settling across from me with an iPad. "Then we'll get your formal statement on record. You doing, okay?"

"No," I said honestly, taking another drink of water. "But I've stopped hyperventilating, so that's progress."

A ghost of a smile touched her lips. "Given the circumstances, I'd say that's a miracle."

She typed something on her screen, then glanced at me again. "You said you didn't know the woman you found in the ditch."

"Right. I've never seen her before. I mean—I'm just arriving in town, and I don't know anyone."

"Well," she breathed. "Her family reported her missing. Name's Claire Landry. She lived about three blocks from where you crashed. She's a frequent night-owl and stays up late, and too often she's holding a drink in her hand. Comes up missing but eventually shows up. But usually, she's alive, and someone finds her asleep, like at the old bar next to Duval's Lounge."

The air went still around me, and my clothes glued to my skin, like Saran Wrap. "Missing?" I repeated. "As in... she wandered off? Or something happened to her?"

"We're still piecing that together. But she was last seen at Duval's bar. You know it?"

"No," I whispered. "I don't." But my heart thudded, and I remembered my online map searches, where I had memorized the streets and the surrounding area of the French Quarter. "Wait, that's next to The Blue Door."

The sergeant turned her head a little to the side, squinting one eye. "That's right. She sleeps there more than she should." She paused. "But you said you didn't know Remy Duval's bar?"

I cleared my throat. "I'm a bit of a perfectionist and like to know my way around, so I'd forgotten I mapped out my part of the town—where my place sits."

"You place? As in The Blue Door?"

"Yes, I'm the new owner," I said, wondering if this trip was a mistake.

I took a drink of water, gagging, spitting the water like a spray as my emotions showed up unannounced. When my life unravels, it prefers to do it theatrically, without notice.

Laveau continued without a blink, "Witnesses say she'd been there with someone, though details are fuzzy. Remy's place is... a lively establishment. People don't always keep track of who comes and goes."

I blinked several times. The dots connecting in my head were unwelcome, crooked, and far too close to home. "So, she left Remy Duval's lounge," I said slowly, "and then ended up... in a ditch?"

"We don't know that she walked from there," Laveau replied carefully. "We only know where she was found."

I rubbed my forehead. I had come here to restore a bar into a jazz cafe, not to get tangled in a local tragedy on day one. But I didn't say that out loud, my compassion barely intact, and I didn't want the sergeant to think I didn't care.

As if summoned by my fraying nerves, a loud voice bellowed down the hall, "Sergeant! Tell your chairs to stop tryin' to murder me!"

Laveau sighed. "Oh Lord. He's awake."

The source of the commotion shuffled into view: an older, tall, Black man, lanky, with a mustache that curled as if auditioning for a movie role. His hair was pulled into small twists, half of them leaning left like they'd given up on life. His shirt read, *I Pace Myself... Mostly*, and he pointed accusingly at the metal chair in the holding area.

"That thing pushed me," he complained to the officer escorting him. "I told y'all, Windex don't fold up that easily."

I blinked. "Windex?"

He snapped to attention as if I'd called roll. "Winston Dupree is my Christian name. People call me Windex. Because I bring the shine, baby." He wiggled his eyebrows. "And also cause I used to clean windows at Duval's Lounge before they fired me for making slick surfaces on the floor with too much of my spray. Their words, not mine."

I stared. Not moving and not responding.

He grinned wider. "You look like you need a blessing... or a nap. Hard to tell."

Laveau pressed her fingers to her temples. "Mr. Dupree spent the night here after stumbling around Royal Street and insisting he was searching for the perfect note on his washboard. He wasn't successful."

"I found a note," Windex protested. "It was sharp."

Laveau ignored him. "He's harmless. Loud, but harmless."

"I'm artistically misunderstood," Windex corrected. "Big difference. And I'll need my washboard back wherever you put it."

I opened my mouth, then closed it again, because honestly, what reply could survive that?

Windex squinted at me. "Hey. You're the lady whose car hit the woman. The one from the ditch?"

I stiffened. "I—I didn't hit her. She was there already."

"Oh, honey, I know," he said kindly, dropping his voice to something surprisingly gentle. "Word travels fast in here. Claire practically lived at Duval's Lounge. He gave her plenty to drink to silence her after she sized him up. He didn't like it. So, he kept her drunk. Then she'd meet her boyfriend at the rundown Blue Door, and I'd see them—mostly cause I was drunk, too."

Laveau shot him a warning look. "Mr. Dupree, you will not—"

"I will not," he echoed, hands raised. "My lips are zipped. Zipped-ish."

He leaned on the wall in the doorway, watching me with curious, too-perceptive eyes. The eyes that saw truth where other people saw noise.

"You look like someone carrying forty pounds of guilt on a five-pound frame," he uttered, apparently unable to remain quiet for long.

"Thanks," I said dryly. "I'll put that on a T-shirt."

He chuckled. "I'm just sayin'—that woman wasn't your doing. Sometimes life drops us into things because we're meant to be there. Even when it looks chaotic."

I wasn't sure if he was messing with me or ministering to me. Maybe both.

"Mr. Dupree," Laveau cut in, "Sit down. And be quiet. Please."

He plopped into a nearby chair and immediately groaned. "Why do these chairs get so many opinions?"

I snorted before I could stop myself, and Laveau shot me an amused side-eye.

She leaned forward. "Now, Ms. Vaughn. Back to you. We'll need your written statement. Before that, do you have any connection to the Duval Lounge? And I was going to ask about The Blue Door too, but you've answered that part."

The question made my chest tighten.

"Not Duval Lounge, but The Blue Door," I said, my words low, "belonged to my dad. He sang there years ago with my aunt Celeste. I was a girl, barely in school. And now, I—I'm here to restore it."

Laveau's eyebrows lifted, but not unkindly. "So, this trip has family roots."

"Yes." My throat tightened. "Deep ones."

Windex perked up from his chair. "You revivin' The Blue Door? For real?"

"Yes," I said cautiously.

He pressed a hand dramatically to his chest. "Praise the Lord and warm up the trumpet section! That place has been dead too long. We've been needin' a spot with soul again."

Laveau gave Windex a raised eyebrow that said *no,* and he gave her a look that said *yes, anyway.*

Then he turned back to me and pointed. "You—Miss Wrecker Lady—are gonna need a band."

I blinked. "I haven't gotten that far. Right now, I need my car to start again without the honking bird in the backseat."

"Good news," Windex declared proudly, "I can get you a band in forty-eight hours."

I frowned. "Are you... a musician?"

He struck a pose. "I'm a *curator* of sound. I connect with talent. I gather the gifted. I assemble the musically wayward. And also, I play a mean washboard."

"A washboard?" I repeated.

He nodded solemnly. "The soul's rib cage."

Laveau scratched the bridge of her nose. "Ignore him."

"Ignore me if you must," Windex said loftily, "but you'll thank me later if you'll let me."

He pointed at me again, not with sarcasm, but with a strange seriousness that settled between us like truth.

Windex announced, even though no one asked. "That woman in the ditch? She was at Duval's the night before. Lots of people saw her. But lots of people might not want to talk about it today."

My breath hitched. "Why not?"

He drawled, "Remy sees everything. But Remy don't always talk."

Before I could ask what that meant, Laveau stepped in.

"That's enough, Mr. Dupree. You are not part of this investigation."

He shrugged. "I'm part of the neighborhood. The neighborhood always knows something."

Laveau sighed. "Ms. Vaughn, please come with me. Let's finish your statement."

My phone buzzed, and I pulled it from my pocket, and it showed repeated texts from Renee, which I didn't respond to—not yet.

I followed the sergeant toward a small interview room, heart heavy, mind spinning. Claire Landry. Missing. Last seen beside The Blue Door. And the town is already whispering. And me, walking straight into a restoration project with ghosts and grief and unanswered questions clinging to its walls, and now this, a dead woman in a ditch. And an old Black man who knows something.

Behind me, Windex called out, "Hey, Miss Wrecker Lady!" He pointed at me with a wink. "You ain't here by accident. Even the pelicans know that."

I shook my head, half exasperated, half unsettled.

And he added, softer this time. "Claire deserved someone to find her. You showed up. She would thank you, if she could."

Then he leaned back, put his hands behind his head, and said to no one in particular, "Now somebody tell me when lunch happens in this place, cause jailhouse coffee don't minister to my soul."

I couldn't help it. I smiled—a weary, broken, rain-soaked grin, my stomach aching for food, too.

I rehearsed my statement in my mind, knowing I'd said the same thing to at least four officers by now. So ready or not, as the mystery of Claire Landry and The Blue Door braided itself together in my day, one difficult thread at a time.

3

The Cousin I Never Knew

THE SIGN FOR CHARTRES STREET slid into view, and my stomach knotted the way it always did when the past rode shotgun.

I tightened my grip on the steering wheel of the green rental—a compact sedan so outdated it still had a CD slot and smelled faintly of crayons and cigarettes. My poor Honda was sitting in some lot with a bent fender, a flat tire, and a warped engine, and pelican feathers in the backseat, waiting on an insurance adjuster. So, for now, I had this washed-out green thing that looked like it had already lived three lives and regretted them all.

"All right, Daddy," I whispered. "I'm back. Let's do this."

A sleepless night at the hotel near the police station hadn't done me any favors, either. Every time I closed my eyes, I saw Claire Landry's body in the ditch, her pale face, the pelican blinking at me from my backseat like some weird, feathered witness. Add the police questions, Cal's worried voice on the phone, and Winston "Windex" Dupree giving me his continued, unsolicited encouragement at the police station, and then add in the sergeant assuming we had something in common, well, resting and sleeping were not exactly on the menu.

But The Blue Door waited, whether I was ready or not.

I turned into the narrow one-way, missed the address by half a block, then circled the alley like some confused out-of-town driver, which, to be fair, I was. Memorizing a map wasn't the same as driving through traffic.

When I finally rolled past the right cluster of buildings, my heart gave a painful little lurch as I pulled to a stop.

There she was.

The Blue Door sat wedged between a shuttered souvenir shop and a half-lit bar called Duval's Lounge. The door itself was more flake than paint these days, yesterday's blue peeling in tired curls. To the right were four sets of windows, the only way light could seem to get inside.

I gazed upward; the second-story windows sagged behind rusty ironwork, and a metal staircase clung to the side of the building in the alley. I'd driven through the alley, not once, but twice, noticing the swirling staircase drooping like a question mark. Half the bricks behind the stairs were chipped; the other half pretended everything was fine.

This place had survived hurricanes, rising water, and the passage of time. Now it had to survive me.

Parallel parking in the green relic took my usual five attempts and three gentle taps on the bumpers of the SUVs in front and behind me. When I finally nudged into place, I sat there catching my breath as today's rain eased into a drizzle, leaving the air heavy and metallic like iron, river mud, and the faintest hint of something fried down the block.

I killed the engine. And silence didn't show up.

The faint thump of jazz drifted from the French Quarter a few blocks away—trumpets, laughter, that loose second-line rhythm that made the whole city feel like it was breathing in time. I let it bleed into me and imagined the musical beats my dad once walked to, the *shadow life* he lived here without me.

"Hi, Dad," I muttered. "Miss me?"

I climbed out, straightened my T-shirt, and grabbed my tote bag from the passenger seat. Inside were my sketches and scribbled notes: a fresh stage layout, an iced-tea bar footprint, tables positioned by the window to catch the music and light, and menus featuring blueberry recipes for those who love brunch.

I also had a paper sack with two blueberry muffins, purchased at a bakery a few blocks from the dreary hotel from last night, because if I'm going to face generational trauma, I'm doing it with carbs. And I wanted to compare their taste to the ones my kitchen will serve.

The neon sign for Duval's Lounge buzzed to my left as I faced the door, throwing pink light onto the wet pavement at the corner. One letter flickered in and out like it had commitment issues. Sergeant Laveau had warned me about my neighbor, Mr. Duval, "cordial, but not your friend," and told me to keep things polite and distant.

"I'm ready for you, Mr. Duval," I said under my breath, smacking my Spearmint gum. "You and your moody neon."

The key to the door felt heavier than it should have as I pulled it from my pocket. When I slid it into the lock, the splintered door groaned as if the building recognized me and wasn't sure if it approved.

Inside, the air hit me like a damp handshake. Wood rot. Mildew. And something faintly sweet, like spilled bourbon sunk into decades-old floorboards. Not that I should know that scent, but in Calvin's not-so-sober years, bourbon had been one of his choices.

Dust floated in the thin light leaking around the shutters. The ceiling fans drooped from the beams, their blades motionless and furry with neglect. My shoes creaked across the floorboards.

I trailed my fingers along the bar top. The varnish flaked under my touch, as if the place were shedding old stories. On the counter behind the bar, a potted plant, half-dead, littered the shelf with brown leaves. I moved the plant to a windowsill, grabbed my bottle of water from my bag, and gave it a drink.

In the back corner, the stage waited, small, barely enough for a three-piece band and a dream. An upright piano lurked at one end, off to the side, its finish cloudy, keys probably sticking, but the sight of it hit me square in the chest.

Dad used to play here. His fingers had moved over keys like prayers. And Celeste—his half-sister, my aunt, I never knew existed until last year—had stood on this stage.

She had poured her voice into the smoky air until she died in the Mississippi River when I was five, back when I lived in Texas with my aunt and uncle. She was murdered by Gus Tiller, one of my dad's old business partners. And to think, my Uncle Harlan was in on it somehow. Horrible to think one's relatives get mixed up in such things.

I stared at the piano until my throat thickened. "We're gonna bring you back, Blue," I whispered. "One note at a time."

A floorboard creaked behind me.

I spun around, my heart pounding.

Nothing. Just dim light, shadows, the faint glint of a stairwell door off to the side of the stage, which I hadn't fully noticed before now.

Still, something in me bristled. Someone had been here recently. The air didn't feel entirely abandoned.

I turned toward the front door again, shaking off the eerie feeling, when a man's voice slid out from the darker corner near the stairs.

"You lost?"

I froze. My paper sack slipped from my hand, and my muffins hit the floor with a sad little thud.

A figure stepped into the sliver of light from the window's hazy beam. He was tall, with coffee-brown skin that glistened slightly from the humidity and braids that brushed his shoulders. Around my age, maybe a little older. His eyes—dark, sharp—studied me as if I'd walked into the wrong song.

"I'm not lost," I said, forcing my voice to stop wobbling. "I'm home. Sort of."

He tilted his head. "That so? Not many folks call this place home."

"I'm restoring it," I said, tightening my grip on the key like it might suddenly morph into a weapon. "The Blue Door belongs to the Vaughn estate now. I'm Emory Vaughn."

The name seemed to hit him like a drumbeat as his jaw clenched, then eased into something that wasn't quite a smile and wasn't quite a frown. "Vaughn," he mumbled.

"Yes." I kept my chin up. "And what are you doing on my property? And how did you get in here?"

He didn't answer that. His gaze flicked toward the staircase, then back to me. "Guess you don't know me. Not that you'd have reason to."

"Should I?" I asked. My heart thudded harder. I took half a step back without meaning to.

He drew himself up a little. "Name's Kermit. Kermit Delacroix."

The last name dropped into my stomach like a stone. "Delacroix?" I repeated the word, catching in my gut.

"You heard me." His mouth twitched. "Might as well cut to the chase. I'm Celeste's son. All grown up."

It felt as if the room tilted. My arms did a ridiculous windmill thing as I tried to make my brain catch up.

"She... she had a child?" I blurted. "A son?"

"Yeah," he said, matter-of-factly. "That was me. Still is, far as I know."

I sank into the nearest chair by a table, my knees having decided they were done taking part in standing upright. The seat wobbled but held.

"No one told me," I whispered. "Not Aunt Diane. Not Uncle Harlan. Nobody said a word about you last year. Or ever."

He observed me, then crossed the space and sat across from me like we'd planned to meet for chicory coffee. His bronze skin caught the weak light leaking in through the shutters, and his braids brushed the collar of his shirt when he nodded.

"Just cause my mama sang in a bar," he hissed. "Doesn't make her a bad parent."

"I didn't mean she wasn't," I blurted. "I just—this is all new. How do I know you're telling me the truth?" I asked, pushing my chair back a little. "I didn't know she... that I..."

"That you had family here?" he finished. "Welcome to the club. We don't get to pick our relatives. We survive 'em."

He sniffed and wiped his nose with the back of his hand, then gave me a measuring look when he caught me staring at his arm.

"Yeah, my daddy's Black," he said, a touch of challenge in his voice. "Mama was white. And I grew up somewhere in between. Took me a while to figure out I don't have to choose sides. I get his color and her music. That's enough."

I shook my head. "I'm not staring at you because of that," I said. "It's just that my entire family tree is booby-trapped with secrets and shadows."

"Sounds about right for the Vaughns," he said dryly.

He stood, walked over to the crumpled paper sack on the floor, and picked it up, offering it back to me. "You dropped this."

"Thanks." I opened the bag out of habit. "Muffin? Blueberry."

He smirked. "Not a blueberry fan. And not a fan of strangers rolling in here thinking they're about to take over."

"Strangers?" I sputtered. "This is my building."

"This is my childhood," he countered, tapping the table with his knuckles. "I grew up in this place. It's home for me, too."

My throat tightened. "You've been... living here?"

He nodded toward the stairs. "Upstairs. Since way before your last visit. Guess you didn't notice."

Shame pricked at me. "Last time I was here, Gus took my brother and me on a tour. It was right after Dad died. I was... numb. Then everything blew up with the missing women and his journal and—honestly, that trip was nothing but one cloud of sorrow after another."

Kermit's jaw worked at the mention of Gus. "I heard he's in prison now."

"He is." I swallowed. "I'm so sorry about what happened to your mom."

He studied me, and something in his expression softened, just a fraction. "Gus took her from me," he said. "I was twelve. After that, I bounced around Treme with neighbors and friends of friends. No daddy in the picture. Just the music and later, this place."

He walked behind the bar, running his hand along the scarred wood. "Used to stand on a stool back here, wiping this counter while Mama sang," he said. "Your daddy would play for her at the piano. Folks would say Celeste's voice made the lights dance."

A painful ache bloomed in my chest. Pieces of Dad's life were sliding into place, but they belonged to someone else's memories, not mine.

"I wish he'd told me," I said. "About her. About you. About any of this."

"Maybe he thought he was protecting you," Kermit said. "Maybe he was running. People in this city do a lot of both."

He slipped a worn driver's license from his wallet and handed it to me.

"Kermit Delacroix," I said, out loud, just like the card read, and also like he'd said.

"Your dad was good to me," he added. "Flipped nickels in the air for me to catch. Taught me to listen for the beat underneath the noise. Whatever else he did or didn't do, he was kind to a kid who needed it."

Tears burned the backs of my eyes. "He never raised me," I said. "Sometimes I'm so mad at him I can't breathe. Then I hear he was good to everyone else, and I don't know whether to be grateful or jealous."

Kermit gave a half-shrug. "People are complicated. And dead people get even more complicated, cause we put all our questions on them, and they don't answer back."

Rain started tapping against the windows, the wind blowing, a soft, steady rhythm.

"I'm not here to hurt anyone," he added. "Just trying to get by till things turn around."

"I'm restoring this place," I said. "Bringing it up to code, hiring staff, reopening. We'll serve brunch, no alcohol, and let the jazz roll in like sweet blueberries. That... that means you'll eventually have to move. I don't know when, but it's coming."

He nodded slowly, as if I'd just confirmed a weather report he already knew. "Yeah. I figured."

"I'm not kicking you out today," I added quickly. "I just… need time to think. To sort this out."

"You and me both," he said. "Claire and Lucien will have to find a new place for their rendezvous."

I shrugged. "Are you talking about Claire Landry?"

"The one and only. Heard she's missing."

"Well, she's… dead. The police found her in a ditch yesterday. Or I did, swerving from the pelicans on the highway. My car crashed near her, and I tore up the underpinning of my Honda."

"You… saw her?" He scratched his arm, his eye twitching.

"I did." I swallowed hard. The picture of Claire in the tall grass is not something you forget in a day.

"Lucien's gonna be…"

"…going to be what?"

"Oh, nothing. Another poor soul gone too soon." Kermit said, folding his arms.

I wanted to ask a million more questions—where he'd been, how he'd survived, why he'd chosen to live over the ghost of his mother's stage—but before I could, movement at the front window caught my eye.

A familiar, lanky silhouette peered through the glass window, cupping his hands around his face to see inside.

"Oh no," I muttered. "Of course."

The door creaked open, and Winston "Windex" Dupree stepped in like he owned the copyright on dramatic entrances. The seasoned, tall Black man from the police station, with warm brown skin, a mustache with more personality than some people's entire faces, and twisted hair that seemed to lean whichever way the humidity pushed it, held a washboard and stroked a note.

Today, he'd upgraded from his *I Pace Myself, Mostly* shirt to one that read *Got Jazz?* in cracked white letters.

"Well, well," he said, looking around with open delight. "The Blue Door breathes again. And look at that, and who is already kissing up to Ms. Vaughn."

Kermit stiffened. "Stop meddling, Windex," he said under his breath.

"You know him?" I asked.

"In passing," Kermit said. "He passes a lot."

Windex pressed a hand to his chest. "I am a man of many streets, thank you. And this one called me this morning. As for Kermit, we go back a few years. You might say."

He looked at me.

And I held my breath.

"Long story short, the police let me go. Public intoxication, blah blah, misunderstanding, eternal injustice, etcetera. Anyway, I got to thinkin', if Miss Vaughn here is really bringing back The Blue Door, she might need a local liaison."

"A what?" I asked.

"A helper," he said. "A translator. A walking, *do not get ripped off* sign. Also, a band wrangler, eventually. But we'll get there."

"I didn't ask for—" I began.

He held up a hand. "You didn't have to. You look like a woman who keeps a color-coded planner and still ended up with a dead body, a car wreck, and a pelican in her backseat in under twenty-four hours. The city is telling you something. You gonna listen or nap?"

I prepared a snappy comeback in my mind, but nothing came out. Because he wasn't wrong. My life was unraveling in front of me, and every time I grabbed the loose threads, three more slipped through my fingers.

"I'm fine," I said, because that's what control freaks say right before they crash into the secrets controlling the present. I pulled out some gum. "Spearmint, anyone?"

"You're in over your head," Windex replied, not unkindly, more like agreement. "Good news? Music has survived most hurricanes. Bad news? Also, it's also where the snakes live and slither."

He clapped his hands once, loudly, making Kermit yell, and I jumped.

"First things first," he said. "This door lock? Trash. That back-alley spiral staircase with a door? People use it as a shortcut. The one in the back room, leading to the alley beneath it, is stuck. If you want this place safe, we've gotta see what eyes and ears it already has on it."

Kermit snorted. "And you're the security consultant now?"

"I am the neighborhood," Windex said. "The neighborhood knows stuff."

Before I could protest, he strode toward the back, flicking on his phone's flashlight and poking his head through a side door like a man on a mission. I watched him go, my heart swinging between suspicion, amusement, and sheer exhaustion.

"What are you doing?" I called.

"Taking inventory!" he yelled back. "Of hazards, opportunities, and cobwebs. Mostly cobwebs so far."

Kermit leaned his hip against the bar, watching me. "You really sure about this?" he asked quietly. "About reopening? About all of... this?"

I glanced around at the sagging ceiling fans, the scarred floor, the piano in the corner, the ghost of a woman I'd never known, and the son she'd left behind.

I thought about Claire in the ditch, the way Sergeant Laveau had looked at me, the weight in Cal's voice, and Windex proclaiming that pelicans were a sign.

No, I wasn't sure. Not at all.

But something in this city, in this building, in my dad's tangled history, was pulling me in like a tide. Away from the safe, predictable world of the ranch and the riding lessons and my carefully planned calendar. Into a place where jazz and secrets and inconvenient truths lived under the same roof.

"I don't know if I'm sure," I admitted. "I just know I'm here. And I can't walk away. Not yet."

Kermit studied me for a long moment, then nodded. "Then I guess," he said slowly, "You're not the only one who needs to figure out where you belong."

Windex reappeared from the back, dust in his hair and triumph in his eyes. "Good news!" he announced. "I'm sure the roof leaks, the wiring's sketchy, and the back door is held shut by pure stubbornness—but this place?" He spun in a slow circle, taking it all in. "This place wants to live."

I exhaled, a shaky little laugh escaping with it. "Good," I said. "Because I'm thinking I came here to figure out if I do, too."

And for the first time since Claire Landry, the wreck, the station, and the pelican, I let myself admit it: My world was no longer under my control.

I sent Cal a text: Can't believe what I'm uncovering about Dad's life here. Wish I could say it feels like home, but it doesn't yet.

Cal texted back with an immediacy that knotted warmth into my chest: I'm here whenever you need to talk. Do I need to come down there?

I texted back while Kermit and Windex chatted off to the side: Let's just say, I've found out we have a cousin, and he lives at The Blue Door.

4

My Happy Face?

KERMIT RUBBED HIS HANDS ON his jeans, avoiding my eyes. "I should let you settle in," he said finally. Then, without waiting for my response, he headed toward the stairs and climbed them, steady, his gait sure, his footsteps heavy, the kind that carried more story than steps.

The piano off to my left drew my attention, as if a deliberate clink of a piano key played a note—but no one sat at the piano. Yet, the note floated around me like a memory I needed to hold on to.

The door creaked open at the top, then clicked softly shut behind Kermit as he disappeared to the second floor.

I turned to Windex, asking the man who had previously landed in jail a personal question. "So, is Kermit really Celeste's son?"

"Sure thing. Watched him grow up listening to her sing, until he was about eleven or twelve. She died in the Mississippi River."

"You're sure."

"I'm sure when I say it. My memory don't fade," Kermit said, pulling on his whiskers.

I sighed, my life altered by Windex and Kermit, and now I'll need to adjust my checklist. Neither was on the list for today, but now Kermit's written in at the bottom, like a ghost from the past that wasn't a ghost, but simply a cousin. And Windex, well, he's just loud. But he might help with a band down the road.

Before I could breathe a full sigh, Windex disappeared and reappeared from the back hallway, holding a dust-covered broom as if he'd just rescued it from captivity.

"I got a feelin' about this place!" he announced. "But I also got an errand. Important business. Neighborhood business. Classified." He tapped the side of his nose, then spun the broom like a baton. "Don't you worry, Miss Blue Door. I'll be back before the paint dries."

"What paint?" I asked, bewildered.

"The metaphorical paint," he said, already halfway out the door. "Same kind your life keeps spilling."

And he handed me the broom and darted out the door, with just a flash of a smile and the door shutting behind him.

Suddenly, The Blue Door was quiet again. Too quiet. Which is precisely when the ache in my chest reminded me that the silence never stays silent for long.

By late afternoon, the off-and-on storm finally broke, and the light returned in ribbons, slipping through the dusty windows like grace that hadn't given up.

I'd already eaten both blueberry muffins, which felt like poor planning but excellent coping skills. And I'd made a mental note; my muffins were so much better.

I'd cranked open as many windows as would budge on the first floor, letting damp air flow through The Blue Door. Dust motes twirled in the beams of light like lazy dancers, and for a heartbeat, I could almost see a small boy behind the bar, wiping the counter with a rag, eyes fixed on the woman singing from the stage.

Celeste. Kermit. My dad at the piano. Kermit's childhood was lived in the spotlight of a life I never knew existed.

I set my beat-up laptop on the bar. I opened my spiral notebook, the one full of scribbled dreams and half-baked plans for the cafe version of this place: blueberry pancakes, waffles, muffins, chicory coffee, and comfort food for souls who'd wandered too long and needed somewhere soft to land.

This would not be a bar, not under my watch. This was going to be a morning-and-midday refuge: brunch and jazz. Coffee and prayer disguised as conversation—a place where people could breathe.

I drew a little rectangle on the page and wrote in all caps: BAND—WINDEX.

The cafe would obviously need its own original band. Jazz standards, some blues, a little gospel sneaking in at the edges. Music in tribute to Dad and Celeste. Music to tell this building it wasn't done yet.

I hadn't typed a single word when a voice called from the front doorway, bright and lilting and so alive it bounced off the walls.

"Emory Vaughn! Well, look at you! Girl, you made it!"

I turned, already smiling, grateful for a human who wasn't tied to my past.

A woman stepped inside as if she'd been poured from New Orleans sunlight. "It's me, Renee Baptiste. I'm your official guide and sidekick while you're here. And why don't you answer your phone? I've called and texted. Girlfriend, answer when I call. It could be important."

I shied away from my snarky answer and said, "Okay, I'll do better." And I pushed away from the bar, relieved. "Hi, I'm Emory."

"Yes, I know," she said, laughing as she came closer. "You look just like your pictures. Josie sent me an entire folder of you. I suppose she didn't trust my imagination. She labeled them, too: 'Angry Emory,' 'Happy Emory,' 'Worried Emory,' 'Sad Emory,' and 'Deep-Thinking Emory.' Honey, I got a folder for all your moods."

"I really need to work on my poker face," I said. "Apparently, my emotions do community theater."

I offered her my best happy face on purpose. It probably came out more like "mildly frazzled but trying."

Renee wore a sundress covered in little yellow flowers, her blonde hair twisted up haphazardly, as if she'd pinned it while doing three other things. Her smile was big enough to rival the city itself. She moved like someone who'd survived hurricanes and kept going anyway—both the weather kind and the "owning a hotel in the French Quarter" kind.

She walked farther into the room, her heels clicking across the warped floor. She inhaled, wrinkled her nose, and announced, "Lord have mercy, this place smells like history and no telling how many bad decisions. I remember peeking in the windows here as a young girl. Played on the corners, in the alleys, grew up here. It was safer back then. Or so it seemed."

"I've got a lot of work ahead of me," I said. "I hope this isn't one of my bad decisions. If so, it'll fit right in with the rest of my life."

She laughed, then impulsively threw her arms around me, hugging like we weren't strangers.

"Josie told me you were stubborn," she said, pulling back. "Insisted on driving from Wyoming—*Wyoming*—all the way down here. Said you were about to turn this ghost bar into a blueberry dream."

"That's the plan," I said, glancing around at the sagging ceiling fans and peeling paint. "Though I think I'm currently heavier on ghosts than blueberries. I might need more faith than furniture."

"Good thing I came stocked," she said. She dug into her purse and pulled out her own notebook. "I've got contractors, painters, and one miracle worker who can fix plumbing without robbing your soul. Mostly."

I chuckled. "You're a gift."

"Don't you forget it," she said, twirling in the open space. "Now, tell me—who's the man upstairs?"

My smile faltered. "You met him?"

"I parked in the alley," she said. "I was coming up the side, and he was heading down the spiral staircase out back. Looked at me like I was trespassing in his memories."

"That's Kermit," I said. "Celeste's son."

Her lips parted. "No," she breathed. "You mean Celeste Delacroix? Your aunt? The one who died when I was, oh, nine or ten?"

"Yes," I said. "Apparently, I drove to New Orleans to meet my cousin. Did you notice? He's a little darker than I am."

She gave me a look, equal parts gentle and firm. "Girl, this is New Orleans. We've got every color of skin the Lord ever thought up. All of it is beautiful. Don't you forget *that*."

"I didn't mean it wrong," I said quickly. "It just... caught me off guard. Nobody told me she had a son. Nobody told me I had family here."

Renee's gaze softened. "Well, I can say this: whatever shade he is, that man's got music in his bones. He was humming when I passed him. Some folks hum to themselves. He hums like he's in a band, and he already knows the set list."

"I think he's been living here for a long time," I said. "Upstairs. Way before my last visit."

She crossed her arms and studied me. "You sure you're ready for this, sugar? You're stirring up ghosts. And in this city, ghosts stir back."

I smiled, though the weight of her words pressed in deeper than I wanted to show. "Then I'll serve them coffee and muffins and pancakes until they behave."

She laughed, but those wise eyes didn't quite let go. "You really believe you can redeem this place?"

"I have to," I said. "It's all that's left of my dad's music. And Celeste's story deserves peace. I can't change what happened in the Mississippi River, but maybe I can change what happens here."

Renee reached out and gently lifted my chin, so I'd meet her eyes. "Maybe your story deserves peace, too," she said. "This place used to shine. I can't wait to see what you do to the building."

Outside, a trumpet started up—slow, soulful, full of an ache with hope braided in the notes. I stepped to the doorway, drawn as if there was a string tied to my chest.

Across the street, under a narrow awning, a young Black boy stood, holding a trumpet, blowing music into the wind. His case lay open at his feet, with a few crumpled bills and a handful of coins scattered inside. The horn gleamed in the late light, and when he played, it felt like the city itself breathed through him.

Renee slid up beside me. "That's Treme's own, Miles Delacroix," she breathed. "Folks around here say he was born playing in rhythm."

My heart jolted. "Delacroix?" I repeated. "Did you just say—"

"Uh-huh," she said. "Oh my! I let it slip. Oh goodness. I've been caught. So yes, that's Kermit's boy."

My words caught in my throat, and I stared at Miles, at the way his cheeks puffed, at the way the notes flowed out like something older than he was.

Renee flashed a smile that was just a little too wide, a little too bright.

"You already know Kermit, don't you? And Miles?" I blurted, the pieces clicking in my tired brain. "You passed Kermit on the stairs in the alley, and you're acting like he was a surprise. Okay, if we're going to do this, no secrets. I cannot handle any more secrets."

She ran her fingers through her loose strands of hair by her ear, sighing. "Guess you caught me," she said. "Not saying all I know is a bad habit. I'm used to keeping my own secrets sometimes, and well, yes, I know Kermit. We grew up together. These days, he plays sax sometimes down on Frenchmen Street. Sad soul, that one. Won't bother you much. And Miles? He's ten. Sometimes he plays out here when school's out, or he's got something on his mind."

I ran my fingers through my bangs. "I don't like it when people don't tell me the truth. I can handle the truth."

"Sorry, Girl. It's a bad habit of mine," Renee said, sighing.

Miles's music lifted, floating across the street like a prayer. For a moment, I could've sworn I heard a hint of *Blueberry Hill* tucked under the notes, like the song was peeking around a corner.

I held my breath.

How many layers could one building, one street, one family history have?

"I'm thinking," I said slowly, "That selling The Blue Door might've been a safer, saner option."

"Safe is overrated," Renee replied. "So is sane. But you may change your mind, you know."

I watched Miles play, my chest tight. "Shouldn't he be in school or something?"

"It's Saturday, Sugar," Renee said, smiling. "Time's weird when you're this tired."

She glanced at her watch. "I've got to run, got too many people to answer to today. But I've got your room all set at the hotel, the Royal Straight Hotel, two blocks over—Room 222. Since I've inherited the hotel, I'm living up to my parents' ways, mostly, as I keep the hotel spotless and maintain accounting ledgers for Dad's old acquaintances. That accounting degree is coming in handy."

"What? Your dad's old buddies?"

"It's just a side job for me. I kept only a few of my father's accounts. The extra money helps me stay up to date with the ongoing maintenance of the hotel and keeps me safe in this town." Renee coughed. "I meant to say, a clean hotel keeps customers happy."

I cleared my throat, unsure what seemed like a slip of the tongue.

Renee smiled. "Oh, I gave you a room with twos, because two is a good number. Feels like a second chance."

"Alright," I said, with a long, drawn-out sound, my Texas drawl hanging on. I'd picked up that Renee enjoyed being in charge, but so do I.

She pulled a plastic key card from her purse and pressed it into my hand. "Here you go. I'll see you tonight. Got to make the rest of the hotel sparkle for the guests. You're not my only project, you know."

"Project?" I said lightly.

She grinned. "I'll add you to my favorites list." With that, she darted down the sidewalk toward the Quarter, her heels ticking against the pavement, hair catching the light.

I stayed in the doorway, listening to Miles play until my throat stung.

**

That night, before walking to the Royal Straight Hotel, I sat on the stage floor near the bar with a single candle flickering beside me. The rest of the room was swallowed in shadows, and I pulled Dad's old journal from my bag, the one that had dragged me from Dallas to New Orleans to Denver and finally to Cody, Wyoming, last year.

I flipped to a page smudged by time and my own thumbprints.

I read aloud, "The Blue Door isn't just a place. It's disguised as a song. Where life can live."

The words blurred as tears formed. I traced them with my finger, whispering, "Then let the music begin."

Somewhere above me, a floorboard creaked.

A door upstairs whined open, then shut again.

I glanced toward the stairwell, spine prickling. A shadow shifted, or maybe my imagination went into overtime.

For half a heartbeat, I thought I heard a woman humming. Soft. Low. A tune that nudged at my memory but never fully formed.

"Celeste?" I whispered. "If that's you... I'm trying. I really am."

The faintest thread of melody drifted down, something like the notes Miles had played outside, but twisted, new. I couldn't tell if I was hearing the past or reinventing it.

"You can rest now," I said, voice shaking. "I'll finish the song."

The candle fluttered once, then went out.

Darkness rushed in like a curtain drop. My heart thudded so loud it seemed too big for my chest.

"Okay," I muttered, fumbling for my phone. "We are officially done with ambience."

I turned on the flashlight on my phone, scrambling to gather my bag, Dad's journal, and my laptop. "First thing tomorrow," I told the empty room, "I turn on the electricity. Oh, wait, tomorrow is Sunday. So maybe Monday. And the second thing? I need light bulbs."

I locked the front door behind me and stepped out into the damp night, not sure it would keep out the alley traffic. And the city's noise swelled around me: laughter from Duval's Lounge, distant horns, the clink of glasses. The pink neon sign buzzed to my right like an irritated hornet, throwing pulsing color across the sidewalk.

I glanced up, and there, in a second-story window of The Blue Door, Kermit's face appeared. His braids hung over his shoulders, his eyes fixed on me, unreadable. We stared at each other for a long second; I squinted up into the darkness, and he looked down like he was weighing something he hadn't decided about yet.

He thinks he's home.

But he's not. Not anymore.

That's what the rational, control-loving part of me decided just as the wind kicked up as I hurried to the outdated green rental parked on the street.

The storm was regrouping, clouds stacking, air thickening. I hopped in, tossed my bag onto the passenger seat, and set Dad's journal gently on top.

I slid the key into the ignition, then froze.

Something white was wedged under my windshield wiper.

I hadn't seen it when I approached the car. Maybe I'd been too lost in my thoughts. Perhaps it hadn't been there yet. My fingers tightened on the steering wheel.

You're being dramatic, I told myself. It's probably a parking ticket. Or a flyer for a swamp tour. Or coupons for beignets, which, honestly, you deserve.

I exhaled, switched off the ignition, and got back out.

The wind whipped my hair into my face as I reached for the paper. It was folded once, no logo, no color, just cheap printer stock paper gone limp from the damp air.

I unfolded it and felt my stomach drop.

Three words. Black marker. All capital letters.

STOP DIGGING EMORY.

The surroundings went quiet in that strange way they did in Wyoming before a storm, as if sound were pulled back like a tide.

Someone knew my name. Someone knew what I was here to do. And someone didn't want me doing it.

I swallowed hard and looked around, scanning the street. Neon from Duval's sign blinked in the puddles. A couple laughed as they walked by, not giving me a second glance. A man smoked in a doorway half a block away, his face shadowed.

Nobody looked like they'd just left a note on my car.

I breathed out slowly, the paper crinkling in my hand. "Okay," I whispered, more to God than to myself, "Dad, help me do this. Please."

Fear crawled up my spine, hot and slow. Underneath it, something else stirred too: anger, maybe. Or resolve. Or that stubborn Vaughn streak that refused to let a three-word note tell me where the story ends.

"I'm not just restoring a bar," I said firmly, touching Dad's journal when I climbed back into the car. "I'm rebuilding a battleground."

Where some died. Where some lived. Where some sang, and others played.

Where Gus Tiller once ruled. Where my dad made music on the piano. Where Celeste lived and lost her life's song.

Where Kermit grew up and lost his mother, where Miles now played on the corner, carrying a melody forward he didn't even know belonged to our family.

Oh, how broken are the steps of my life—and theirs, too. But somehow, life kept walking anyway.

Jazz still played. Miles still blew his horn. Kermit still hummed. I was still here, heart pounding, fingers shaking, note on my lap.

Yes, the shadows of the ghosts of The Blue Door were wide awake.

And now, apparently, so were its enemies.

I turned the key, wipers swishing as the first new drops of rain hit the glass, and the pink neon from Duval's sign flashed across my windshield like a warning light.

I stuffed the note into my journal, like tucking a confession between pages.

"Daddy," I whispered, easing the car away from the curb, "How many secrets did you keep? And how many of them are still breathing?"

I wished he were in the passenger seat. I also wanted Calvin here, complaining about my driving and insisting we turn around. I wished I'd let him come with me.

But my wishes don't always come true.

Most of them live inside my head.

Only to haunt me when I sleep.

Room 222 waited for me at Renee's hotel.

A bed. A door that locked. A night where, if I were lucky, I might sleep for over twenty minutes at a time.

As I drove away and circled to the hotel, I glanced into the rearview mirror.

The Blue Door stood in the distance, dark and patient.

Kermit lingered in the window upstairs.

And a face watched me from the door of Duval's Lounge, not clear, but it appeared to be a man.

I whispered, "This won't just be a renovation. This was a war for what would live here on Chartres Street."

I inched along, knowing someone had just officially declared themselves on the opposing side of my plans.

5

Debts Don't Drown

I DANCED DOWN THE STAIRS the next morning, ready to conquer the day, prepared to take on the world. Renee Baptiste called to me from behind the counter in the Royal Straight Hotel lobby, her voice lifting over the clinking of keyboard keys from the two clerks on either side of her, and the inaudible murmur of guests.

"Let me show you the quiet side of New Orleans. You could use a little peace after that long drive, the accident, and the… unexpected news of finding out you have cousins here. We'll enjoy Sunday before your work keeps you too busy to see the beauty of my city."

I sighed, my day already interrupted by my new bubbly friend. But I could use a breezy courtyard moment or two to sit or take in the shade of an old oak tree, or even maybe a judgmental cat watching me sip chicory coffee.

What she meant, apparently, was cemeteries.

"Sugar, this is where the city does its truest talking," she said an hour later as I parked the outdated green rental down Basin Street, her in the passenger seat, the morning sun spilling across marble like it had been practicing all night.

We had passed tour groups, iron fences, and a stone wall that hid most of St. Louis Cemetery No. 1. The French Quarter was just beyond it, a hum of brass, fryer oil, and vendors calling out like carnival barkers. But the wall dampened it all to a steady heartbeat: boom... boom... boom.

New Orleans never stopped, not even for the dead.

Renee glanced at the parking place I'd just squeezed into. "You'll never get this spot again. This is a miracle."

"I'll add it to my gratitude list," I said, under my breath. "Along with not dying from the migrating pelicans."

My Honda was still sitting in a city lot somewhere with a busted front end, and a file number, and the scene of the wreck played on repeat in my mind like a crime show rerun. The ditch, the pelican in the backseat, Claire Landry's body under a white sheet, and Sergeant Laveau's firm demeanor telling me I could go, but not to leave town. But to call her if needed.

"Not a suspect," she'd said. "But very much a witness."

Witness. I wasn't sure I liked that word.

I grabbed my tote bag from the back seat; the strap was worn just right against my palm. Inside, I'd tucked Dad's journal, a bottle of water, my laptop, and a pad and pencil— like I might take notes on how to talk to ghosts.

"You sure this isn't… invasive?" I asked as we walked toward the gate. "It's like we're visiting other people's grief and turning this place into a tourist attraction."

Renee slipped on her orange-rimmed sunglasses, which matched the orange stripes on her sundress, and smiled. "You don't come here to invade. You come to listen."

We stepped through the iron gate into a stone city of almost silent people. Tombs rose in rows like tiny houses, stacked and layered, doors for the already gone. Names, dates. Crosses and shells. Angels with cobweb shawls. The plaster was sun-bleached and cracked, but the place buzzed faintly, like a stage hum before the first note.

"This is where people keep their promises," Renee whispered. "Where they tell the truth when they're finally brave enough."

"What does that even mean?" I asked, following her down a narrow path, wondering if she was giving me more than a history lesson.

"Josie told me you don't sleep much. She said that you're having nightmares about your daddy, and they keep you up, and you dream about those missing women. So, I figured, a soothing walk with the dead might help."

"I'm not convinced cemeteries and *soothing* go in the same sentence."

The path narrowed and widened in odd places, as if the cemetery breathed. Renee walked ahead like she'd grown up playing hide-and-seek here, her heels clicking softly. Moss clung to brick and plaster, refusing to let go.

A man in a lightweight jacket brushed past us, giving Renee a second glance, and his broad shoulders and quick stride told me he had somewhere urgent to be. His black skin, shiny in the sun, and his overgrown eyebrows shadowed his eyes as they cut to me as he passed, sharp and assessing, lingering just a second too long on my face.

"That was… intense," I murmured.

Renee didn't look back. "Cemeteries make people weird," she said lightly. "Some come here to remember. Some come here to forget."

My chest loosened with each step. The chaos of the past two days—wreck, police station, pelican, Kermit, the note on my windshield—settled in layers that hadn't quite organized themselves yet.

"The tombs are stacked," I said, trailing my fingers along one. "That's odd."

My tote slipped, and Dad's journal tumbled out, thumping against my shoe.

"You brought your daddy's stories," Renee said, tipping her chin toward it.

I bent to pick it up. "I carry this everywhere. Josie probably told you. It's like having Dad with me without… actually having him."

"She did," Renee said. "Said you hold it as if all your answers live inside it. Baby, the past isn't where you'll find your peace. It's in today."

"It belonged to my dad," I said. "The pages have already given me answers, about him, about Celeste, about those women who died. This journal led me here. You come to the cemetery to listen; I read my daddy's words."

"No need to get testy." Renee arched one perfectly shaped brow, pulling down her sunglasses. "I'm just saying, maybe it's time to let the journal rest a little."

A ding on Renee's phone made her stop walking, and she sighed, with a bit of a growl. "Well, it seems Sunday isn't a day of rest."

"What do you mean?" I asked.

Renee tapped in a response on her phone. "Oh, nothing. Just my past bothering me today." And she cut her eyes over her shoulders twice.

A flicker of movement caught my eye. The eyebrow man from earlier stood a few tombs away, half-hidden by a taller vault, watching us. When he realized I'd seen him, he turned his head toward the far wall as if he'd only been admiring the architecture.

"Who is that man?" I whispered. "He keeps staring."

Renee glanced. "Oh, him? No one. Maybe someone. Not anybody we care about." Her hand brushed my shoulder. "You're trapped in the past, Emory. It's time to walk ahead and live."

"You realize you're the one who brought me to a cemetery."

She smiled. "Details. This is to help you face your life, not run from it."

"I'll write that down for later," I muttered. "Right after 'stop finding bodies' and 'avoid pelicans.'"

She snorted. "Sassy fits you."

We stopped before a large white tomb with a wide flat top, plaster cracked like old knuckles. Visitors had left offerings—beads, coins, a tiny toy trumpet, a single cinnamon stick tied with ribbon. Grief brushed the back of my neck, enough that my eyes stung.

"People bring small things when words are too heavy," Renee said.

"What do you bring?" I asked, half-teasing, half-curious.

"Time," she said. "And a good listening ear. Both are in short supply."

I ran my gaze along the edges of the tomb, where cracks spidered across the surface. In one crease, something bright caught my eye—a tiny shard of color wedged into the plaster, like the tomb had swallowed a secret, a spot that mysterious man touched before scooting away.

I reached up and tugged it free. Blue chalk. Just a thin stick of it, the same blue as the door on my building. "Blue," I murmured.

Renee noticed. "It's your color," she said.

"I see that. It's the color of the door where Dad played piano, where Celeste sang, where people walked in on two legs and ordered something to drink. It's like the city branded my family with blue paint."

"You really gonna run a cafe on a song?" Her voice teased, but there was no mockery in it.

"I'm going to run it on love," I said. "And pancakes. And waffles. And muffins. And jazz. But mostly love."

She nodded as if she approved. We moved deeper into the maze of tombs, the air cooling in pockets, carrying the faint scent of fried dough from some far-off fryer.

"People used to mark Marie Laveau's tomb with an X," Renee said, pointing toward a guarded corner. "To ask for favors. Now they don't do that so much. I bring flowers and respect instead. I leave my bad decisions here, too. The dead don't owe us anything."

"Wait, the sergeant at the police station, is she related to this Laveau?" I asked, squinting at the tomb.

"Could be a relative. That name goes way back. Who knows? Might not be, though," she answered.

"Did you grow up playing here, too?" I asked. "You seem to know this place way too well."

"Yes, ma'am," she said. "My brother and I used to sneak in here when we were kids. I'd hide; he'd never find me. I learned patience here. Learned to read dates and let them change me."

"Dates?"

Renee stopped by another tomb, plaster peeling back to show brick beneath. "Look here. It's the same pattern every time. The imprints show where someone was born with a dash, then where they died. The hyphens are where their story lives. So, eighty years for that one. And that little dash is where all the living happened."

"The hyphen?" I asked.

"Uh-huh." She tapped a name. "You want your cafe to succeed? Then live within those dates. And be a woman who survives. Make your life mean something."

I swallowed. "So, is that a question for you or for me?"

"For both of us. I'm sorting through a few things in my business, and breaking free from them isn't easy, here in the French Quarter. Sometimes this place swallows me whole. But life calls us to change the future with our choices today."

I squinted as she ran her fingers along the tomb, and I processed what Renee meant as she spoke to me, but her words also seemed to be for her, too.

A crow called from the wall, a single, judgmental caw that somehow made me smile.

We started down a narrow lane where tomb walls pressed in on either side. A child's plastic toy car sat at the base of one vault, and a rosary hung in a crack.

Everything whispered.

Up ahead, a man wearing a suit turned a corner too quickly, like he didn't want to be seen. As he passed a crumbling tomb, his hand brushed the plaster, slipping something into a broken seam, and he glanced back at me.

"Who is he? He's watching us, too." I said, feeling paranoid and uneasy.

"He's harmless, and cemeteries aren't for everyone," Renee said lightly, but her shoulders were tenser now. "Don't chase shadows. Not today. Shadows come in all forms. Just stay close to me."

At the next tomb, the plaster had peeled back, revealing raw red brick. Wedged in a crease, where the man had just touched, I saw something—a folded slip of paper.

"Is that... for me?" I asked.

"Only one way to know," she said, her tone light, but there was a warning buried in it.

I set my tote down and reached for the paper. It came free easily. Not weathered, not old. Recent.

I unfolded it carefully.

Two words, written with a heavy hand: DEBTS DON'T DROWN.

Below the words, a faint ring, like a glass had once been set on the paper. Beside it, a rough sketch—just a rectangle with a curved top and three stacked panels.

The Blue Door. Stripped to the bone.

My stomach dropped and then clenched. I handed the note to Renee.

"Hmm," she said, eyes narrowing behind her sunglasses. "Somebody wanted you to find this."

"No kidding. It was that man. And I don't have time for these games," I snapped. "Friday, I find a dead woman in a ditch and end up at a police station. Last night, someone left a *Stop Digging* note on my car. Now I get cryptic tomb mail? No, thank you." I spun around as a man, a woman, and their toddler scooted by, the dad holding tight to his daughter's hand.

"Don't worry about the note. Someone wants to scare you off," Renee said, not looking at me, but beyond my head.

"What are you looking at?"

"Oh, just the man who most likely left you that note at the tomb. But he's gone now."

"See, this is beyond weird. Renee, I'm not digging. I drove to New Orleans. I didn't plan any of this with Claire Landry, and I don't know what this all means."

"You walked into this by coming. Besides, our steps are guided by a destiny we don't always have a say in. But remember, the musical notes in a song or the words on a piece of paper, they don't get to tell you who you are or what you do."

We stood in silence for a moment.

Outside the wall, a snare drum rolled a crisp pattern—tat-tat-tat—like a parade getting ready.

Renee folded the paper and slipped it into my tote without asking. "It's possibly a warning. It could be a threat, or someone trying to clear their conscience. In this city, sinners leave breadcrumbs, too."

"Debts don't drown," I repeated.

"You won't drown if someone throws you a rope," she said.

I countered with my response. "I don't need a rope. I have a plan. I have the money. I can make this happen. I don't owe anyone anything." The protest came out small and childish, even to me.

Renee didn't argue. She just walked, and I followed, the path shifting under my feet like the whole cemetery had tilted a few degrees.

Near the exit, a tour group shuffled in with a guide waving a brochure like a parade flag. Renee threaded her arm through mine and steered us out onto the street, into the clatter and spice of the Quarter.

"Come on," she said. "The dead whispered. Now you need the part where the living shouts, so your bones don't rattle."

We walked straight into the city's bright noise, a brass band on the corner pushing air like it could inflate hope; a woman selling beignets from a stall, powdered sugar drifting like snow; a man in a Saints jersey promising the best oysters on earth if we'd follow him inside.

At one corner, a few blocks over, Renee gestured to the stone building with ferns that towered over us. "This place hosts an annual jazz festival that draws folks from all around. See there?" She pointed to a brass plaque glinting in the sunlight beside the three sets of double doors, its engraving reading: "With thanks to Remy Duval for his generous support of New Orleans jazz."

I shrugged, not sure why I cared about what this Duval man did, other than I knew his lounge being so close to my cafe might be a problem.

Renee went on, "Remy's been a big supporter of the cultural landmark here. Keeps the music alive, they say."

I nodded, although an unease settled in my chest at the name of Remy.

Renee pulled me along, and I bought a paper cone of candied pecans because I am a reasonable woman with a sweet tooth and a complicated past. Renee bought lemonade from a kid who called us "ma'am" so earnestly that I almost adopted him.

"I love it here," I said around a mouthful of sugar and crunch.

"You love the romance," she said. "Wait till the romance sends you a bill."

We turned onto Chartres, and I felt that magnetic pull toward the block where The Blue Door sat, flaking in its faded blue. Part of me wanted to march straight there and pry every secret out of the walls. Part of me wanted to drive straight back to Wyoming and pretend none of this existed.

Renee put a hand on my shoulder. "Don't go inside yet," she said. "Let the place miss you for a minute."

"Wait, I left my rental car back at the cemetery," I said, half turning.

"It'll be there," she said, "And parking spots are scarce. And so are buildings like this one. It's a prime location. And the story you're stepping into? That's the thing you gotta pay attention to."

We ducked into a narrow cafe around the corner with a chalkboard menu, with muffulettas wrapped like gifts, po'boys that looked like they could fix a broken heart. We claimed a corner table. The ceiling fan above us turned in lazy halos.

"This is the part where you breathe," Renee said, sliding a coffee toward me. "Cemeteries whisper. The Quarter shouts. You need both."

"But I've received two notes, in how many hours?" I started.

"You found a note," she said. "And last night, you found another. And before that, you found a body. None of that's small. But your path is charted like the river that runs south; you've come here for your next chapter."

I wrapped my fingers around the warm mug. "What do I do with these threats?"

"You outlast them," she said.

"I'll send Sergeant Laveau pictures of the notes and let her know. It can't hurt."

Renee sipped her coffee, which had more cream than brew. "You should let her know. She is a person who loves the truth."

"And you don't?" I let the coffee slide down my throat as I waited for her answer.

"I do, but it's hard to know who is on your side— sometimes."

"I'll remember that…" I said, the po'boys arriving at our table by the quick-footed, petite waitress.

Renee slid her coffee mug aside. "Emory, just surround yourself with people who love your dream as much as you do. That will help."

"People like you?" I asked, half-teasing.

She clinked her cup against mine. "Josie told me you're the sister everyone needs, just a little much sometimes."

My breath stopped for a second. "A little much?"

"Yeah, she's used to peace."

"I'm sure having my brother and me in her world disrupted that calm," I said, reassuring myself more than Renee.

Renee smiled. "Growing up with a brother who could be as mean as the devil was tough, too. But whoever the Lord sets on your stoop, they might be your family."

Before I could answer, a trumpet flared outside— bright, clean, impossible to ignore. I turned toward the window, already knowing.

Miles stood on the corner, horn lifted, case open at his feet. A small crowd had gathered: tourists with phones, locals with knowing eyes, a nurse in scrubs who'd stopped walking to listen. The notes soared, and the song he chose made me choke.

"I found my thrill…" I whispered.

"On Blueberry Hill," Renee finished, smiling.

"My hill is The Blue Door," I said.

"And Miles and Kermit?" she murmured. "They're your family, whether or not you planned it."

**

We stepped outside and joined the edge of the circle. Miles saw us and flashed a quick, shy smile mid-phrase, holding a note a beat too long because he could. Then he slid into something new, a melody I didn't know that still felt like prayer tugging on both God's sleeve and mine.

A large man stepped close to Miles's case and dropped a folded bill. Broad shoulders, gray ball cap, scar on his chin like a comma. A man from the cemetery. He didn't clap. Didn't smile. Just turned and walked away, leaning on the brick wall nearby.

"Hmm," Renee said under her breath. "It's time I put that one in the file."

"What file?" I whispered.

"The 'don't do me wrong' file," she said. "Thickest one I own."

The crowd thinned. Miles knelt and started stacking coins like little stair steps.

I walked over. "Are you playing for pancakes?"

"For a practice trumpet mute," he said, grinning. "But pancakes are good, too."

"You sound like a lawyer," I said.

"Daddy Kermit says play the truth," Miles said, shrugging. "And truth costs money."

Renee choked back a laugh. "Child, you got sermons in your pockets."

He looked up at me. "You opening The Blue Door soon? Mama said you're trying to save it."

News traveled fast here. Faster than my ability to process it.

"I'm trying," I said. "Miles, can I ask you something?"

"Sure," he said. "What you wanna know?"

I hesitated, then pushed my hair behind my ears. "Do you ever hear music when nobody's playing?"

Renee squinted at me. "That's an odd question."

Miles thought about it. "Music is alive all the time," he said. "Sometimes I hear Grandma Celeste when Daddy plays her songs, when he thinks I'm asleep at The Blue Door. It's like a humming in the walls. Like when you hold a seashell to your ear and pretend it's the ocean."

A shiver rippled over my arms. Renee bumped my shoulder, reminding me I was still connected to a dead body, a wreck, and an investigation, and for me, those notes felt like threats.

"You, okay?" she asked.

"Yes," I lied. "No. Maybe. Ask me after the grand opening of The Blue Door."

Miles counted his coins, snapped his case shut, and slung it over his shoulder. "I'm going home," he said. "Mama's making red beans."

"What's your mother's name?" I called.

"Naomi."

Renee waved, her manicured red nails flashing. "Tell Naomi I said hello."

I tugged on Renee's arm. "You know all of them, don't you?"

"Yes," she said. "They're neighbors. And family. Put those neighbors and family together in this town, and they'll fuss, fight, feed you, and save your life. Eventually, you'll see."

"Where can a girl get her nails done? I've thought about it, but life on a ranch doesn't allow for those brief splurges of primping." I asked, caught by the sparkle on Renee's hands, then gazing at my nails—clean, but clipper-trimmed, no polish.

"I know a girl a few blocks from here. She just fixed me up, ripped off two of them the other night… so she did mine just yesterday. Can't work in a hotel and invite guests in with sloppy, unkempt nails." She held her hands out in front of her, admiring them.

"I'll add that to my list for the grand opening: get a manicure."

As Miles trotted off, I glanced back toward Basin Street, and my mind wandered toward my wrecked car, the notes, the woman in the ditch, the detective's card in my pocket. Toward the cemetery and the words scrawled on tombs. And landed on *Debts don't drown. Stop digging, Emory.*

The city had spoken twice now. In stone. In ink. In trumpet notes and sideways looks from strangers. I came for a simple renovation—one encouraged by Josie, who was convinced I needed a change of scenery.

Yes, The Blue Door would get a coat of paint. A good cleaning. New lights. A cook and, yes, even a band.

However, I've walked straight into family ties I hadn't asked for, and warnings I wished would go away. A manicure wouldn't fix the uneven hangnails of life.

For the first time, it hit me that this wasn't just a trip to restore a bar and turn it into a cafe.

This was an invitation into a story I couldn't walk away from anymore. Josie may have pushed me some. Cal may have tried to talk me out of it. But with a mindset of finishing the task, I'm determined. This is happening despite the interruptions and those who wish I'd go home. But seriously, home in Wyoming was lovely at first, but lately I've become anxious.

Last year, a road trip to Cody solved three murders, something I never counted on, and landing there was a diversion from Texas life and my emotions, because before that, life was a blur of disconnected moments of longing for my dad and my mom.

As a girl, I wished my mother had lived so she and my dad could tuck me into bed, only to grow up with an overbearing uncle, Harlan, a not-so-kind man, and an overprotective aunt, Diane.

So maybe New Orleans can become the place I'll call home if everyone lets me mark off my list and open a cafe. I flew into town like a pelican migrating south, for the atmosphere and the romance of the lights. They are calling my name, so staying here might be worth considering if things go as planned, which hasn't quite begun that way.

I sent Cal an update via text, the unsettling messages making me chew through my gum faster than usual: Things are getting weirder here. I'm understanding why Dad never spoke of this place; it's layered with mystery.

I followed up by taking photos of the two notes and sent them to Laveau, but she didn't respond. Not that she had to.

Cal's answer came back: Do you need me there? It sounds like things are spinning. Keep me updated. Please.

I texted: I'm fine.

I added to my response with another text: I've walked off the worry of yesterday. I hope. Tomorrow's Monday. A fresh start. I'll keep you in the loop.

Yes, Sunday had gotten away, and for me, loneliness falls at sunset, no matter if the Mustangs roam or the rivers cascade.

No matter if the saxophone plays or the trumpet sings.

No matter what the Mississippi River says when the moon rises into the sky.

Sergeant Laveau texted back: Don't go out alone. Make sure you keep watch.

And I texted her: Okay.

But I knew I had arrived alone. So, my plans to honor her text might not come to pass, as I'm not calling Renee every time I step outside.

Chapter 6

Head in the Sand

ROOM 222 HAD GOOD INTENTIONS but not excellent follow-through; the bed was soft, the air conditioner hummed like a lullaby, and the blackout curtains did their level best. My brain, however, had other plans and kept replaying the last forty-eight hours.

Wreck. Ditch. Claire Landry. Pelican in the back seat. Police station. Windex Dupree. Kermit upstairs. Miles's trumpet. Renee Baptiste. Men at the cemetery. Debts don't drown. Stop digging, Emory.

My mind became a curated highlight reel of the last few days, on repeat.

Sometime around dawn, Monday morning, I finally drifted off, and when I woke, sunlight was leaking around the edges of the curtains like the day was apologizing for being late.

I stared at the ceiling and had a very mature, very reasonable thought: *Nope. We're not doing this today.*

I rolled over, grabbed my phone, and checked the time. Not too late, not too early. Just enough space to pretend this was a typical trip, in a normal city, doing everyday things, without bodies or notes or distant cousins.

I kicked off the covers and swung my legs over the side of the bed. "Okay, Emory," I said out loud. "Today is about cafe stuff. Nothing else."

The bathroom mirror was unkind but honest. My eyes looked like I'd borrowed them from someone who'd been crying on and off for a week. I washed my face, smoothed my chestnut hair into something less tragic, and pulled on jeans, a blue T-shirt, and my tennis shoes. Blue felt appropriate. It matched the door and my entire emotional situation. And then I brushed my teeth. Added a little foundation and blush. And popped in a piece of Spearmint gum.

I opened my tote on the bed. Dad's journal lay on top, weighty as always. The *debts don't drown*, note peeked out from between its pages. And the *stop digging* note sat crumpled in the side pocket where I'd shoved it last night.

I stared for a second, then decided.

"Absolutely not," I muttered.

I took both notes, folded them together, tucked them deeper into the journal, and slid the journal to the very bottom of the tote under my laptop, and beneath a stack of menu ideas I'd printed from Pinterest. If denial had a filing system, I'd nail it.

On top of everything, I laid my color-coded notebook on the bed—the one labeled: BLUE DOOR CAFE PLAN, DO NOT PANIC.

I flipped it open.

Today's list:
1. Meet with contractors.
2. Get quotes for electrical and plumbing.
3. Sketch the stage layout for a jazz band.
4. Have the piano tuned.
5. Start menu draft (chicory coffee, tea, pancakes, waffles, muffin lineup, etc.)
6. Do *not* get involved in any investigations.
7. Be thankful for Kermit. And Miles. At least, try.

I underlined numbers six and seven three times and circled them for emphasis.

The phone vibrated in my hand as if the universe wanted to argue. On the face of my phone, my brother's eyes showed, and his silly grin. "Cal?" I asked, though at first, I considered letting it go to voicemail, and guilt answered for me. "Hey, big brother," I said, trying for light.

"Hey," he said, his voice tight with that controlled calm he used when he was worried. "You, okay? You sound… tired."

"You know me," I said. "Thriving on chaos and Spearmint gum."

"Em," he warned.

I sighed. "I'm okay. Really. I survived the wreck, the pelican, the police station, and my rental car is a lovely shade of tortoise green."

He let out a breath that was half laugh, half groan. "Sergeant Laveau called last night."

My spine straightened. "She... what?"

"She said she wanted to confirm she had your emergency contact info right, and that you're not a suspect, but you're important to the investigation. Those were her words."

"Yeah," I said, my nervous energy tingling beneath my skin. "She told me not to leave town. Apparently, that's what happens when you trip over a dead woman."

Silence stretched between us.

Then Cal offered his brotherly advice. "The dead woman was someone's daughter or sister, maybe. Be kinder."

"Sorry, I'm just tired."

"You could come home," he said finally. "Let the city keep its secrets. Let the bar rot into the past, and we'll figure something else out to honor Dad. A bench. A plaque. I don't know. Something that doesn't involve notes and corpses."

The ache in my chest swelled. I thought of the ranch, my horse, Star, and the mountain air that smelled like pine and dirt and not like bourbon-soaked floorboards.

I imagined waking up in my room, hearing Aunt Diane humming in the kitchen, going out onto the porch, Cal talking to his horse, Renegade, and me riding my Mustang into the valley to quiet the noises in my head.

Safe. Predictable. Solid.

Instead, I said, "I can't just leave. I'm on the deed. Paid back taxes. I legally own The Blue Door. And I promised myself I'd do this for Dad. That compass he tossed into the trash can from outside the bar all those years ago, that Amos, his old friend, saved and gave to me. It's a sign."

"What kind of sign?"

I swallowed hard. "That broken compasses can point in other directions."

"That's not a sign. That's my sister making up stuff."

"I'm not making it up. The compass belonged to Dad. It's brought me here to honor him."

"Fine, but you also promised yourself you wouldn't die of stress by forty," he said. "How's that going?"

I rolled my eyes, even though he couldn't see it. "Look, I'm not investigating anything. The police can handle Claire's case. I'm just here to renovate. Make pancakes and muffins. Restore the building. Get my car fixed. Then I'm out."

"Emory…"

"I mean it, Cal," I insisted. "I don't have to dig into every mystery that walks by. I did that already with last year's road trip and the missing women. I'm retired from trauma." Those words spewed from my mouth, but if I were to tell the truth, solving those crimes came with a certain adrenaline rush.

He was quiet for a long time. "You can say that, Em," he said. "But this place is tied to Dad and to Celeste, and now to that woman in the ditch—so you know you won't leave this alone."

"You're mistaken." I cut in, sharper than I meant to. "I'm tired today, but when I get some sleep, I'll be better. I want one thing in my life that doesn't bleed when I touch it."

The words hung there between us, raw and honest.

"Okay," he said finally. "Okay. I hear you." His voice softened. "I just… wish I could be there. You know. Run interference. Bring snacks."

"You being here would make it harder to leave if I need to," I said. "One of us has to be functional back home."

"Who says I'm functional?" he asked, and I could hear the smile trying to come back. "A few years sober doesn't mean four years sane."

"It's more than some people have," I said gently.

"Fine. I'll stay here, help on the ranch, and keep Aunt Diane from worrying herself into a new dimension. You just—"

"Stay out of trouble," I finished.

"And call me," he added. "Every day. Or I'll start calling the hotel and asking for my emotionally unstable sister in Room 222."

I snorted. "You would."

"In a heartbeat," he said. "I love you, Em."

"Love you too," I said, throat tight.

When the call ended, I stared at my reflection in the dark TV screen.

Head in the sand.

That's what I wanted—a day where the biggest problem I had was whether to consider serving a Tuesday special of banana pancakes or lemon-blueberry.

I wanted a life where my dad hadn't disappeared into secrets and distance, hadn't left journals behind instead of memories. A childhood where he'd been there, hands on the piano keys and on my shoulders, not just on other people's stories.

I wanted the ordinary life I'd never had and could never get back.

Instead, I had a rental car, a rundown bar, and two threatening notes sharing space with my to-do list.

"Pancakes," I told my reflection. "Start with pancakes."

The walk to The Blue Door felt almost normal, if you ignored the part where I scanned every block for gray ball caps and scars and glanced over my shoulder with each step.

The city was awake in a different way on Monday morning. Delivery trucks blocked lanes, restaurant workers hosed down sidewalks, and a sleepy brass player practiced scales on a balcony with his hair standing up as if it hadn't caught up yet.

Inside, The Blue Door smelled like yesterday: dust, old wood, faint mildew, and the ghost of spilled liquor. The air had a thickness to it, as if all the lives lived here had left something behind that refused to clear.

"Today," I told the room, "We focus on paint chips and not on death. Deal?"

The room did not answer.

I set my tote on the bar, dug out Dad's journal, and— before I could change my mind—slid it into a cabinet under the counter. I placed the two notes beside it, as if I were putting away dishes I didn't want to see.

"There," I said. "You can stay here and marinate. I've got work to do."

I spread my sketches across the bar. Stage layout, table positions, a spot where the espresso machine would go, and how to make sure whoever sat in the back corner still felt close to the music. It felt good to think about angles and light and sound instead of motives and last sightings.

The front door creaked open.

"If this is a ghost," I said, without looking up, "I am not in the mood."

"Ghosts don't knock, Blueberry Girl," Windex's voice announced. "They just rearrange your furniture."

I glanced up to see Winston "Windex" Dupree filling the doorway, grinning like hospitality and chaos had a child, and it was him. He wore a faded T-shirt that said *JAZZ IS A VERB* and carried a paper bag that smelled suspiciously like donuts.

"You brought a peace offering," I said. "You may enter."

He strutted in and set the bag on the bar. "Two beignets and a plain donut," he said. "The donut is for balance."

I tore open the bag and smiled. "Bless you," I said. "I didn't have breakfast. Just nerves and hotel coffee."

He perched on a barstool, spinning halfway around to survey the room. "So," he said casually, "you heard any more about the lady in the ditch?"

I froze mid-bite.

"No," I said, dusting powdered sugar off my fingers. "And I don't need to. That's the police's job. Mine is pancakes."

He raised an eyebrow. "Sergeant Laveau stopped by my block this morning," he said. "Asking questions about Claire.

She also went to Remy's bar. Asking things. Making folks uncomfortable."

I squinted at him. "How do you know that?"

"Because I hear things," he said. "I talk to people. And also, because drunks talk too much when you play the right chords."

"I'm not a detective," I said firmly. "I'm not investigating Claire. I'm not investigating anyone. I'm renovating."

He studied me for a long moment. "You keep saying that," he murmured.

"Because it's true."

"Or because you want it to be."

Before I could snap back, there was another knock at the door. Sharp, official. The knock that didn't ask permission so much as announce its presence.

I set the donut down and wiped my hands. "If that's my sanity, tell it I'm busy."

Windex slid off the stool. "That's the police," he said. "They knock like that when they already know the answer."

I opened the door to find Sergeant Laveau standing there, hair pulled tight, expression neutral, her green eyes taking in everything behind me.

"Ms. Vaughn," she said. "Mind if I come in?"

"Sure," I said, stepping aside. "We're open for business to law enforcement and semi-strangers with donuts."

Her mouth almost twitched, but she let it pass. She clocked Windex with a glance.

"Mr. Dupree," she said.

"Sergeant," he replied, tipping an invisible hat. "I was just leaving."

"No, you weren't," she said mildly. "But you can sit."

He did.

She turned her attention back to me. "We're still working on Claire Landry's timeline," she said. "I wanted to touch base with you in person and see if you remembered anything else."

I shook my head. "I never saw her before the ditch. I swear. I just… landed on her. Literally."

Her gaze softened a fraction. "I know this is hard," she said. "You did the right thing calling 911."

I hesitated. "Did she have family?"

"A sister here," Laveau said. "A brother in Lafayette. They're on their way."

Guilt stabbed me. I imagined someone getting that call and coming to identify the woman, the one I'd met only as a body in the grass.

"We have witnesses who say Claire was last seen at Remy's bar," Laveau said. "Right next door to your place. With someone."

"We keep hearing that," Windex muttered. "Remy's— where you go to drink and forget who you left with."

Laveau ignored him. "I also got your text that you received a note on your car and at the cemetery," she continued, looking at me carefully. "Stop digging, Emory. Want to tell me about that?"

My heart thumped harder. "It was on my car," I said. "Under the wiper. I didn't see who left it."

"Do you have it?"

"Yes," I said. "It's… under the bar, on a shelf." I moved intentionally, as if any sudden movement might make this feel more real than it already did. I reached into the journal and grabbed both notes, handing her the one from the car.

She read it, jaw tightening. "And the other one?" she asked.

I blinked. "This one is from the cemetery."

"Yes, Renee also called me and told me you found a note at the cemetery."

I shot an incredulous look at the ceiling. "Of course she did."

Laveau studied both notes and said, "Someone wants you to think you're in danger," she said. "Or wants to scare you off from whatever they think you might find."

"I'm not trying to find anything," I insisted. "I'm trying to open a cafe. That's it. No mysteries. I'm finished with family secrets and unsolved cases. I'm done."

Laveau looked around at the sagging beams, the stage, and the piano in the corner. "Places like this have long memories," she said. "People talk. Maybe Claire heard something at Remy's. Maybe she asked the wrong person the right question."

"That's not on me," I said, heat rising in my face. "I didn't even know this place existed most of my life. I didn't know my dad played here until last year. I don't want—" My voice broke. I swallowed. "And if Claire came here, I wasn't even in town to see her. And I don't want this to be my life."

The sergeant slipped both notes into an evidence envelope. "You're not to blame for what other people did," she said. "But you're here now. And whoever wrote these knows that."

I exhaled shakily. "So, what do you want me to do? Close the place and run home?"

Her eyes met mine, steady. "That's your call," she said. "I can't make it for you. But I will say this—if you notice anything else out of place, if anyone bothers you, you call me. Right away. And don't go poking around Remy's alone."

"Wouldn't dream of it," I said. "I'm allergic to sticky floors and bad lighting."

She let out a breath that might have been a laugh. "Stay safe, Ms. Vaughn."

After she left, the room felt heavier.

"You, okay?" Windex asked quietly.

"No," I said. "But I have a plan, and I have a list. It's what I do."

He nodded, but his expression said he didn't believe me.

I sat on a barstool and stared at my notebook. "I want simple," I said to no one in particular. "I want an ordinary life. Is that too much to ask?"

Images crowded in, like shadows, with Dad at a piano with me pressed against his side, learning chords instead of reading about crimes; birthdays at The Blue Door with music and cake instead of long drives and unanswered questions; Cal and me growing up with a father who stayed put, who didn't leave journals instead of his presence.

A life where The Blue Door was just a cafe with decent pancakes. Where Claire Landry was at home, not in a ditch. Where Celeste was still singing.

I blinked hard and pulled myself back to the present.

That was the plan. Renovate. Rebuild. Refurbish. Pretend the notes were just some messed-up prank. Let the police handle the investigation. Stay on my side of the line.

I picked up a pen, flipped to a clean page, and wrote at the top:

TO-DO: MAKE THIS PLACE NORMAL.

Underneath, I added:

- Call electrician
- Order paint samples
- Research coffee suppliers
- Ignore ghosts
- Ignore threats
- Ignore the man with the scar and the gray cap
- Get a manicure

Outside, faint but unmistakable, a trumpet line floated in from the street, someone practicing scales, bending notes. Miles. Maybe. Another musician. Possibly.

Windex moved to the windows. "Streets are busy with music today."

I closed my eyes for a second, letting the sound wash over me.

I wanted to stay safe, small, and far away from trouble.

But trouble, it seemed, had already written my name and followed me here.

7

Enemies & Allies

AFTER A STRING OF PHONE calls and appointments set for several contractors to come out, like adding a new commercial kitchen, which, somehow, got left off the list, Renee held my arm in hers, her heels the click of grace as we shuffled outside to the sidewalk.

Even with plans in place, I still half-wished the city would let me back out quietly. I hadn't truly weighed my decisions, just jumped at the chance, knew Dad's inheritance money could make it happen, and had to be busy doing something productive—to make a difference, to shut down the noise inside my head.

The Blue Door squatted behind us now, stubborn and watchful, wedged between the trinket shop and Duval's Lounge like it had been assigned this exact spot by history and dared anyone to argue.

I glanced back once—to make sure the door was closed, to reassure myself that nothing had shifted while we stood outside as I wrestled with ghosts. Not that it mattered, the locks in the alley on both doors were broken.

"Renee," I said, nodding toward the trinket shop as we moved outside, "Who owns that place?"

The windows were dark, crowded with masks, tarnished mirrors, strings of beads, and objects that looked like they'd lived several lives already. A hand-painted sign in the window read *OPEN*, through the door.

She didn't answer right away.

"Someone," she said finally. "No one. Depends on who you ask."

"That's not comforting. Whoever owns that place is my neighbor."

She cleared her throat. "Hmm, the place changes hands. Folks don't keep it long."

"So, who runs it now?" I asked, pulling on her arm.

As we slowed, the bell inside the shop jingled once.

We both stopped.

The door hadn't opened.

The bell hadn't been touched.

A shape moved behind the glass—just enough to disturb the reflection. Not a face. Just presence.

"Did you hear that?" I started.

Renee took my hand. "Don't stare," she whispered. "That place notices curiosity."

I stood just outside my front door, and it was as if the shop leaned closer, trying to memorize me. And I glanced down, as something else caught my eye.

Black scuff marks on the sidewalk were evident on the concrete just beyond The Blue Door's threshold, where a patch of grass had grown in the crack, with small black smears from maybe shoes, like someone had slipped and caught themselves.

I turned back and moved closer to my door; the lock plate bore a fresh scratch, too, that I didn't remember from before. Or maybe I'd been too rattled to notice.

Either way, the tiny hairs on my arms rose.

"Renee," I said, pointing. "Someone's been trying to get in, but we both know you can get in from the alley, too."

"Well," she said, scanning the block. "Let's hope nobody tried the back way."

A metal scraping pierced the air, my ears objecting, and I covered them with my hands. The sound came from next door at Duval's Lounge through an open window. And ice shifted with the sound like a metal scoop dropping ice into glasses.

Then laughter—too sharp, too knowing.

A round man wearing a freshly ironed white shirt leaned out the door's entrance to Duval's Lounge and held a cigar like it was his sword.

Renee leaned in close to me. "That's Remy Duval. And he's trouble."

"I gathered," I said, knowing trouble followed me lately.

Remy shuffled toward us, sleeves rolled, tie loosened, gray whiskers shadowing his jaw. His eyes skimmed us like inventory.

"Ladies," he said pleasantly, like a blade wrapped in silk. "Early stroll on a Monday evening?"

Pam Kumpe

"Just walking," Renee replied, charm reinforced with steel, but Remy touched her arm, and she jerked it away.

His gaze settled on me and lingered. "Ms. Vaughn."

"Mr. Duval," I said politely, my toes curling. "Nice to meet you."

He nodded toward the scuffed threshold. "Looks like your part of the street is gaining fans. Careful with admirers. They get possessive."

"Like creditors?" I asked.

Renee's glance flicked to me—approval and caution braided together.

"Debts are just love notes with due dates," Remy said.

"And what's owed is owed," I replied.

"Always." His smile widened. "Repaint that thing another color besides blue, and I might forget to hate it."

"I'll paint it the color of mercy. And blue is my favorite color."

His eyes sharpened. "Mercy's expensive. Debts must be paid."

"Regret is expensive too," I said.

Renee nudged me, a jab with a polished fingernail.

Remy laughed once, a hollow growl. "See you around."

As he passed the trinket shop, he flicked his eyes toward its window, and the bell over the door chimed again.

Then he went around the corner, the other way.

We stood there, listening to the hum of his world seep under our threshold like fog.

"You feel that?" Renee asked.

"Yes."

"That's not weather."

I placed my palm against The Blue Door. The wood was warm; the paint flaking under my skin.

I turned to Renee. "I'm not leaving."

"Good," she said. "Then we make you unmovable."

We turned to go, and that's when the trinket shop door creaked open.

Not dramatically.

Not like an invitation.

More like a sigh.

A man stepped into the doorway, tall and lean, posture guarded. His tan skin carried the same warm undertone as Renee's. His hair was threaded with a shade of dark blond, pulled back tight behind his ears.

He held a cup of coffee in one hand and a string of beads in the other.

"Still pulling folks around town by the elbow, Renée Baptiste?" He asked, almost as if he knew the answer. His voice was calm, edged. "City's got legs. People can think for themselves. Give folks some space and let them breathe. Remember, losing someone you love changes everything."

Renee stopped cold and spun. "Lucien," she said. Not sharp. Not warm. Just true. "Didn't know you were open."

"I'm always open," he said. "Just not always welcoming to certain women in heels and painted nails and too much makeup."

His gaze slid to me, curious now. Measuring. Not predatory like Remy's, more surgical.

"And you must be the Vaughn girl," he said. "The one with the blue door and the long shadows."

"I didn't realize I was famous," I said.

"You're not," he replied. "But buildings talk. And yours has been clearing its throat."

Renee's fingers tightened on my arm. "Lucien, don't."

"Don't what?" he asked mildly. "Tell the truth? Or remind you we share blood?"

I glanced between them. "You're related?"

"Unfortunately," Lucien said.

"Estranged," Renee corrected. "By choice."

"By survival," he said evenly.

The bell jingled behind him, though no one touched it.

Lucien nodded toward a piece of blue chalk now resting on the windowsill of The Blue Door. "That ain't mine," he said. "But it's a warning."

"A warning from whom?" I asked.

He met my eyes. "From someone who wants debts paid."

The street behind us swelled with sound—brass and laughter—as a second line rounded the corner.

Lucien stepped back. "Be careful, Emory Vaughn. This city loves redemption stories. But it collects interest."

Then he disappeared into the shop. The door closed. And the bell stayed silent.

Renee didn't speak until the first trumpet cracked the air from someone down the street. "That," she said quietly. "Is my brother."

"And he knows more than he's saying," I replied.

She nodded once. "He always does."

"And you knew he was my neighbor," I said, my tone cracking with accusation.

"I try not to say his name."

The city answered before I could say more.

Brass lifted the air. Parasols twirled.

Strangers refused to stay strangers.

Someone pressed a strand of beads into my hand.

Someone laughed as if they'd been waiting all day.

"A second line," Renee grinned. "Come on, Emory. Let's get your life to dancing."

"I don't dance."

She didn't listen.

Joy swept past Duval's door without permission. Remy now stood stone-faced in the doorway again, tipping his hat as if he were in charge of the parade.

As the marchers curled away, the world tilted into alignment.

The dead had whispered.

The living had shouted.

And The Blue Door stood in the middle—waiting.

"City of the Dead," I murmured.

"Loudest place in town," Renee said. "Now go write your menu and your action plan."

"My action plan?"

"You'll need locks that don't lie," she said, nodding toward Duval's bar. "He and his friends don't scare, and you might secure a lawyer with teeth and a hymnbook."

I smiled despite myself, spine finding steel. "I can make another list. I do like to write my plan."

"Make two."

We stood on the sidewalk a moment longer, not having gone far at all. "This place can be redeemed," I said.

"So can people," Renee replied. "Or most." And she glanced at her brother's trinket shop. "Some are beyond hope."

"Now that doesn't sound like the Renee I met a few days ago," I said, moving my bangs out of my eyes.

"Well, with my brother, Lucien, he's like a cat that's outlived its nine lives. He's scratched and clawed many times, too many. So, space helps, and I stay away from him."

Behind us, The Blue Door breathed, and I hung on to stubborn hope, one I plan to implement by serving up jazz with blueberry pancakes.

I thought I heard a low woman's hum, a piano warming up, and a river practicing forgiveness.

For one suspended beat, the city held its breath with me.

Then the bell above the trinket shop door trembled—a thin ripple of a sound.

The opening of a song, maybe.

Back inside The Blue Door, the air was warmer than outside—a warmth that remembered bodies and wanted more of them. A fresh group of dust motes lifted like they'd been waiting, and I'd caught them mid-flight, but more appeared with each swing of my hand.

I walked the floor slowly, each creak another verse in a song I hadn't learned yet. When I reached the narrow nook beside the stairs, where the wall bowed like it was exhaling—I stopped.

Something fluttered.

A thin brown ribbon caught on a nail head.

"Nylon?" Renee said, plucking it free. "Cassette tape?"

My throat tightened. "My aunt Diane said my dad recorded everything. Reel-to-reel. Back then, he would have used cassettes. Most were lost, I'm sure." I hesitated. "Celeste's music, too."

Renee dropped it into my palm. It curled there like a question mark.

And just like that, denial cracked, and my life's reel broke into pieces of stray relatives and people who don't want me here, made me question coming to New Orleans.

But I wanted pancakes and paint samples. I wanted control. I wanted an ordinary life where secrets don't hum in the walls.

Instead, I had a neighboring bar owner with predatory eyes and a cassette tape in my hand.

"Wait," I said, staring at the wall. "Last year, when Gus showed Cal and me this place, we went down an old staircase. Underground."

Renee nodded. "Right here, next to the wall leading to where your kitchen will be. There's a lever that moves the flooring, and the stairs go to the basement. Kermit has shown me boxes down there. Old instruments. Records. Sheet music."

My heart skipped a beat, having forgotten the basement room from the orchestrated tour Gus gave last year.

"That's where I found Camille Thornton's silver Concho from her saddle. She was my dad's fiancée in Wyoming, and she's never been here. And his having it in Louisiana, tucked inside a box, incriminated Gus."

Renee exhaled slowly. "Celeste, Camille. Lila. Their lives were too short. But it seems a lot of the evidence that put Gus away was… circumstantial."

"True, but a conviction happened despite it." A tear escaped before I could stop it. "You know their names?"

"Yes, I've read every news story about Gus during his trial," Renee said, swallowing hard.

"I did, too. I noticed how some reporters made the women appear less-than-innocent in their part."

"People love a good-bad girl story, I suppose."

I cleared my throat. "My uncle Harlan wasn't too innocent in his dealings with Gus, either. My aunt struggled to find her joy this past year, and now I'm here doing this— and for what?"

"For your dad," Renee said, nodding.

I changed the subject. "Did you see how Remy looked at the scuffs on the sidewalk? It's like he knows what happened there."

"That man thinks the world owes him," Renee said. "Stay out of his way."

I clutched the piece of cassette tape ribbon between my fingers, not realizing I'd twirled in like a rubber band— knowing the past held answers on tape, somewhere.

Chapter 8

What Are You Afraid of?

I COULDN'T FALL ASLEEP OR stay asleep.

Not because of the music and laughter outside—New Orleans never apologized for being awake—but because my nightmares arrived like a spiral staircase with no landing. Each step pulled on my heart, stretching it farther than it should go, tugging memories into shapes they'd never held in real life.

The Blue Door creaked and slipped into my dreams like it remembered everyone who'd ever laughed or lied inside it. Faces blurred. Voices overlapped.

And when I opened my eyes, all I could see was my daddy's face—young, tired, smiling like he knew something I didn't.

Around midnight, I'd given up pretending rest would come and slipped from the Royal Straight Hotel and walked the few blocks to The Blue Door, the city quieter now but never silent. I pulled the old stool up to the bar, set a bottle of water from my bag on the counter, and lit the same candle from the other night, happy that the matches were on the shelf beneath the bar. The flame flickered, bending and wavering like it knew secrets, too.

I pushed the lever that opened to the basement and pointed my phone toward the downstairs, turning on the flashlight. I stepped slowly, the creaking of each step, lowering me to the underground area.

"Nothing but old boxes. Storage of the past. Perhaps a place to keep our kitchen supplies. But it's so out of the way, an awkward room at best."

I went back up, when my dad's words echoed from his journal: *You can't rebuild what you don't face.*

I didn't know if he meant walls or wounds. Besides, he never faced me, unless it was a holiday or birthday—and then sometimes he missed some of those.

My bitterness showed up like a broken compass, and I wiped the tear from my eye.

The candle sputtered on the wick.

Then something thumped on the second floor, upstairs.

Not a pipe. Not the wind.

A footstep.

Slow.

Purposeful.

I hesitated, then curiosity, stubborn, bossy, dressed up like faith, nudged me toward the stairs. Each step groaned beneath my weight, the sound too loud in the quiet.

Halfway up, I caught a scent I hadn't noticed before, old tobacco and lemon polish, layered like a memory someone had cleaned but never quite erased.

The upstairs hallway stretched, narrow, faded wallpaper curling at the edges. A door at the end stood open, warm light spilling through from a flashlight propped on a small table. I'm not sure why I'd waited to check out the second floor of the bar, only that by finally climbing the steps, I might find answers I can't seem to see in the daylight.

"Kermit?" I called softly.

Silence.

Inside a room, a saxophone gleamed under the beam of light from the window, polished, loved. A cot sat against the wall. An old record player rested nearby, the cord resting on the floor waiting for electricity to bring it to life, and a Louis Armstrong album sat halfway out of its sleeve.

Kermit Delacroix sat in the corner, adjusting his mouthpiece.

"You move quietly for someone who doesn't belong here," he said without looking up.

"I didn't mean to intrude," I said. "I couldn't sleep and came over here to think. Then I… heard something."

"Walls talk at night," he replied. "They gossip more than the Quarter."

I noticed a worn Bible on a shelf. Music books were stacked beside it, and the dent near the bell of his sax was shaped like a thumbprint.

"So," I said carefully. "You really are living here? But you're going to have to leave. And I'll need your key. I need a clean slate. Maybe this won't work out, with you staying here."

He snorted. "Back door doesn't lock, and the rope loops around the casing to keep it pulled tight. Been that way since I got out."

I coughed, fully aware of the two entrances in the alley and their inability to keep folks out. "What did you mean by 'since you got out'?" I asked.

His face tightened. "Angola. Six years. Got out two years ago."

The word *Angola* shifted the room.

"I'm sorry," I said, knowing it wasn't enough, and hearing that my cousin served time didn't make my heart stop from pounding like a hailstorm in winter.

"This ain't my actual long-term home," he added. "But I keep the ghost of my mama's past company. It tips better than people."

I hesitated, then asked the question that had been pressing on me since our first meeting. "What really happened to your mother? I mean, what do you remember?"

He met my eyes. "She trusted the wrong man."

I wiped my nose, the itch of my questions growing. "Gus Tiller was slick. Lots of those types around."

"Hey, you pointing at me, now?" He asked.

"No, it's just that we barely know each other."

Kermit sighed. "True. Not my fault. Not yours. Our paths only crossed now because of your dad's journal."

"Wait, you know about the journal?"

"News travels. I listen. I watch. I take notes." Kermit touched his saxophone, like he loved music more than people. "You know, Gus made promises to my mama. Made money. And made her dead."

I swallowed. "And you remember him?"

"Yes, he took her away from me. You don't forget that. I was twelve and angry," he said. "Still am."

Kermit played a few haunting, low, and long notes. The same ones Miles played after *Blueberry Hill.*

"That song," I said. "Is it hers?"

"Yes, my mama wrote it," he replied quietly. "Called it *Blue Shadows.* I don't remember the words, just the sound."

Then he told me about the tin box, the one he pulled from behind his cot.

"Before she died, my mama told me to hide it. She said that if anything ever happened to her, this box would explain why. When I got out of prison, it was the first thing I had to see, besides my boy, Miles."

"Why a tin box?" I asked, yawning, not sure if sleep called me or if his story made me worry if he might be a little slick, too.

He opened the lid and pulled out a photograph of Celeste and a Duval's Lounge matchbook with words scribbled inside: Debt paid. Keep your mouth shut.

"The notes just keep showing up. They're wearing me out," I snarled. Then I squinted, glancing at a beautiful photo of a woman wearing a red gown on the stage at The Blue Door. "She was..."

"...my mama," Kermit said, his voice cracking.

"But the matchbook? Why would it have Remy's bar logo on it with such a note, if Gus was her killer?"

"Remy and Gus go way back. Money favors. Even got myself trapped in Remy's laundering game, which put me in jail for a time. I'm done with him and his schemes."

I moved to the window, and the light outside was blue like sorrow. I glanced down at the street, and the late-night drinkers were still out, laughing, staggering, and hanging onto each other.

"Hey, Kermit, tell me about Lucien?"

"His mind is good. His reactions, well, not the best. He gets mixed up, yells a lot, causes a ruckus, then hides out. Let's just say when I went to prison, he should have too."

"So, should I be afraid of him…"

Kermit interrupted me. "Or should you be afraid of me?"

"Stop that; you're not helping when you say those things." I barked.

"You need new locks. And it might be a good reason to keep me close. We are family," he snickered.

"True. Neither of us had a say about how that happened or unfolded, did we?"

"Nope, life doesn't come with a handbook for picking out your relatives."

"I would have picked my brother, Calvin. You'd like him. He's annoying but has a good heart."

"Never had a brother. Or a sister. Or a dad. Just a mama for a short time." Kermit joined me by the window. "Emory, it's really time for you to lock your doors. Remy's watching you. And so is Lucien."

"What? So, both of my business neighbors have it out for me?" I laughed, a slight chuckle, a pretend sound of bravery, because the shadows from both sides of The Blue Door were casting darkness at my feet, as if fingers of the past were grabbing for me.

A panic inside rose from my shaking knees to my shoulders, the kind that jerks you awake from sleep, and it sends me running when I'm wide awake.

"I've got to go. This is too much. I just wanted to open a nice cafe and bring jazz to the stage."

I skipped every other step on the stairs, stumbling on most of them. I wasn't brave. I was overwhelmed. And for the first time since I arrived in New Orleans, leaving felt like survival.

Chapter 9

Of Lights and Noise

DOWNSTAIRS, THE CANDLE ON the bar flickered, the wick nearly gone, and I blew it out, turning to face the flickering of yet another set of lights.

Through the windows on the first floor, the ribbon of red and blue strobes stopped me in my tracks.

I stood there staring at them, the city already dressed in moonlight, and something was off, and I bumped into the chairs next to the front door, and I called, "Kermit?"

He stepped out from behind me, having followed me downstairs. His eyes were bloodshot, the first I'd noticed. "Police are coming."

"What?"

"I saw them fighting," he said. "Lucien Baptiste and the woman from the ditch. Claire."

The words landed like bricks.

"I watched them from my room upstairs. She pulled away. Lucien grabbed her arm. He slapped her. She fell to the sidewalk, and he pulled her to her feet."

"What? And now, you tell me this?" I pushed Kermit like a cousin would, slugging his shoulder to make the world stop throwing surprises at me.

"Stop hitting me. I'm not your punching bag."

"Sorry, you were the closest thing, and I swing and ask questions later."

"Poor Calvin. You must have hit him a lot growing up." Kermit grinned, his teeth reflecting the flash of lights outside.

I clasped my hands. "Sorry, some habits are hard to break."

"Tell me about it." Kermit inched next to me. "As for Lucien, he hit her. She fell. But he's not a killer. He helped her up, too. He's loud and in your face sometimes, but only if you push him. He gambles with his money more than he should, too."

"So why are the police here? What is going on?" I asked, the nightmare of staying awake, worse than going to sleep.

Kermit went on, "It's all on the cameras, and my face is there in the window upstairs, too. Windex said it was on the streets—about the cameras."

"So, they've come for you? Or Lucien?" My arms extended wide, like propellers.

"Don't hit me, please." Kermit flinched, his face like a boy who'd endured the pain of life's slaps too many times.

"Sorry, what is the truth here?" I demanded, my body shaking with fear at what I might learn.

"I'm still on supervision. Wrong place. Wrong time. Puts me back inside prison."

"But the cameras should clear you."

"They will show part of this story, but not all. Across the street, the cameras at the T-shirt shop caught Lucien pointing at me as if I were involved."

"Wait, how do you know this?"

"Windex told me earlier when I was playing my sax with Miles at the corner. He overheard them talking at the police station since he got picked up for sitting in a fountain to wash his clothes, using his washboard to clean his shirt."

More sirens approached, and the street held patrol cars beyond each corner.

I moved to the sidewalk and into the shadows, with Kermit remaining inside the bar.

Sergeant Laveau stepped from her patrol car, calm but final. "We have surveillance footage," she said. "And a witness."

Kermit joined us before she asked about him. "I'm her witness. I'm ready to give my statement."

And he followed her to the open door of the patrol car and curled into the backseat like a child watching his life unravel.

Next door, the incessant knocking of two officers continued on the trinket shop door. They called Lucien's name, and the night hummed with noise like oversized crickets were set loose at midnight.

I lingered by the streetlight as a few suits went inside The Blue Door, to make sure Lucien wasn't in my place. They left after a few minutes.

Movement. Shadows. Red lights. The Blue Door. The trinket shop. Confusion. Shouting and too much noise.

Renee arrived, unsteady, wearing purple house shoes, flamingo-printed PJs, no makeup, hair in a ponytail, and tears streaming down her face over a partially fresh scratch mark on her cheek. "I just heard that my brother is involved in Claire's death. Seriously, what is wrong with my brother?"

"What happened to your face?" I asked, pointing.

"It's nothing. Make-up keeps it covered. Ran into an old fence plank in the alley behind my hotel." She ran her fingers over the scratch and took a deep breath.

Lucien was arrested within the hour.

Handcuffs. No resistance. No eye contact.

Only a slight jingle from the bell to his trinket store when he exited with the two officers.

Kermit rode with the sergeant, and his glance told me more than I wished; it was as if he knew who killed Claire Landry.

Renee collapsed into a chair inside The Blue Door, the moon lighting her face through the window, her ashen color paler than it should be, the scratch mark bright red, like her nails, as if grief had knocked her knees out from under her.

"I can't believe this is happening."

I didn't respond.

She wept. I sat. And we talked a little.

Shuffled footsteps from people checking out the excitement soon slowed outside, and by five in the morning, we were still sitting there, half asleep, worried, numb, and lost in the layers of life.

"I've got to go see what they have on my brother. I can't just sit here. I can't believe he's ruining our family name." Renee's hand went to her mouth. "Lucien. He's my brother. I've got to help if I can."

She rushed to the door, only to crash right into Windex.

"Nice flamingos," Windex said, grinning, and he held his washboard close and reached for his head as if another hangover lingered.

"Stop with the jokes. I need to help my brother." Renee growled.

Windex snapped, a low response. "Since when?"

I marched up to him. "If you're going to work here or help me, get a jazz band together; that bottle you find needs to disappear. I will not have you coming to my cafe drunk."

Windex played a rough sound on his washboard. "Yes, Boss Lady."

"I'm serious."

"Yes, ma'am," Windex said, nodding and announcing, "Lucien may seem guilty. But Kermit knows what he saw. Claire's death goes deeper than the shadows that seem to fall in the French Quarter. And maybe the local drunk knows more than them all."

Windex's words hung in the air longer than his washboard notes.

Renee remained frozen mid-step near the door, her hand gripping the frame as if it were the only thing holding her upright. "What do you mean by that?" she demanded, her voice sharp but trembling underneath. "What do you know?"

Windex scratched his chin, eyes squinting toward the street as if he could still see the patrol cars that were long gone. "Folks talk when they think nobody's listening. And cops talk when they're tired. And people talk loudly when they think they've already won."

**

The sun rose and morning came as it does each day. The night blurred into another memory I didn't want, and for some reason, Renee never left to check on her brother.

Kermit slid into the room, startling me, appearing from the shadows, and crossed his arms. "I know Lucien didn't do it? Claire was alive when she left Lucien's side."

"Wait, the police let you go already?" I interrupted.

"Yes, it's a revolving door there." Kermit turned to Windex. "Tell me what you know."

"I'm saying," Windex replied slowly, "That guilt don't always show its face."

Renee let out a sound that was half laugh, half sob. "My brother has been in trouble his whole life. He always thought he could outthink consequences. But murder?" She rocked her head. "Claire was irritating, yes. Nosy. Always digging, always asking Lucien for money. But killing her? That's not Lucien."

"You didn't see his face that night. Someone paid him to rough her up," Kermit said with confidence.

"No, he's not that kind of man." Renee spun toward him. "Lucien wouldn't take money to hurt his girlfriend."

"What? Claire Landry was Lucien's girlfriend?" I screamed, not sure why everyone thought it was necessary to keep me out of the loop. "Why hasn't anyone told me this?"

Kermit shrugged. "It wasn't for me to tell."

Renee let out a long sigh. "He's a blemish. A bad seed in our family. But Lucien isn't a killer."

Kermit didn't flinch. "Hey, Ms. Renee, remember how Lucien pushed you off the slide in the park when we were kids? And you beat him up."

"Stop it. He's always overreacted." Renee shouted, her southern squeal like a pelican's honk. "I'm tough when I need to be."

"My point, exactly," Kermit said.

I winced at what they weren't saying.

Two officers passed by the window, and the four of us stopped talking, walked outside, and marched behind them like a parade with horns and drums, to see where they were going.

Renee gasped and rushed forward before I could stop her. "You have the wrong guy. My brother wouldn't kill anyone."

The officer turned back. "That's not what the footage shows."

Windex mouthed, "The footage shows what they want it to show."

Renee clutched the officer by the arm. "My brother is many things, but not a killer."

The officer's voice dropped. "The truth will come out."

Windex whispered in my ear. "You think Claire was alone that night? You think she didn't owe people? You think Remy Duval didn't know she'd been asking questions, trying to blackmail him to pay off her gambling debt and that of Lucien's?"

I pushed Windex aside. "That's enough."

Windex played a tune on his washboard and leaned on a street pole. "The Blue Door's been boarded up for a reason, Emory Vaughn. The shadows live on."

"Well, it's time for them to fall," I said, wishing I knew how to make that happen.

The officers disappeared inside the trinket store, and the chime above the door remained silent. And I took notice that silence can tell you a lot about the present.

Renee scooted back inside The Blue Door, collapsed against the bar on a stool, shaking now, panic fully unleashed. "This is my fault," she sobbed. "I brought you here to New Orleans. And I've let my brother stay hidden with his mental state for too long."

"You didn't bring me here," I said, squinting.

"I did. I knew The Blue Door was an eyesore, and Josie and I talked about how you needed purpose and she needed space—that you'd moved into her world and life was too chaotic."

I gulped. "My new half-sister told you that?"

"Oh, gosh. Since college, we've always told each other everything. We were trying to help you. She said your lists, organization, and planning were too much. So, she said, that you should remodel The Blue Door, and she planted the idea, and I told her I'd help."

"This entire thing was to get me out of Josie's hair?" I gulped at the idea of Josie's scheme with Renee.

Renee added, "Lucien has met Claire here at The Blue Door to hide their relationship. With you opening a cafe, they could break up. She gambled away her money, his, Remy's, and even the money I loaned Lucien. She was a liability. And now she's dead. Dead. This is horrible."

"Stop it." I searched for the words, but Renee's release of how much I drove Josie crazy in Wyoming hit too hard. I swallowed every harsh response and dug deep, trying to find words that would please not only my Aunt Diane but also my dad.

None came out. Silence spoke instead.

Moving beside her, I whispered. "Secrets don't stay buried forever. They surface. Always do."

Kermit spoke, his voice steady but heavy. "Claire didn't die because of Lucien. She died because she knew the wrong thing and said it too loudly."

Windex nodded. "And because somebody wanted an example."

The sun of the new day crept higher, spilling light across the worn floorboards of The Blue Door. And dust floated like witnesses who had seen too much. Like peeling paint from a wounded life, where you end up wishing for sleep.

Renee wiped her face, straightening slowly. "I'm going to the station. I won't let them railroad Lucien."

"I'll come," I said.

She looked at me, eyes red but resolute. "No. You stay here. Someone has to hold this place steady." She touched my hand. "I didn't mean to make it sound like Josie's mad at you. She's adjusting to you being in her world. She wasn't ready for a new brother or sister. Or for the past to speak of such horror for her own mother, Camille's death."

I turned to Kermit and knew precisely what Renee meant. No one picks their family. And no one has a handbook for figuring it all out either.

Kermit nodded. "She's right. The truth must find light."

Renee paused at the door, turning back. "If Lucien didn't do this... then who did?"

Windex tapped his washboard softly, a rhythm like a heartbeat. "The kind of man who smiles while he waits."

We all knew who he meant.

Remy Duval.

But then, in the silence, I pieced together an idea of clues that were now adding up in my mind—but telling them to anyone meant waiting for the right time.

A chilly breeze brushed across the land, and The Blue Door stood silent, listening.

And for the first time since I arrived, I understood the game I'd been pulled into. It was about surviving the truth once it came out. And now, there was no going back, not now.

Besides, a flight out of New Orleans to see my half-sister Josie doesn't seem so inviting, right now, thanks to Renee blurting out how the two of them brought me here to give Josie some space.

So, I'll give Josie her space. And I'll have mine.

Besides, I'm ready to sort through a few things that are keeping me here now.

Because when everyone thinks I'm not listening, I am.

Chapter 10

Shifting Sand

THE FOLLOWING DAY, I GRABBED hotel coffee in a paper cup, after sleeping most of the day before, and for the first time in a while, all night. I carried my bag and plans with me to The Blue Door. And I couldn't help but think that threats don't always arrive by invitation. And people you trust could be accomplices, guilty of a crime, or both.

Sometimes threats show up folded neatly in white envelopes, tucked under a candle, and possibly carried by people you know or just met.

I sat alone at the bar for a long time, trying to breathe after finding the Polaroid sitting under my candle. My heart was racing and pounding with a boom of irregular beats, and I'm sure someone would have heard it if I weren't alone.

I hadn't moved since I set my coffee on the bar and picked up the envelope with the photograph inside. It's as if whoever snapped the picture had been standing close enough to breathe me in. But who put it there? And when?

Kermit? Windex? Renee? Police officers? The front door to The Blue Door was locked, but it's no secret that the alley is the entrance to this place—for anyone.

So much for private property.

I hated the thought of not knowing.

I turned the photo over again.

The Blue Door at night. My silhouette. With the candle.

The timing gnawed at me. Whoever took it watched me. Knew when I'd be alone. Knew where the light would fall.

I tucked the photo into my notebook and forced myself to stand because fear likes stillness. It grows best when you don't move, but a creaky sound across the ceiling from above, followed by the soft patter of footsteps, deepened the unsettling chill in my bones.

I called to my dad, not that it mattered. "Please, walk with me through this. Please."

The morning passed in small, practical tasks. I called the roofer to double-check his scheduling with me. And I found a locksmith for today. As for the electrician, he sighed when I described the building and said, "Honey, we'll pray first, then we'll work."

Kermit returned midmorning with Miles, who planted himself on the stoop just outside on the sidewalk with his trumpet and played like the street needed reminding that it was alive.

I watched him from the window, something warm and heavy settling in my chest. This—*this*—was what I wanted: music in daylight. People lingering. No secrets.

Except secrets were already here.

They lived in the walls. In Renee's pauses. In washboard songs. In pink neon signs. And in trinket shops. And in alleys.

That afternoon, Renee came back with iced coffees and a clipboard, all efficiency and charm, her smile back in place, as if she'd pressed reset. Her makeup was flawless.

"Locks ordered," I said. "I've got cameras coming, too. Well, we've got to get the electricity on first."

"Good, so you called my guys? The ones I trust?"

"Yes, all set," I said.

She handed me my coffee, and our fingers brushed. Her nails were freshly painted—deep plum, glossy. Too glossy to miss. But they matched her purple sundress.

"You got your nails done, I see."

"Yes, my hands are my life. With them, I make a great impression, or... I don't."

I remembered the scratch on her cheek and the way she'd said she *ran into a plank* without worrying about whether it might scar, as she's so put together.

"Emory?" she prompted gently. "You with me?"

"Yeah," I said. "Just thinking."

She nodded as she understood. Like she always did.

"I'll be back in a bit," and she was gone.

And that was the problem.

Renee flitted in. And often dashed out. Her polished look sometimes came with erratic behavior.

Windex unsettled me next when he arrived late afternoon, sober, quiet, leaning against the counter of the bar like he was weighing whether to speak or leave.

"You ever notice," he said finally, "how some people show up right when you need 'em?"

"I do, so are you talking about yourself?"

"Nope, just an observation I've made."

I wiped the counter with my dust rag, hoping to add a shine to a day that already had lasted too long. "Maybe, when people show up, it becomes a friendship."

He smiled, but it didn't reach his eyes. "Sometimes. Other times, it's called management."

I paused. "Management of what?"

"Situations," he said. "Outcomes. Ms. Renee is good at managing people. I expect."

"What does that mean?"

"Nothing, never mind. Windex thinks out loud too much."

Before I could ask more, Renee swept back in with a contractor, showing him the room to the side where a commercial stove would go, counters, and a refrigerator big enough to walk into. She was laughing, directing, and smoothing.

I argued. "Renee, I have someone for the kitchen."

"But this guy, he's the one you need."

"But…" I again tried to stop her, but when Renee's set loose like a friendly tornado, you get out of her way.

She'd brought me another iced coffee to give me a caffeine boost, and the moment passed with her orchestrating my plans, even rewriting them, but it didn't leave me at ease.

Plans for the kitchen were set in stone. The electrician readied his team, and before sunset, I remembered the photograph in my tote, which reminded me that being alone at The Blue Door might not be a good idea, especially at night.

Oddly enough, Renee never mentioned Lucien or her visit to the police station, or if she even went, and neither did I.

That evening, after everyone was gone, I sat with my notebook open and wrote facts. Not theories. Not fears. Just facts.

Fact number one:

Renee knew about the alley.

Fact number two:

Renee knew Claire.

Fact number three:

Renee's face had an unexplained scratch.

Fact four:

Renee had access to the entire block,

the cameras, and the people.

And fact number five:

Renee was always one step ahead of danger.

I stared at the list until my chest hurt.

Then I closed the notebook.

"No," I said out loud. "She's helped me too much. I need a good night's sleep so that I can think clearly."

I thought of the way she'd linked arms with me. The way she'd pulled me through the crowds. The way she'd said *baby* when I shook.

People who hurt others don't do that.

Except sometimes they do.

**

Back at the hotel, I slept poorly, despite how worn out I was and how every inch of my body shouted with aches and pinpricks of irritation beneath my skin, a sure sign of exhaustion.

In my dream, I was standing in the alley behind The Blue Door. The light flickered. A woman cried out. And when I turned, Renee stood there, her hands stained dark, her voice calm.

You should've listened to the chorus.

I woke up shaking, drank some water, and curled up under the comforter, staring at the ceiling until my eyes closed. But I was still awake.

And the patterns emerged—not dramatic ones.

Quiet ones.

Renee always positioned herself between me and the street. Renee always answered questions before others could. Renee always redirected fear into productivity.

"You're safe," she'd say. "I've got this handled. Trust me."

And I did.

And good old Windex and Kermit had planted doubt in my mind already.

"You notice," he said one evening as we replaced a warped board under the stage, "how she never asks what you're thinking?"

I frowned. "She asks all the time."

"No," he said gently. "She tells."

The board came loose with a crack.

Then Kermit looked up at me. "You ever been hit by someone who said they loved you right after?"

My throat tightened. "Why are you asking me that?"

He shrugged. "Just saying. Love and control share a language."

I rolled over in bed, thinking about those conversations, asking questions, and thinking some more.

Soon, I was up and outside, in the dark, alone, and in front of The Blue Door. The streetlights shone a path for me, but the alley called me to take a walk.

I rounded the trinket store, and the alley smelled like damp stone and old oil. I stood where Claire must've stood, possibly behind my place or Lucien's store after her altercation with him, and I surveyed the area.

I walked off the steps from Duval's back door to my fire escape staircase, to the trinket store and back, and replayed possible ways the night had unfolded for Claire Landry.

Timing. Access.

A hard place to land. Where she might hit her head.

My phone buzzed with a text: *Hey girl, where are you?*

I stared at the screen longer than necessary.

I'm taking a walk, I typed.

Her reply came instantly.

Good. Don't like you being out alone at night. I saw you leave the lobby.

I slipped the phone into my pocket, my heart pounding—not with fear.

With grief. For Claire.

And for myself.

Because somewhere between beignets and blueprints, between prayers and promises, I realized something I wasn't ready to say out loud. Because possibly, the safest place I'd wished for in New Orleans might be the most dangerous one.

And the person who'd held my arm so gently through this city might also hold tightly to something sinister.

Something sharp. Criminal. Hidden. Nearly exposed.

Something that isn't filled with heels, smiles, and friendship.

I wasn't ready—not yet—to let the truth finish its sentence. What if I'm wrong? What if I am chasing the wind and lost in the whirlwind of confusion?

I sent Cal a text: Maybe I need you here.

11

Miles and Celeste's Music

THE LAYERS OF THIS TRIP thickened like maple syrup. Cal was constantly texting. Me responding. And things had gotten quieter.

So, the next two weeks flew by as if a winter storm was settling in for the long haul. My road trip to get here landed me in a mix of shadows, with doubt, and caused me to look over my shoulder at every turn.

I've taken several tours of the cemeteries and the French Quarter, memorized the one-way streets, and attended street bands to search for someone who might like to play at The Blue Door.

Windex assured me he could find me a band, but releasing that to his control wasn't within me, yet.

I'm processing how my intrusion into Josie's world in Wyoming set this entire renovation project into motion, and how even here, I had family I'd never met, which now, have kept my emotions off-key without a tune.

And someone wants me gone?

But the notes stopped. The street was quiet.

Life was almost normal.

Which doesn't make sense, given the threats I faced when I first arrived.

The building had sat abandoned for years. Sat. Closed up. Shut down. Dark. No business pursuits inside. Why does my coming here bring Duval out of the woodwork? Or his cronies? Or someone else, for that matter?

I needed time to process everything.

Renee seemed to understand; she had pictures of my worried face on her phone, thanks to Josie, so she wasn't pushing me—just giving me insight into what I might encounter.

One minute, I'm putting her on the list of people not to trust, only for Renee to be a light when other trails go dark.

Renee met me in the lobby as I pushed the door open.

As if she'd forgotten to follow up with me, she said, "I'm sorry about my brother. I should have told you Lucien doesn't like new people or me butting into his life."

I grinned. "Renee Baptiste. You're one of a kind."

"Well, actually, I'm two. Lucien's my twin brother."

"What? But you told me you had an older brother."

"I do. It's Lucien. He's ten minutes older than I am."

I almost laughed, thankful that Renee seemed to be letting her guard down.

She took a call on her cell phone and rushed off behind the counter at the hotel, waving. "I'll be back. The water pipe broke in a bathroom on the third floor. I've got a mess to contend with."

One second, Renee's pushing my buttons. The next thing she's smoothing out my life. I'm torn between who to trust and what to think, and whenever I consider the entire Claire Landry death, my insides churn with questions.

The morning broke like jazz—slow, uncertain, and slightly out of tune, and now, I'm on a mission. For answers. For truth. For my survival.

I'm ready to implement some decisions on the rebuild. The surrounding pressure might squeeze in, but I'm not giving up. Not yet.

I could sense that The Blue Door woke up when I came inside. The floorboards popped like knuckles; the pipes hissed like stage applause, and somewhere upstairs, Kermit's saxophone hummed a single note before fading.

A bar with rhythm. A bar with history. And maybe, a bar with a warning. Unless the ghosts moved away during the last few days.

But soon, it will be a jazz cafe. A menu with blueberries. And a place for tourists to sit, relax, and enjoy some peace.

I stood at the counter, my sketches of how the cafe should look before me, and said, "Good morning, Dad. Good morning, Celeste."

It became a habit, like a prayer, to greet my aunt and my dad when I came into this building. I talked to them as if they could hear, and I wondered if maybe they did. "You'd probably hate that I'm turning this jazz club into a pancake cafe. But you'd love the syrup bar. And the band, if I can find one."

Outside, the street was waking, too. A brass band's warm-up scales floated from somewhere near Jackson Square, all trumpet trills and trombone grunts.

The city stretched, yawned, and got ready to charm or chew up whoever walked its sidewalks.

Lucien's shop remained closed. And I hadn't noticed Remy Duval watching me. Or anyone, for that matter. Except Kermit.

He shadowed me a lot, not that I've told him I've noticed. His constant worry came with remarks like, "Emory, things are quiet. But truth reminds the past it must tell what happened."

His riddles kept my pulse racing and my anxiety high.

That's when I heard it, so faint I thought I imagined it.

A trumpet. Not the rowdy kind that strutted Bourbon Street, but a smaller, cleaner sound. The kind that told a story instead of selling one.

The sound came from inside The Blue Door—somewhere.

I turned, wiping my hands as if they were wet, even though they weren't. My pulse quickened. "Kermit? Is that you?"

No answer.

The music lifted, tender and precise. Each note slid into the next with that sort of breathless perfection you can't teach; it just lives in a person.

I moved across the main room toward the stairs. The light was golden through the slats of the off-kilter door, dust dancing as if it was keeping time. And there, standing on the stage barefoot to my left, trumpet in hand, was little Miles Delacroix.

"I thought your daddy took you with him."

"He did. Something came up. So, I came back. I came in from the alley and took the staircase. Daddy made me a copy of his key the other day, said you got new locks."

"Okay, I guess that's fine. By the way, your daddy is helping renovate this place."

Miles smiled but didn't answer.

He looked small but steady, his back straight, his focus absolute. The trumpet shone in his hands as if it belonged there, and the melody he played, soft, aching, hopeful, cut straight through me.

It was the same melody he had played on the street; the one Celeste wrote called *Blue Shadows*.

Miles hit the high note and held it. It trembled in the air, pure as forgiveness. And a small piece of the ceiling tumbled to the floor.

And I jumped. "Well, we'll fix that, too."

Miles continued to play his trumpet, and the notes lifted in the air as if they had something important to say and weren't waiting to be invited. The tune rang out the way scripture does when it finally makes sense.

I exhaled. "Miles?"

He spun around, almost dropping the trumpet. "Sorry, Miss Emory. Am I playing too loudly?" His grin was all dimples and nerves. "Daddy Kermit said I could play here anytime."

"Don't you have... school?"

He shuffled. "Spring break."

"It's not spring. It's late October." I grinned.

"Then winter break?" He said, wincing.

"Are you skipping school?" I asked, ready to call Kermit, since I'd gotten him a cell phone so we could communicate the way cousins should.

"Maybe. It happens sometimes. I don't see Daddy much. And I come here and spend the day with him. Mama won't let him come to our house too often. Even though he's back, she doesn't want him." Miles sniffled. "But I do."

"Well, your daddy should be proud of you. Not the skipping school part, but the music part," I said, leaning against the wall by the staircase. "You just gave the first concert in our new cafe."

He laughed, a bright, quick sound. "You like jazz?"

"Yes, I love music. It's my life. I play the guitar."

Miles looked around. "Where is your guitar?"

"I left it behind in Wyoming. For when I return." A slight ache ran through my entire body, the kind that tinges your skin with regret. "I should have brought it."

"Yeah, music makes me happy," Miles said.

"Me, too."

Miles put his hands up, blocking the glare from the windows behind me. "I can barely see you."

"With no electricity, it's pretty shadowy in here. The electrician is finishing up soon. He's gotten most of the wiring fixed or replaced." I glanced up. "But it looks like I might need new ceiling tiles over there."

"It's dark upstairs, but Daddy Kermit doesn't seem to mind," Miles said, tiptoeing to the stairs. "I'm going to see if he's back. Okay?"

Before I let him go up, I said, "Miles, I think the walls were listening. You are very talented. I've never heard a young man your age who plays so well."

He stopped and looked back at me. "Mama says music runs in my blood."

"She's right. And I love the rhythm of the song you just played."

He glanced toward the hallway by the top of the staircase, then back at me. "Daddy Kermit says *Blue Shadows* was Grandma Celeste's favorite. Said she wrote it when she was sad. But no one knows the words to it."

"Your grandma's voice was like honey poured over heartbreak. Or so I've been told. Your daddy said she wrote this song for someone she loved."

Miles licked his lips and played a note. "Someone like family?"

"Maybe. Or maybe it's a song about the love you never get to keep."

He seemed to think on that, brow furrowed. "I think it's about coming home."

Miles responded with a deeper answer than I expected for a ten-year-old, which caught me off guard. "Why's that?"

He shrugged. "Because when I play it, it feels like somebody's saying, 'Your daddy made it back.'"

I nodded, my sense of sadness for Miles showing up with a burn in my chest, a wish for my daddy to make it back, knowing that part of my life was over.

Miles went on, taking a step up the staircase. "My daddy was gone too long, and he finally came back."

The way he said it—simple, certain—sent a chill through me.

He lifted his trumpet again. "Wanna hear the ending? Daddy Kermit says nobody knows how *Blue Shadows* ends exactly, cause Grandma never finished it."

"I'd love to."

He started again, this time slower. The first few notes fluttered like breath, soft as memory. Then he paused, lips pressing together, eyes closing as if listening for something only he could hear.

And then he played the next part, gentle, unexpected, a shift that made the hair on my arms rise.

"Where'd you learn to do that?" I whispered.

He lowered the horn, blinking. "It just... showed up. Daddy says I have the gift."

Before I could ask more, Kermit's voice thundered from the stairwell. "Miles!"

The boy flinched. "Uh oh."

Kermit came downstairs and touched Miles on the shoulder. "I told you to wait outside for me. That I'd be right back. I didn't want you to bother Ms. Vaughn."

"I was just—" Miles started.

"I said outside, boy." His tone cut sharper than it needed to. The warmth drained from the room.

"Hey," I said, stepping in. "He wasn't hurting anything. Just playing his trumpet for me."

Kermit turned to me, jaw tight. "He's a kid. He doesn't understand what that song does to me. I had business to take care of, and the boy needs to mind me."

"What does the song do?" I asked.

122

He sighed, dragging a hand down his face. "That song opens doors that should stay shut."

Miles's eyes widened. "Daddy, it's a good song. Grandma would want us to finish it."

"Yes, she would, but it's a memory that bleeds," Kermit said. His voice softened, but the hurt beneath it was still raw. "You go wait by the corner store, Miles. Get yourself a soda." He handed him some change from his pocket.

The boy hesitated, then looked at me. "It's okay, Miss Emory. Daddy Kermit gets... twitchy."

Miles put his trumpet into its case and slung it over his shoulder and slipped out to the sidewalk, the door shutting behind him with a small, hollow thud.

Silence.

The kind that hums with everything you didn't say.

I crossed my arms. "You didn't have to bite his head off."

Kermit sank onto a stool. "You think I don't know that? But you didn't hear it."

"Hear what?"

"The rest of it."

I frowned. "The song?"

He nodded. "I heard it. I did. Miles finished the song."

"I love the haunting way the song makes me feel," I said, trying to reassure Kermit.

He hit his fist on the counter. "Celeste wrote *Blue Shadows* and said she'd finish it when forgiveness came. When I heard Miles play that ending—" He looked at me, fear flickering in his eyes. "She's here, Emory."

I stared. "Here as in memory, or—"

"As in here." He tapped his chest. "As in I heard her humming last night. Thought I was losing my mind."

My pulse quickened. "I've heard her, too."

He froze. "When?"

"Several times."

We looked at each other, the air between us tightening with something neither of us wanted to name.

Then Kermit stood abruptly. "I gotta go talk to Miles, apologize." He charged up the stairs, returning with his sax, and headed for the door.

"Where are you going?"

"Jackson Square. I play there when the ghosts get too close—I'll take Miles with me. We're gonna play. He can teach me the ending."

"Kermit—"

"Don't follow, Emory." He stopped in the doorway, the light cutting across his face like a line between past and present. "If Celeste's music woke up, it ain't just her that's listening. I'm tied into something I'm trying to get free of."

And he left before I could breathe another word.

After he was gone, I sat at the piano at the end of the stage, touching the worn ivory keys. They were yellowed with time, but they hummed faintly under my fingers, like static before life shocks you and sends you to your knees.

I pressed one key. A soft note echoed, then another, like someone else's hands resting atop mine. The melody came unbidden, slow, deliberate, full of longing.

Blue Shadows.

With my photographic mind and sense for music, I can play almost any song once I hear it. And my fingers tapped out the notes on the keyboard from the song Miles had played earlier.

Tears pricked my eyes before I even realized I was crying. I whispered, "Your memory is so alive, Celeste."

The chandelier above me swayed, just slightly, its glass crystals chiming a faint, perfect note.

I didn't run.

Instead, I whispered into the stillness, "If this song's still unfinished, Celeste, help me play the ending with a jazz band that keeps your memory alive and with comfort food for those who wander."

A faint scent filled the air, jasmine, like perfume and memory. I pressed the piano keys again, so wishing I'd brought my guitar on the trip.

Then the silence came.

I sat there for what felt like an hour, waiting for something else, but the room stayed quiet.

Outside, the sound of a trumpet drifted faintly through the Quarter again—Miles's song, lighter than before.

As the sun rose higher in the sky, Renee arrived with her usual flair, and her water-pipe situation was resolved, and she held a bag of beignets. "I brought sugar," she announced. "How are my ghosts today?"

I didn't even try to hide the tremble in my voice. "And how do you stay so thin? You eat sugar all day long?"

"I have a high metabolism." She said, grinning, and Renee set the bag down and eyed me. "What happened?"

"Miles came by," I said. "He played Celeste's song. I think he's finished it."

Renee froze mid-motion. "Finished it?"

"Yes."

She ran her fingers through her long hair. "Lord, have mercy."

"Apparently, forgiveness is coming." I moved closer to Renee and brushed her blonde hair aside. "Did you look in the mirror before you left? You've caked makeup on your cheek."

"I was in a rush. It's fine." Her expression softened. "Maybe that's part of why you're here."

"What, to see a scratch on your face, one that's not healing and is inflamed?"

"No, to finish a few things left undone."

She sat beside me on the old piano bench for a bit before she said, "Music's just prayer with better rhythm. Don't fear it."

"I'm not sure it's the music I fear," I admitted.

"Then what?"

"It's the silence between songs. And sometimes, it's people."

Renee smiled knowingly. "That's where God tunes His instruments. With our time between the dates on our tombstones."

I looked toward the stage, where sunlight now pooled across the floorboards like a spotlight from the windows across the room. "You think God's tuning me?"

"I think God is getting you ready for the next set."

**

The electrician came and assured me it wasn't as bad as it could be, that only a few more walls needed new outlets and wiring, and that he'd need a week.

And that's when I sensed the wear and tear of my heart, in need of new wiring, too.

The plasterer and sheetrock guy arrived after saying he couldn't, ready to handle the tricky old materials, to plaster and re-plaster, to deal with rotted joists, and to replace and fix the ceiling, and he needed at least a month.

As for the roofer, there's no need to repair; I'm getting a brand-new roof. He'll do that in the next few days.

The wheels were set in motion, and I was ready to move ahead, to block out the ghosts that earlier tried to run me off.

So, as I locked up, I said goodbye to Kermit, who had returned to check in. "Thank you for all your help today. I feel better knowing we can lock up the place."

"Welcome, Ms. Em," Kermit said, sliding up the staircase.

Renee wiped dirt from her cheek. "I'll see you tomorrow, sweety. I've got to see how my hotel is doing. We've got a large party of tourists coming in, and everything needs to be perfect."

That's when I noticed something new taped on the window outside. "Wait, what's with this? I didn't put that paper there."

Pinned beneath it was a business card: Remy Duval, Proprietor at Duval's Lounge.

On the back, in a looping script: "Some songs don't belong to the living. And debts don't fully go away."

My fingers went stiff, and I looked up and whispered, "Lord, I need more than music now. I need armor to fix this place up. Help me survive Remy Duval and his monsters."

I tossed the business card into a trash can on the curb, and a soft breeze brushed past me, and the pink sign at Duval's Lounge flickered at the exact moment.

"I'm ready to face you. I'm ready to finish what I've started. And trust me, Mr. Duval, you can't stop me."

A man across the street stepped from the shadows. The one with a comma scar on his chin and knowing eyes. He snapped his brown knuckles like a high-school bully and didn't move.

I shouted. "Go on, now. Nothing to see here. You'd best be on your way."

12

Pancakes and Promises

IF HEAVEN HAD A SMELL, I THINK it's the scent of butter and sugar caramelizing on a griddle. Several weeks flew by, like a brass band strutting by, the parade of accomplishments checking off daily from my list.

And not once did I take a day off from following my list, except to eat Thanksgiving dinner at Naomi's with Miles. And even Kermit was there, along with Windex, and plenty of their other friends, who I think most of them came to stare at me.

Now and again, the man with the scar on his face watched me from across the street, but I'd noticed it happened when Miles was nearby. And I wondered if he watched Miles or me.

And I yelled at him. Twice. But it didn't faze him.

But so far, things are on schedule for the cafe.

Sort of.

Cal thought I'd call it quits before now, but I'd sent him updates and photos and fibbed to him about getting plenty of sleep.

His last horse-riding lessons for the season in Cody wrapped up, and he encouraged me to find myself, complete the project, and return to Wyoming before Christmas.

I patted my chest, glancing around the cafe. The Blue Door Cafe didn't just *stand* in the middle of this block on Chartres—it *leaned*, like it was eavesdropping on every conversation that ever passed its windows. The shutters were crooked but proud, painted the color of twilight, a blue so deep it felt like it had swallowed a hundred sunsets. Eight shudders. Four polished windowpanes. Light enters the cafe like sunshine.

And a new sign over the painted *mercy* door, The Blue Door Cafe.

Inside, the air hummed with stories. The wooden floors were scuffed but now polished, and decades of dancers who'd tapped, swayed, or stomped their way through heartbreak and hallelujahs in the bar were a part of the history.

The stage, small but mighty, sat beneath a sign carved by Celeste herself, which I'd discovered in the underground room we're using for storage. The sign read, "Mercy Served Warm." It caught the morning light just right, gleaming like gold in a stroke of grace.

The old bar counter stretched the length of one wall, a remnant from the jazz days, but instead of whiskey and gin, the shelves behind it now held mason jars filled with lemons, mint sprigs, and syrupy blueberry preserves.

Renee insisted on the fresh lemons and mint sprigs. "This place needs lemonade that can heal a soul, along with iced tea."

So, The Blue Door Cafe would pour sweet tea so strong it could wake the dead and serve it in mismatched glasses rescued from thrift stores and estate sales. Lemonade and tea. What a combo.

On the counter, a chalkboard listed the day's blessings: Blueberry Pancakes, Blueberry Waffles, Beignets with Honey Drizzle, and Mercy Blue Biscuits.

Round tables filled the main room, each one clothed in faded linen, the color of river fog, crowned with a single plastic daisy in an old coffee tin. Chairs mismatched, some creaking, some steady, like the customers who'd soon sit in them.

Everything on the menu leaned toward a brunch full of blueberry delights, but Miles had told me we should have at least one dessert. "Pecan pie is my favorite. Daddy Kermit says it's music to your mouth. Crunchy and sweet and full of sugar."

"Well, then, pecan pie it is," I'd said. "Some folks might stop by for music and just pie. My aunt Diane has the best recipe for pecan pie, too."

Miles licked his lips and ran up the stairs to tell Kermit. "We'll have pie soon. Real soon, Daddy."

And when the skillets come alive, and hiss in the kitchen, and the smell of butter and sugar meets the steady hum of a saxophone warming up, the place will come alive.

Renee's friend, Chef Silas Dupree, tall as a streetlight and twice as steady, accepted the job when I offered room and board upstairs.

"So, are you and Windex related?"

"We're part of the Treme families from across town. And yes, we're brothers. I'm seven years older. My music's in the kitchen. Windex, found his on the stage."

Renee had reminded me that Silas was black before I met him, as if that even mattered now.

"Renee, you're the one who told me all skin colors are beautiful. And I believe it. I need a superb chef to make my recipes sing."

"He'll do that and more," she assured.

So now, the kitchen would pulse like a heartbeat—skillets sizzling with bacon, spoons clattering, butter whispering secrets to the pan. Silas had tested recipes out on the contractors over the past month. All were approved, but those breaks slowed progress because of frequent stops to taste the food.

His sleeves were rolled to the elbows: a faded tattoo peeking out, an anchor with wings. He stirred a pot of blueberry syrup so rich it looked like melted gold. And preserves were his specialty.

When we met, he said, "You must be Emory," without turning. His voice was a low hum, part gravel, part gospel. "Renee said you're the one who'll turn this bar into a blessing."

"I'm trying," I said, brushing dust off my jeans.

He tasted the blueberry syrup with a spoon, added his own twist, and nodded once. "Tryin' is how miracles start." He handed me the spoon. "Taste that. It's hope with butter."

I smiled. "You a chef or a preacher?"

"Both, on a good day," he said, wiping his hands on his apron. "I don't serve alcohol, don't cuss at the eggs, and don't rush a pancake. Grace takes time, just like batter."

Then he grinned, a flash of light in the dim kitchen, the side room with the back door, that now had commercial appliances and a fridge that took up most of a wall—as a walk-in one wouldn't fit.

"Now, let's make this city remember what mercy tastes like," Silas said, running his hand over the new stove.

I installed a fire extinguisher on the wall by the broom closet—just in case, hoping he didn't burn any food.

Now, each day, children run by, peeking in the front window, and even the walls seemed to sway to the beat, as if the entire building remembered joy and was finally willing to believe in it again.

The sound was pure *New Orleans*, a mingling of redemption and rhythm, cinnamon and jazz, second chances and syrup. And of course, blueberries.

And Kermit, my faithful cousin, who was always helpful and ready to run an errand or assist with a task, became a loyal and dear friend.

Just yesterday, I told Kermit. "I couldn't have done this without you. Your touch. Your knowledge of what goes where, when it should, or how it should look; that's made this special."

He smiled. "I'm ready to play with the band. This cafe will bring in a lot of tourists." Kermit said, wiping the beads of sweat from his brow, his eyes flicking over his shoulder.

"You, okay?" I asked, his nervousness more pronounced, and lately he has acted twitchier, constantly glancing back as if someone were behind him.

"I'll be fine. Miles is gonna be fine. Naomi's letting me actually come inside, sit in the living room, and talk with her. I see things differently now."

"That's great. I'm so happy for you."

Outside, some tourists walked past without a glance, but those who stepped close read the sign and nodded, as if they wished the cafe were open—and it will be soon.

Something about my little cafe—its daisies on the tables, its music, its heart—had a way of whispering, *Sit down. Let grace feed you.*

Renee hugged me. "You did it. Mercy, girl. Almost three months. That's a coffee break in New Orleans."

"I'm so eager to see what's next. We've made such progress," I smiled. "After my cancer scare last year, every day is so important. Each breath is a gift in this life."

"I've tried my best to get you out and about," she said. "Josie told me you don't sit much. And boy. She's right."

"I know. But time is short. You never know what's coming."

"True, girl. So true." Renee said, running her hand over the table by the window. "Life's full of surprises... and consequences."

"What did you say?" I asked.

"Oh, nothing. Just overthinking too much lately."

I almost didn't ask, but knew it was long overdue. "So, what's the latest on Lucien? I heard he made bail."

"Yes, he's charged with second-degree murder, has a curfew, an ankle monitor, and must stay in New Orleans Parish."

"Whoa! How did he make bail?" I asked, without taking a breath.

"I paid it. He is my brother. He's family," Renee said, sighing and wiping her cheek with her hand.

Lucien was indeed out on bail.

Not innocent.

Just released.

And somehow, the entire case surrounding Claire's death still wasn't adding up completely.

Renee changed the subject, which is why I hesitated to even ask about her brother.

"New Orleans has a heartbeat; mixed with jazz, sirens, laughter, tears, and sin. But you'll add your touch with more jazz, brunch, and blueberry muffins, pancakes, waffles, and even blueberry bacon and sausage."

I grinned. "I don't remember telling you about the bacon and sausage."

"I listen closely," she said, smiling.

By nine o'clock that morning, the place smelled like Saturday mornings when I was growing up at my Aunt Diane's house and sounded like hope with Silas humming and perfecting our menu in the kitchen.

Renee had brought gifts: a battered waffle iron, two cast-iron skillets, and an optimism large enough to hang wallpaper with.

"Sugar, if this place doesn't rise like a biscuit by Easter, I'll eat my hat," she declared.

"I'm not waiting for Easter. By January, we'll be so busy. I can't wait. This will be the most popular family cafe in no time." I said, assuring myself more than her. I laughed, though my nerves buzzed beneath the humor.

The day moved fast, rising with finishing touches and last-minute ideas. I thought about the day I'd first arrived, those first hours when an invitation to leave town made more sense than staying. And now, the cafe is almost ready.

I had found no notes or warnings in weeks. Even Remy Duval hadn't popped out to bother me.

But as for Celeste's ghost, whether real or just the ache of memory, it wasn't leaving me alone.

Renee noticed me staring at the doorway. "You're spooked, baby."

"Haunted," I corrected, rubbing my neck. "There's a difference. Spooked, you can run from. Haunted stays and rearranges the furniture."

She arched a brow. "Well, you're in the right city for both."

"I keep hearing Celeste's voice, or it sounds like it could be her. But I know it's just my imagination." I said, tugging on my ear.

Windex slid in. "Morning, ladies. I heard this here's the new cafe that's gonna save New Orleans one pancake at a time," he said.

"That depends," I replied. "Are you here to eat, or to clean windows?"

He winked. "Depends on what's dirtier, your windows or your reputation."

Renee whooped. "Now that's a man who belongs here."

He took a bow. "I've been cleanin' souls with rhythm since '82. And I've brought a couple of my friends to try out for the band."

"Windex, you're the best," I said, knowing a few weeks ago I might not have ever uttered that, but I hadn't found a band in all my searching.

Renee leaned over. "Windex is the best washboard player this side of the Mississippi. Used to play with Papa Galloway and the Bayou Saints."

"Used to," Windex said. "Till they fired me for playin' louder than the trumpet. A man's gotta know his volume, they say, but I don't."

I smiled despite myself. "So, your friends are looking for work?"

"Yes. Payment in money. And in pancakes or promises."

"I can feed them after they play and the tips belong to the band, and yes, we'll match any salary they could get elsewhere," I said, not prepared to lose them to another place before they started.

The trombone player smiled. The one next to him marched to the piano. And the third said, "Let me get my drums."

I grinned. "So, Kermit and Miles? They'll play with you, too?"

"Absolutely, Blueberry Girl. We got us a band." Windex played a few notes on his washboard, and he grinned. "Then we got a deal."

And just like that, Windex became part of the Blue Door Cafe Jazz Band, a rhythm keeper, philosopher, and walking comedy show. He tuned his washboard with bottle caps on stage and drummed a beat with spoons, filling the empty cafe with life. He even carried an old cassette tape player, plugged it in, and played it along with old jazz tunes, adding his touch.

The band took to the stage within the hour to practice, and I glanced around. "But where's Kermit? He is a part of this band, too—along with Miles, and now they're a no-show?"

Chapter 13

Kermit's Past Hits the Present

BENEATH THE EXCITEMENT OF the nearing grand opening, and the music, the recipes, and the laughter, something darker hummed when Kermit slipped out the front door about two hours ago without a word.

I needed him to run by the hardware store for a long extension cord, too, and now he has band practice. But he hasn't answered his phone.

"Has anyone seen Kermit?"

A collective answer of no made my heartbeat race, and by late afternoon, the street outside was alive with foot traffic: locals, tourists, musicians, and a few folks who didn't belong anywhere but the corners.

Renee had gone to fetch more flour, and more blueberries, and Windex, and his band performed for an imaginary crowd without a trumpet player or a saxophone player.

I checked the time on my phone again.

"Kermit's not answering my calls," I murmured.

Windex didn't look up. "Musicians don't do late, they do unpredictable."

"He always calls," I said. "Something's off. He's been so reliable."

Windex paused mid-strum on his washboard, studying me. "Then trust that gut, Miss Emory."

I managed a half-smile.

Windex raised his eyebrows. "Then go fetch him. He's probably at Naomi's house. I'll watch the door. You go find your sax man."

"Thanks, I won't be long." I charged outside, crossed a few streets, cut through an alley, and headed to Naomi's place.

I spoke to no one but the clouds forming in the sky. "What could keep Kermit? I've gotten used to his presence. He's like a brother. Arguing with me. Suggesting changes. Offering wisdom. And applauding the progress."

Treme pulsed with midday heat, the kind that makes air shimmer. Winter was coming. But not today. It was unusually hot, and I'd made this walk a few times now, to Naomi's apartment, a second-story flat above a corner store, the type with laundry lines stretching like spider webs and laughter spilling out of open windows.

Naomi answered the door with Miles glued to her hip, both of them surprised. She was beautiful in the quiet way that pain makes people attractive, strength etched in her cheekbones, and a hint of grace in her tired eyes.

"Emory? Everything okay?"

"Have you seen Kermit today?"

Her smile faltered. "Not since last night when he brought Miles home. He said he was playing the late set in Jackson Square and then joining Windex at the café today."

"So, you haven't seen him at all?" I asked, thinking maybe he's spent the afternoon with her, and she wasn't saying.

"Now, you know he stays at The Blue Door. He doesn't stay here. Hasn't for a long time."

Miles tugged her sleeve. "He promised to take me for beignets and to practice with the band."

Naomi crouched to his level, smoothing Miles' shirt. "Maybe he got busy, baby."

But the lie sat wrong between us.

I pulled out my phone. "I'll check the square."

"Be careful," she said. "There've been fights down there lately. Kermit got into a scuffle one day. Some men have been asking questions about who rightfully owns The Blue Door. And Kermit, he don't like it. He swings with a fist when he shouldn't."

"That's wrong on every level," I said, my voice higher than I meant, but firm like a faithful Vaughn.

"Old ghosts," she said, voice low. "But some ghosts got friends who ain't dead yet."

I snarled. "Like Remy Duval?"

"Maybe," she said.

The closer I got to Jackson Square, the louder the city grew: brass bands, vendors, street preachers, tarot readers, carriage rides. Life and decay, sharing the same stage.

Kermit wasn't at his usual spot by the fountain. His case wasn't there either—only a crushed paper cup and the faint echo of another saxophone lingering in the air.

I turned toward the cathedral. Two officers stood by the steps, whispering to a man beside a bicycle.

I recognized him.

Remy Duval.

He saw me before I could hide, his mouth curving into a smirk that didn't belong anywhere holy.

"Miss Vaughn," he said. "We keep meeting at inconvenient times. I see your cafe is coming right along."

"What are you doing here?"

"Checking on business." His tone was too casual. "One of my suppliers has been playing *street musician* when he ought to've been paying debts."

My stomach dropped. "You mean Kermit."

He shrugged. "That man owed money to more people than just me. It catches up eventually."

The officer beside him said something I didn't hear, but I saw them glance toward the river.

I ran through the crowd and pushed my way, and my heart was pounding so hard I could barely breathe. The Mississippi River came into view, gray and merciless under the high sun. And people stood clustered near the railing, with the hanging vines and banana plants, camellias beginning to bloom. I pushed past them.

And there, half caught in a tangle of driftwood along the levee, was a saxophone. Gold. Dented at the bell. A pelican sat on the rotted log, flew off when I got near, and circled back for one more honk.

It must be Kermit's sax.

The sight of it cracked something deep inside me.

I charged to the shoreline, beyond the English Ivy and a row of Magnolia trees, and the ferns lacing the walkway, ready to snatch the sax when the officer from before caught up, breathless.

"Miss, you can't be here. We need to secure this area."

Sergeant Laveau showed up from nowhere, putting herself between the officer and me. "You're needed over there," she ordered, pointing the suit to the crowd crossing the yellow tape.

"Go, take Kermit's sax. It's evidence, but it won't solve this case if it stays at our station. It'll mean more to you."

Laveau created a diversion by calling over two other suits, and they marched along the shoreline as I rushed to the instrument.

She returned for a second and said, "His body was found… earlier. They took Kermit to the parish morgue."

The world tilted. And I couldn't inhale or exhale.

I charged for the sax, grabbed it from the swollen river's edge, and ran up the embankment, cutting between the crowd of people, disappearing down an alley, running like I'd stolen the sax instead of rescuing it.

The city noise dulled to a heartbeat I could barely hear, and as I rounded the corner, I bumped into Remy again, and his voice floated from behind me, smooth as poison. "Seems debts really drown folks sometimes."

I turned back and slapped him before I realized I had.

The couple walking by gasped.

A small girl cried.

But Remy only smiled. "Careful, Miss Vaughn. Anger's a dangerous tune to play."

I wanted to scream, to break something, to undo the river. But all I could do was cry, "Kermit didn't deserve this."

Deep down, I knew the truth that would drive the rest of my days in New Orleans: Someone murdered Kermit Delacroix. And I was going to find out who.

I rushed to The Blue Door, hurrying past a lone observer of my tears, and the knowing gaze of an orange cat on the windowsill offered its long, sad meow.

Could it be the same person who thought Claire Landry knew too much—whatever 'too much' meant in the world of jazz, the French Quarter, the trinket store, and Duval's Lounge?

**

That night, I stared at the saxophone on the bar at the cafe, and oddly enough, no one came for it or chased me down.

The candlelight flickered off its gold body, glinting with small flashes as I'd turned off the lights to sit in the shadows of sorrow.

A faint echo of a saxophone's trill drifted from outside somewhere in the French Quarter, a gentle and mournful wail, as if Kermit played his last song.

It's nearly Christmas, and I'd just met Kermit in early October, and grew to care about my cousin, who is now gone because of the corrupt hands of those who think they control my destiny and my joy.

In some ways, they're right, but justice has a name, too—it's Emory Vaughn. And someone has to pay.

Windex sat nearby on the piano's bench, quiet, after refusing to leave me completely alone. His fingers played something sad on his washboard, and he tapped a random note on the piano's keyboard, which sounded like someone crying.

Renee returned with sandwiches, but didn't speak, and the air was too thick with overwhelming unhappiness.

Silas had retired upstairs to give me some space.

I whimpered, almost like a child, my shoulders shaking. "I should've stopped Mr. Duval. But why Kermit? What did Kermit do to warrant this?"

Renee sighed. "New Orleans teaches lessons to all of us. Hard to swallow. Harder to understand. And sometimes, people are trapped by the past of their family."

I glanced away, taking in her words, not sure what to make of her response.

Windex wandered up to the bar. "Remy's not the kind you stop. Kermit had plenty of folks after him for things he'd gotten caught up in. I'm not so sure Remy Duval did this. Other people own part of this town too, or think they do."

I traced the dent in the sax with my thumb. "Kermit told me I'd opened doors that should stay shut. Maybe that's what got him killed."

Windex nodded slowly. "Then we find who left him in the river."

I cried, "But to think, his mother died in the Mississippi River, and now he has the same horrible death—this has to stop."

Renee wrapped her arms around my neck. "Sweet girl, this may be out of our hands."

The cafe door creaked open behind us, and Naomi entered with Miles clinging to her hand. Her eyes were red, and her steps were heavy. "He's gone," she said.

I moved to her, and she collapsed against me, sobbing. And Miles buried his face in her dress.

Naomi whimpered, "Ms. Em, I was trying to let Kermit back into my life. I should have stayed clear and look, now, he's gone."

When Naomi pulled back, I cupped her face in my hands. "I'm going to help you find who did this. I promise."

She nodded through tears. "Then you'd better start fast. Because I'm sure that whoever killed Kermit isn't done."

The room went still.

Miles sniffled and hugged his mama's leg.

And Windex shouted, low with a sad note. "Lord, have mercy."

Outside, thunder rolled low over the city, like drums in a funeral march. And as lightning flashed through the windows, I saw it: the shadow of a person, taping a note to the glass of the window outside.

I charged to the sidewalk, the rain splattering on my face like pellets from a gun, and I hollered, "Come back here. I'm calling the police."

Windex showed up next to me. "Ma'am, come inside. It's not wise to shout at the wind."

"But look." I grabbed the note, which had the words *Debt Not Fully Paid* written on it, possibly with a Sharpie. *Keep your mouth shut. Leave town.*

I stared at the words until they blurred, whispering, "I'm certainly not leaving New Orleans now."

**

Back in my hotel room, sipping Earl Grey tea after a hot shower and after eating six chocolate chip cookies, I took my father's journal and Kermit's saxophone and laid them side by side on the bed.

And I prayed, a long-overdue prayer, something I forget until I panic. Or until my world falls apart.

I prayed for truth to rise from the shadows, for justice to echo through the music, and for the courage to follow the trail even if it led straight into the dark.

Kermit Delacroix deserved more than silence, and his untimely death has now left behind another child who has lost a parent in this cruel world.

I shouted, "Life is so unfair. Kermit deserved a song that ended on a high note." I moved to the window and pushed the curtain aside. "And I'll make sure his song continues."

I dialed my brother's number on my cell. It was time to bring him up to speed on the tragedy surrounding the cafe and our cousin, and to let him know I was mistaken and he was right. The nightmares at night are trying to stay with me during the day. And I need my brother.

And no matter what Cal says, he's not convincing me to leave Louisiana and run back to Wyoming.

My dad left The Blue Door to us, not that I'd ever expected to renovate it and make it sing again.

But now that I do, The Blue Door Cafe will open as planned.

I have the deed.

I have ownership.

And I have rights!

I shouted, "Kermit! The Blue Door Cafe's grand opening is for you."

I texted Cal: Another death in the river. I need you to get a plane ticket and come to New Orleans. And now.

14

The Bar Next Door

GRIEF HITS DIFFERENTLY IN New Orleans.

It doesn't whisper. It wails in brass and thunders through the rain. It dances through the streets in black umbrellas and second lines, pretending to be a celebration but bleeding just beneath the rhythm.

By morning, the city had moved on—it always does—but I hadn't.

I moped around the lobby of The Blue Door Cafe, staring at the dented saxophone now lying on the bar, having brought it back to the cafe to mount it above the stage. The brass had lost its shine overnight, dulled by the humidity and the truth.

Windex polished it earlier this morning, before he left for Jackson Square, whispering something about giving it a proper farewell.

Silas had a list of fresh fruit to buy and a coupon for sugar, but before he left, he said, "Ms. Em, I found this old floor plan in my broom closet on a shelf. Need it for anything? Seems it shows how this place was built. The stage has some old compartments in the flooring, too."

I glanced at the sketch, tossing it into the trash. "We have new plans. Won't need that," I said, as Silas left for the market.

Renee had promised to call a lawyer she trusted to help us pursue Kermit's redemption.

And now, inside The Blue Door, I was alone.

The silence inside the building felt heavier than before, like the walls knew what had happened and didn't want to talk about it.

Outside, the sky was gray, the gray that looks like a bruise that hasn't healed.

Naomi and Miles were most likely at their apartment, surrounded by neighbors, casseroles, and condolences.

Miles had cried in my arms yesterday before they left, and whispered, "We were going to be in the band together."

That one sentence had torn something right down the middle of me.

Now, I needed answers. For Miles. And Kermit.

I stepped to the sidewalk, locked the front door, and marched to the alley, circling past the trinket store, stopping to pause, and wondering where Lucien might be, and what he might know about Kermit's death. He was out on bail after all.

I made my way down the narrow alley in back, moss taking over the backside of the buildings behind my strip, and I marched to Remy Duval's bar, ready to round the corner from the back to circle the block—although I'm not sure why that became my goal.

Right beneath my alley staircase, a shiny object made me pause, and I reached for it. "Wait? This is nothing but a... but a broken, red fingernail?"

My world spun in circles, and the heel-clicking, sweet-talking Renee Baptiste, with her polished nails, became the center of attention for me, and knowing that sent me on a trail that circled back to Claire Landry and Lucien Baptiste.

I stuck the broken fingernail into my jeans pocket to see if Renee had lost one, not sure if it meant anything.

I froze when a delivery truck inched along past me, stopping at the back door of Duval's Lounge. The driver, with long hair, a white shirt, and jeans, holding an oversized envelope, stepped out, went inside, and did not actually deliver any beer marked with the truck's logo.

"Hmm, maybe I should hang out here more. No telling what I'm missing," I said, beneath my breath as the truck left the alley, turning right.

I spoke to the wind, putting my hands in my pockets, my fingers touching the red nail in my left pocket. "This can't be Renee's. It's been weeks since Claire's death, unless it got stuck in the pebbles and has been here the entire time."

The alley smelled like rainwater, cigarettes, and more bad decisions, wrapped in vines that took over the windowsills and bricks.

Once out front, at Duval's bar, I noticed his neon sign still buzzed, flickering DUV L'S LOUNGE, like the place couldn't decide whether to exist—the letter A, dark like the day.

I took a deep breath and walked in.

The bar was dark and half-empty, smelling of whiskey, sweat, and something sour beneath it. The bartender, a heavyset man with a tattoo of a crawfish on his forearm, looked up from polishing glasses.

"Morning," he said flatly. "We're not open."

"I'm not here for a drink." The soles of my shoes stuck to the floor, as if last night's party had ended messily, and I was surprised that the place's interior wasn't shinier or cleaner.

The bartender repeated his words. "We're not open."

I glanced at the man to my left, nursing his drink. "You served him, you must be open."

Remy's voice came from the back, smooth as the whiskey he might pour, and the bartender poured me a drink, anyway. "Here, Miss. You need this."

I pushed the glass away. "No thanks. I'm not interested in your poison."

Remy joined us. "Let her waste it, Beau. I enjoy watching ambition die slowly."

He stepped out of the shadows, wearing a crisp white shirt, no tie, and his sleeves rolled up. He smiled like someone who had read the Bible once and didn't care for the ending.

"Miss Vaughn," he said, mocking, but politely. "My condolences."

"Spare them." I kept my voice low. "You were seen talking to Kermit before he died." I made that part up, but he didn't know it.

"I talk to everyone. It's a habit."

"You threatened him."

"I offered him work."

"He's dead."

Remy's smile faltered, just a flicker. "Unfortunate. Tragic, really."

The man to my left downed his drink, and he shuffled, uninterested, his over-the-top wobble interfering with my stance. "Excuse me, can you give me a little room?"

He nodded, "Sorry, LeBlanc meant no harm." And the man slid to another stool.

I turned to Remy, raising my voice. "Kermit's death was convenient."

Remy downed the drink that sat in front of me. "You sound like a woman looking for someone to blame."

"I sound like a woman looking for the truth. Kermit was my cousin. Did you know that? My cousin. And when you mess with my family, you know the phrase, you're messing with me." I shouted, as if noise made me appear more in command.

He leaned in closer, so near I could smell the whiskey on his breath. "Truth's a funny thing in this city. It's always drunk, always talking too loudly, and always ends up face down in the river."

My pulse jumped, but I didn't flinch. "Maybe this time, it'll crawl back out and survive."

Remy's eyes narrowed. "Careful, Miss Vaughn. The Blue Door's got ghosts enough. You ask too many questions, and you might meet the kind that answer back with trouble."

"I have already started asking questions."

That caught him. For just a moment, something in his expression shifted—a flicker of recognition—or fear.

Then the smirk returned. "Enjoy your blueberry pancakes, Miss Vaughn."

I turned to leave, but he added, "Oh, and tell Naomi my offer still stands. She'll need help now. And I've got a soft spot for widows."

I spun around. "Leave her alone. She's got a son to raise."

His grin froze. The air between us thickened like humidity before a hurricane.

Beau wiped a glass clean and set it beside five others, watching. The jukebox hummed to life on its own, spilling a low blues tune into the tension.

"Goodbye, Miss Vaughn," Remy said finally, his voice a velvet knife.

I left before the words in my throat turned into something sharp enough to regret.

Outside, the air hit like steam, the rain starting again in soft sheets. Across the street, LeBlanc from the bar tipped his hat and moved on, and I walked the sidewalk back to the cafe, not taking the alley, as I own my place and my face doesn't need to hide in dark places.

When I stepped back inside, the phone behind the counter rang, the one Windex pleaded with me to keep—a landline for those who remember them.

I froze.

No one had this number. Not yet.

I answered. "Blue Door Cafe."

A man's voice rasped through the static. "You want to know who killed Kermit?"

My stomach flipped. "Who is this?"

"You already know."

"Remy?" I asked.

A low laugh. "Keep digging, Miss Vaughn. You'll find more than music. Check your walls. If you find something, let it fall away and stay in the past."

The line went dead.

I stared at the receiver, pulse hammering.

Check my walls?

I looked around—the once peeling plaster already covered with new sheetrock and paint, the water stains gone, the chipped places hidden behind the new covering.

My dad's old journal flashed in my mind. A note he'd written once, scrawled in his messy script: *Sometimes the truth hides in the past on the stage.*

Two hours later, I had a screwdriver, a flashlight, and a hunch when two spots on the wall didn't quite match up behind the stage. I pried a small section loose, exposing the wooden frame.

Something was wedged between the studs.

A metal tin.

"Seriously. Why didn't we see this during the renovations, when this section was off-center?" I shook my head, knowing this corner of the room was the darkest, so maybe it never showed itself in the shadows—until now.

I pulled it out carefully and set it on the floor. Inside was a cassette tape, its ribbon half-unwound, with a label written in faded ink: Celeste and Ben.

And beneath it, a photograph: Celeste in a party dress, little Kermit, and a much younger Remy Duval—all smiling.

My breath caught.

Remy had known Celeste pretty well from the looks of the photo. Did he once work with her? Maybe loved her. I don't understand. Maybe Remy helped Gus kill her?

I turned the cassette over, and on the back, written in faint pencil, were three words: Proof. If needed.

My pulse quickened.

I grabbed Windex's cassette player from the table, tightened the reel, and popped the tape in. It crackled, hissed, and then—it must have been Celeste's voice that I heard next.

"Remy, if anything happens to me, you'll know why. Everyone will know it's you and Gus. You think this city forgets, but it doesn't. They resurface, just like the truth."

Static.

Then a man's voice—Remy's—low, angry. "You talk too much, Celeste."

A muffled thud. A crash. The tape stopped.

I sat there, frozen.

Remy Duval hadn't just killed Kermit's mother, Celeste. He'd silenced her along with Gus—and now, years later, he'd silenced her son, Kermit.

And now I was worried that I was next in line.

I tucked the cassette into the tin, hid it behind the flour sacks in the kitchen cabinet, and tucked the photograph into my jeans pocket on my hip.

Silas returned with his sugar. "Hey, what happened to the wall on the stage? That's a disaster!"

"I was chasing a sound, and I think it was a rat. I dug for the little guy, and he got away. But don't worry, I've called the contractor. And an exterminator." I fibbed.

He took my explanation as gospel, but before he went to the kitchen, he removed the screwdriver from my hand. "Emory, you're dangerous with this."

**

That night, I went to Naomi's apartment in my rental car, the green and dated vehicle an eyesore.

Miles opened the door; his trumpet clutched to his chest. "Miss Emory?"

"Hey, buddy. Can I come in?"

Naomi appeared from the hallway, eyes swollen, grief written in every line of her face.

"I found something," I whispered, trying not to let Miles hear, but his eyes told me he's excellent at reading lips. "It's something that proves what happened to Kermit's mother—and maybe Kermit too."

Pulling the photo from my pocket, I handed it to Naomi, and her hand trembled as she took it. "Remy," she whispered. "I knew he was trouble. Kermit always said the past doesn't die; it just changes clothes."

I nodded. "I'm going to the police tomorrow. But I need your help first."

"My help?" Naomi's eyes darkened. "You're playing with fire."

"Then help me bring water." I sighed. "Think of all your recent conversations with Kermit and where he goes during the day. We might track down some clues to his last... moments."

She took a deep breath, her voice shaking. "I'll help. But promise me one thing."

"What's that?"

"Promise me, Miles doesn't get caught in it."

I looked at the boy, his small fingers tracing the trumpet valves.

"I promise," I said. "No more lost songs."

Later, as I drove back to The Blue Door Cafe, the rain came harder, drumming on the windshield like impatient fingers. Streetlights glowed through the mist. And a touch of the cold winter moved into New Orleans.

My cell buzzed, almost as if the sergeant knew what I was facing. I read the text: Let's meet. I have something for you at the station.

An hour later, after fighting traffic and getting caught in a marching band blocking the road, I sat across from Laveau at the police station, a file on the table between us.

"I can't officially give you this," Laveau said, pushing the file forward. "But you should see the patterns, the connections. See the names. One keeps showing up. And it's a mess, but you've got sharp eyes. We have corruption and money laundering and secrets."

I handed her the photograph of young Kermit, Celeste, and Remy from my pocket. "You keep this."

"I'll put in with my other evidence. This could help."

I scanned the file Laveau shared, my heart pounding with gratitude and determination. And I sensed a calm knowing she was on my side. "Thank you," I whispered, finding courage in Laveau's subtle support.

"Be careful. But wait, isn't there a cassette tape you found?"

"Yes, but I've hidden it for now."

"You sure? The water's rising in the river with activity at Duval's Lounge," Laveau said, almost like a warning.

"I'll keep that for now," I said, not sure why I kept the tape, but I did.

As I turned onto Chartres, lightning flashed—and in that brief pink light, I saw him. Remy Duval. Standing beneath the awning of his bar, watching me.

I parked in a spot that barely allowed my car to fit on the street, and I charged from my seat, leaving the rental door wide.

"What's that?" I asked, looking down.

And in his hand, he was holding a photograph.

Of me. In Cody, Wyoming. With Cal at Josie's ranch.

15

The Night of Shadows

I SNATCHED THE PICTURE FROM Remy's grasp, ran away, tripping over cracks in the sidewalk, and sensed my life swallowing me like someone had tossed me into a deep river with rocks tied to my feet.

"Why would Remy Duval have a photo of me in Wyoming before I ever came to New Orleans?" I cried, my breath rattling like static into the night air.

I froze at the entrance to my cafe, glancing back at where Remy grinned from his corner, and I realized night falls faster in New Orleans when you're afraid.

I grabbed my things from the front seat of my car and rushed into the cafe.

The city hummed louder too, brass and thunder trading verses, while shadows stretched across the cobblestones like they had somewhere to be.

Every flickering streetlamp looked like a question I didn't want to answer.

I locked the door behind me twice. Then I rechecked it.

I texted Cal, something we'd done with our back-and-forth arrangements today—his trying to get a plane ticket and me telling him: Never mind, don't come. I'm fine.

I sent a new text to my brother: Please come.

Windex came in from the back alley and offered to stay, but I told him no—I needed quiet. So, he left, and Silas was already asleep upstairs, or at least, I didn't hear footsteps in the kitchen.

I texted Renee, and she had begged me to sleep at her apartment with her, which was actually a suite at her hotel on the third floor.

I promised I would, not sure if my worry about her was warranted, and that I'd be there soon.

Except I didn't go.

I couldn't.

Something about The Blue Door Cafe felt like it needed company tonight, or maybe it was me who couldn't bear to leave it alone.

I brewed a pot of chicory coffee and sat at the bar with my laptop open, replaying the cassette on the player, transcribing every word from Celeste's recording—tapping each word into a document. Every syllable. Every rustle. Every breath.

Her voice trembled through the static, and my heart broke all over again.

"Remy, if anything happens to me, you'll know why…"

She hadn't been pleading.

She'd been warning.

I went to the kitchen for another cup of coffee, the smell of blueberry syrup making my stomach churn, so I grabbed two pieces of bread, popped them in the toaster, buttered them, and put them on a saucer, pouring syrup over the two slices.

"This will help. I need some food."

Somewhere outside, thunder cracked, rattling the windowpanes. I flinched, coffee sloshing over the rim of my mug as I bumped it with the saucer of toast. The storm rolled in heavy and low, the kind that drowned out footsteps, screams, and truth.

I went to the door and rechecked the lock. Secure.

But when I turned back toward the stage, the lights over the piano flickered—once, twice—and all the lights went out.

"Not tonight," I whispered, holding my toast, trying not to bump into the tables with the daisies.

Then I heard it.

Footsteps. Padding upstairs.

Slow. Careful. Deliberate.

Was someone in Kermit's old room?

Or was Silas awake?

I froze, every muscle locked, and dropped my toast, the syrup sticking to my shirt as if I'd taken a bite and missed my mouth.

"Silas?" I called. "If that's you, I swear—"

A thud interrupted me. Something heavy fell. Followed by the scrape of metal.

I grabbed the flashlight from the drawer beneath the bar, the one Kermit insisted I keep since it's dark in the building if the lights go out.

I turned it on and edged toward the stairs, my heart pounding so hard I could taste it. The beam of light shook in my hand, jumping across the wall.

Halfway up, I smelled it—cigarette smoke. Not the sweet kind. The kind that clings to fear.

"Windex? Silas?" I whispered, though I knew better.

The door to Kermit's room was half open. I pushed it wider with the flashlight.

Empty.

The window was open, rain blowing in. The curtain flapped like a frantic bird, and the floorboards glistened wet.

And there—on the cot—lay my dad's journal.

Opened.

Pages ripped out.

My breath hitched. "No... I left that on the bar downstairs by my laptop."

I charged downstairs, pointing the light toward the bar, and the cassette tape and player were gone as well. But not my computer.

I flew into Kermit's room and lightning flashed outside, throwing a quick burst of white across the room—enough to see a wet footprint near the door.

Before I could move, the floor creaked behind me.

I spun.

Nothing.

Just the echo of my pulse.

Then a whisper, close to my ear: "You should've stayed quiet, Miss Vaughn."

I swung the flashlight—caught only a glimpse—a shadow retreating through the hallway. I bolted after it, my shoes slipping on the slick floor.

"Stop!" I yelled, but the word cracked apart in my throat.

The back door slammed wide open to the alley at the spiral staircase, and the wind howled as the shadow tumbled near the bottom of the stairs, then rose and slipped into the darkness.

I ran down the stairs myself; my chest felt like ten people were trying to suffocate me as I tried to breathe. Standing in the alley in the sheet of rain, I could see nothing.

And the shadow disappeared toward the street.

But wait, the window to Kermit's room was open.

Had there been two people in the cafe with me?

By the time I reached the corner, there was no one.

Just puddles and cigarette smoke lingering like mockery.

A flicker of paper waving on a pole caught my eye—taped to the lamppost. A square, small piece of yellow paper, soaked through, but legible enough to read: Next comes fire.

My stomach dropped.

I ran back up the spiral staircase, rushed up, locked the door, and shoved a table in front of it.

Back downstairs, the power flickered again, plunging the room into darkness. Seconds later, it returned, and the lights came on, my heart pounding so loudly I thought it was the drums on the stage.

My reflection in the bar mirror looked like a stranger, eyes wide, hair plastered to my face, terror and resolve warring in equal measure. And blueberry syrup on my shirt.

That's when I heard it—faint but unmistakable—music.

Not thunder. Not a dream.

The piano.

Playing *Blue Shadows*.

Every note soft and slow, like a heartbeat echoing through the wood.

I stepped closer, breath shallow. And that's when I saw Windex playing, smoking a cigarette, the ashtray on the piano, and the cigarette smoldering.

"Ms. Emory, what were you chasing in the dark?"

"Wait, when did you get here?"

"I came in the front door. I knocked. Had to use my key. Thankfully, I had it. I left my washboard, and the piano just called to me in the darkness. So, I played a little."

"Did you see that man run upstairs?" I quizzed him.

"No, just got here. Saw nothing, just jazz speaking to my soul."

I sighed. "So, you know this song?"

"Yeah, it's Kermit's song. Or his mom's song. I'm missing him already."

"Celeste? Did you... by chance, know her?" I whispered.

My next question landed like a saxophone note, as if it might cause the past to rise from the cemetery of an old tombstone.

"I did. She was a favorite of many. She loved an audience, and boy, could she sing."

I sat on the bench next to Windex and hit a key, one note, and the tears came.

Then silence.

And the air grew colder.

A candle on the bar flared up suddenly, tall and blue—and in the flicker, I considered going home to Wyoming.

**

By morning, the police would arrive, take my statement, and treat me like a woman unraveling in fear.

Remy would deny everything, of course. It was probably one of his cronies—men without a backbone.

They'd call it a break-in. Maybe vandalism.

But I knew.

Someone wanted me out. Someone wanted that tape gone, maybe because it named them, or perhaps because it named something worse.

When the officers left and the sun slipped between the clouds, I finally called Calvin. He answered on the second ring.

"Em?" he said, voice thick with sleep. "Did you break your leg? Did you get arrested? You're not answering your texts. Josie had Renee report back to me and said you're wallowing in Kermit's death. And that you were afraid. So now, catch me up."

"I've had someone break into The Blue Door. And I must not have seen your texts," I cried, the tears rushing out like a long-overdue waterfall of pain.

"Cal…" My voice cracked. "He had a picture of me."

Silence.

Dead, heavy silence.

"Who had a picture of you?"

"Remy Duval. A photo of me in Wyoming. Before I ever came here."

More silence.

I pulled the picture from my tote. "Who would care so much about me coming here that they'd have someone watch me before I left Wyoming?"

"I'm not sure, but I'm sure money or property is involved." The protective brother, Calvin, tightened his gaze. "Tell me everything. Right now."

So, I did—all of it. Every scream inside my chest poured out—Remy, the break-in, the missing tape, the threat, the piano, the whispers. Kermit in the river. The sax on the driftwood.

When I finished, Cal exhaled a growl like he was trying not to punch a wall. "That's it," he said. "This is too much. And too dangerous."

I sighed. "But I can't leave now. Miles needs me. So does Naomi. The cafe is almost ready to open. I've finished this for Dad. I must open the cafe."

"Do you want to die next? Emory, you're my little sister."

"I'll be careful."

"You'll be stubborn," he corrected. "And those are different things."

"Cal—"

"Where are you right now?" He asked.

"In the cafe."

"Look at the front window."

Confused, I turned toward the cafe's entrance, gazing through the windows.

And froze.

Standing outside in the rain, jaw clenched, was Calvin.

My brother.

Backpack slung over one shoulder, eyes fierce enough to scare the devil himself.

I gasped, opening the door, pulling him inside, wrapping my arms around his neck. "Cal?! How—"

"You should have read your texts. I'm here to take you home," Cal said, his eyes determined, glaring.

"So, you're on the phone acting like you're thousands of miles away, and you're literally outside?"

"If I'm not firm with you, you don't listen."

"I don't listen because I'm a grown woman and I don't need you telling me what to do." I spouted those words, the farthest things from the truth.

He lifted his hands in surrender. "I took a late flight. Then an early one. And the worst Uber ride ever. I'm not letting you do this alone."

"So, you're staying here with me?" I grinned.

"If that's what it takes. Because if you won't leave, then I'm staying put."

"I could use your company," I said, the tears falling like they'd been trapped for years, and hugged my brother so tightly, I thought I was going to pass out.

"Em, I can't breathe," Cal muttered.

"Sorry, I'm so glad you're here." I stood back, water dripping from my clothes. "Cal, you look terrible."

"You look worse," he replied, pulling me back into a hug that cracked me open.

"I shouldn't have let you come," I said, against his shoulder.

"You didn't," he muttered. "I came on my own. I should have come when you first drove here. I don't know what I was thinking."

"I'm a big girl. All grown up. But I didn't expect this."

When we pulled apart again, his jaw was set like stone. "Show me around, where the break-in happened."

I nodded.

But as we turned toward the bar mirror, something glinted—a smear—written on the mirror with what appeared to be flour.

One word: Run.

Calvin's voice dropped to a whisper. "We're not running. Who wrote that on there?"

Silas called from the kitchen. "I did. You folks are digging up graves that won't leave until you do."

Cal turned to me. "Who's that?"

"My cook. Kermit's friend. Renee's friend. And Windex's brother. He comes recommended. And I like him. He reminds me of Hank back in Cody."

My washboard musician called from across the room. "I'm Windex. If you need a band, a liaison, or a guide around town, I'm your man."

Call nodded, "Maybe your cook could run this place, and you can come home."

"I was planning on Kermit taking that job. But now." My voice cracked. "Now everything's changed."

Cal stepped in front of me, his shoulders broad and protective. "We're staying for the grand opening. If we don't, then they win."

"Exactly. So, seriously, you're staying with me?"

"Yes, I can't let you stop now. This place looks great. Dad would be so proud."

I smiled, a small one that felt like a release. "I must finish what I've started." I swallowed hard, my throat raw with sadness at how fast life changed like the seasons.

Somewhere deep inside The Blue Door Cafe, the idea of running away kept pushing at me, as something old and angry stirred in the shadows.

Windex played a few notes on his washboard.

Cal spun around, his reddish-brown hair waved at me, his need for a haircut obvious to probably only me. "And that must be the washboard musician that plays jazz," he said, pursing his lips.

Windex stopped playing. "This washboard knows the secrets of this entire town. I play; I clean windows. I'm your man."

I introduced Cal to my new friends, the one with music in his bones, and the one with food at the end of a recipe.

Cal shook their hands and turned to me. "I feel better knowing Windex and Silas are here, but that didn't stop the intruders."

"I know, it's just that whoever came inside ripped out pages from Dad's journal and took the cassette," I whined. "Why can't I have a normal and calm life?"

I caught Silas up on the late-night intruder and how I'd called for him many times, but he didn't answer, and he sighed as the air escaped from a teakettle on the stove. "I sleep hard these days. That new bed you got me is great. And well, I need new hearing aids."

Windex played a few notes on his washboard. "Who wants normal? That's for folks who've stopped trying to do good, like you, Miss Em. You've got the good stuff inside your heart. We need that here. We've got jazz to play. I can feel it."

Silas slid toward the kitchen, mumbling. "I've got to get my hearing aids replaced."

My phone dinged. "Cal, it's a text from Renee. She's got you a room at the hotel, and it's ready when you are."

"So, she's been a great help to you, too?"

"Yes, she's gotten in my way some, but that could be my control issues rising. But yes, Renee's been there through everything with me. However, some things with the renovations might have gone faster without her."

Cal nodded. "Josie's great at delegating, too. I've already got a mile-long list waiting for me in Wyoming. But I love giving the children riding lessons. It's a fit for me."

I scratched my ear, thankful that Cal had found his calling up north, where the Mustangs run free. But returning to the North may not be for me in the future.

I hugged my brother. "I'm so glad you're here." I sighed. "But Renee can be a bit much."

And Windex chimed in. "She's a bit too much for most of us."

I remembered the note that said, *fire is next* and broke into sobs. "Cal, what if someone tries to burn down the cafe?"

16

Blueberry Hill

REMEMBER, CAL IS HERE…

That's what I kept saying most of the night, turning to one side, then the other, and I'd roll over in my bed like a log careening down a mountain. In nearly awake moments, I'd reassure myself, knowing Cal's hotel room was close to mine, but grief has a strange rhythm.

Each moment I slept in New Orleans felt like a rerun of watching loggers saw down trees, only for one to get away, crush someone, and do it again the next night. My heart constantly felt the crushing weight of this trip.

And because the rhythm of time doesn't always march forward, it can sway sideways, dip back, and loop around like a jazz song on a late-night street corner, I'm struggling to smile and make my lists count.

By sunrise, the rain had stopped, but the ache hadn't, and my eyelids hung from exhaustion.

I stood on the steps of my cafe now, the morning sun washing the street in a kind of weary gold. My reflection shimmered faintly in a puddle: same woman, a new tiredness, same chestnut hair, now in a ponytail, a little mascara, and smacking gum. My grief itched with a layer of leftover sorrow, but duty called, and my mission could not fail.

Cal emerged from the kitchen, saying there was water on the floor by the water heater, a leak that needed to be addressed. "Did you check the credentials of your contractors?"

"Renee helped me. You know that," I said, moving to the puddled spot by the wall near the closet, and I reached for the mop. "It's under warranty. After all, the water heater is brand new."

"My point exactly," Cal said, taking the mop from my grasp.

I leaned on the counter, and he wiped up the floor, mumbling. "We'd better get them out here before the place floods."

Silas joined us, showing up from the back room where he kept supplies. "Called Renee already. Saw that mess earlier. We don't need no flood. We're about to open."

I smiled, noting the inconvenience of a water heater compared to the work that's already gone into restoring the cafe.

I marched to gaze out the windows by the tables, and the city smelled like chicory coffee and wet earth, and the cafe was quiet except for the clanking from Silas practicing his recipes. And Cal, moaning about my choice of contractors.

Finally, Cal and I poured ourselves some coffee and sat by the table nearest the front door. The steam rose from my coffee, warming my nose, and the first sip—always the best.

"This will be great. It must be. For Dad. For me. And for Kermit." I said, sipping my coffee too fast, burning my lip because I didn't wait for it to cool.

"You've bitten off too much. I should have come sooner and supported you. Besides, you take on projects and dive in headfirst. Not all Emory Vaughn ideas should come to life."

"Now, you're a fine one to say such a thing. You left your job in Texas to work at a ranch with horses."

"I lost my job. All because of your road trip last year, if you don't remember," Cal interrupted.

"But now you teach children to ride horses in Wyoming. How exciting."

"Yes, I love it there. So, let's get finished here, so I can get back to what I love."

"But, Cal, on the good days, I love it here. There's music everywhere. And I love music. I should have brought my guitar with me, but in my rush to get on the road, I left it in my room at the ranch." I sighed, "And now, Kermit won't ever hear me play."

Cal swallowed hard, not commenting on my guitar-whining moment. He glanced toward the kitchen. "So, you've just let Silas move upstairs?"

"Of course, it's perfect. He won't be late for work this way," I said, smiling. "Kermit lived up there, too. Now his room is...empty." I choked on my words, coughing.

Cal reached for my hand. "Sis, we need to prepare for when we leave. Let Silas or Windex run this place, and let's go back to Wyoming."

"I can't leave. The water heater is leaking. And it's under warranty." I squirmed in my chair. "And don't you want to meet Miles? That boy is a part of our family. He's the cutest and smartest little trumpet player this side of the Mississippi River."

"I guess. But, if we keep digging, we're bound to find we're related to people all the way back to the Garden of Eden."

"No, need to be rude. He's a kid who's lost his dad."

Cal sighed. "Sorry, I just get frustrated with the trail Dad left behind, that's all."

"Kermit was Celeste's son. We need to make sure Miles and his mom, Naomi, will be okay."

"Em, you can't save the world."

"I'm not. I'm just trying to be there for my family. Dad didn't always do that for us, but we should." I countered, my coffee warm in my throat.

We sat in silence, except for the conversation from the back, where Silas showed the plumber where the water heater sat, where it leaked, and how fixing this was important for grand openings.

I moved that way, but Cal said, "Silas can handle this. You're not in charge of everything."

I grinned. "I might be."

We finished our coffee, and Cal asked, "So, where is Windex? Shouldn't he be up by now?"

"I'm not the cafe police. Remember, I'm not in charge of the world. And we're not officially open. No one's on a time clock, just yet. Once we open, our hours are 8 a.m. to 2 p.m. each day—a family place with jazz for our minds and blueberries for our souls. And before you ask, we'll be open on Sunday, and the band will play gospel."

Cal shook his head. "A Vaughn family cafe in the Quarter's heart. Who knew?"

I whispered, "Me, I knew. This will be great. You'll see. I'm just trying to find the song in the story."

Cal's presence eased my edginess, and the worry of Kermit's death and the break-in. I thought about how the police had come yesterday, taken photos, and promised to be in touch. They'd said words like *vandalism* and *trespassing.* Not one of them reacted when I mentioned Kermit's murder and the possible connection to my cafe.

Plus, I'd expected to see Sergeant Laveau, but she didn't come; only two suits, who took notes.

Kermit's dented saxophone case sat propped against the bar, and I knew. This wasn't over. The police didn't even ask about the sax; a sign they weren't truly taking me seriously. Or maybe, they didn't know I'd rescued it from the river.

But Kermit's case… it wasn't even close to being over.

Cal tapped the table. "Em, you've got that figuring out the universe stare going on."

I raised my eyebrows. "Just trying to figure out how to help Kermit's song live on."

Just then, the fast-talking, high-spirited Renee arrived with pastries. "Morning, family," she declared.

Cal squinted. "Don't we have plenty of food in the kitchen?"

"Now, Calvin Vaughn, I'm trying to be neighborly. Don't ruin the mood." Renee said, charming him with her smile.

He peeked inside the box. "You're too good to us. Josie told me how you've shadowed Emory all these weeks, helping her, guiding, almost like a sister."

I smiled. "Cal, don't go getting soft on me."

"Well, donuts do help," he said.

Renee tossed a napkin to Cal. "Got to keep the workers fed, even the honorary ones," she teased. "Oh, and the plumber is on the way. He'll make the water heater work or replace it."

I smiled weakly. "He's already here, with Silas in the kitchen."

Silas bellowed, "Water heater is fixed. We're back on track."

Renee smiled, "If you need me, I'm always just a phone call away. Always. Donuts and a plumber. Both fix things in us. Sweets. And hot water. We need both. And friends. We all need friends."

She hugged me from behind, and it wasn't one of those polite, Sunday-side hugs as she pulled me to my feet. It was the kind that holds your ribs in place when your soul's falling through them.

"You slept at all?" she asked.

"Not really. Every time I close my eyes, I hear the piano playing and dream about my dad at the keys, and then I see Kermit playing his sax on the stage, and then I jerk awake. Or the nightmare is about loggers and trees crashing over me."

"If you don't get some sleep, you're going to fall apart," Renee emphasized, her voice at a pitch that brought Windex down the stairs.

"What's all this squealing going on down here? Sounds like a catfight." Windex asked, nodding to Cal, like he knew my brother would agree that Renee could be a little too much.

After handing out breakfast and coffee, Windex and Silas reached for the last two glazed donuts, and we started cleaning.

Windex shook his head, humming. "You like things clean, but clean is overrated. Everything gets dirty again."

Cal nudged Windex. "You know her already, huh?"

"Yeah, she's the Blueberry Girl with more dreams than days to make it happen."

"I'm in the room. Stop talking as if I'm not," I smiled, happy my love for cleanliness was being enforced.

Windex played on his washboard, and Silas went back in the kitchen, organizing his workspace, and I wiped off the residue of those who invaded my world.

Renee scrubbed the tables, humming an upbeat tune, while I sorted through what the intruder had knocked over by the bar: a few of the plastic daisies on the floor, and the placemats, too.

I marched to the piano to wipe it down; the dust was a constant coating that fell from yesterday's woes, and the floorboard under the piano squeaked oddly.

I crouched down and tugged. A corner shifted. And the end popped up.

"Renee," I said, as if she knew more about renovations. "Come here. We'll need to fix this stage; someone might trip on this. I can't believe your guy didn't see this—your master floor finishing man we had to have."

My tone had sharpened, and Windex stopped playing his washboard. "This world's not perfect, Ms. Em, don't forget that."

Cal came to my side. "She's tired, that's all."

Renee answered, too. "Emory's racing through the day as if tomorrow isn't promised."

I sneered. "I just need a little sleep. But we need to fix this flooring."

Cal pushed on the wood, and the board popped loose. "Yes, a nail or two. We can fix this right up."

I plopped down, crossing my legs. "All this hard work. We've put so much into it, and nothing is working. The water heater leaked."

Renee whispered. "It's fixed."

I countered, "But look at this floor."

Cal touched my shoulder. "We'll fix it right up."

And that's when I cried as if the waterfall behind the melting sorrow of winter crushed my heart and poured from my eyes.

No one moved. Not one said a word for minutes that seemed like years, and then I wiped my nose on the napkin

Renee handed me and took the longest breath ever. "I'm fine. Really. Just fine."

Then I saw it. Another small, sealed tin, with spider webs around it, about the size of a coffee can. I opened the can and, wrapped in a cloth, was a note.

"This is crazy. Who hides notes in the floors and walls of an old bar? Who does that?" My voice rose, bringing Silas into the room with what appeared like batter on his hands, and Windex hit a note on his washboard.

I held up the paper, the edge crumbling at my grasp. And the handwriting stopped my breath. "This matches Dad's penmanship in his journal. Look, it says, *for when the hope finds you, you'll have your song again.*"

Windex knelt, his aging knees popping as he reached into the crevice. "Look, there's a 45-vinyl record. The label reads, 'Blueberry Hill: Vaughn & Celeste.'"

My throat closed. "Dad recorded with her?"

Cal pushed Windex aside. "How many secrets does our dad have?"

Renee whistled. "Looks like your daddy had more chords in him than anyone knew."

I choked, "How many hidden tin boxes are there in this place?"

Cal peered over my shoulder. "This is too strange."

Renee touched Cal's shoulder. "Not for New Orleans. Shadows hide at every turn. Some slip out by day when you're not expecting them. Some stay hidden for a lifetime."

I cringed. "Renee, you make this sound so haunting."

"Trust me, girl. I've lived here my entire life. I can't explain how life can twist and turn, or how it churns, in this town. But never be surprised."

I carried the record to the sunlight streaming through the doorway, tracing the grooves with my fingertip. "He must've hidden it before Celeste died. Maybe this is the key to what happened."

Renee tilted her head. "You gonna play it?"

Windex answered for me. "You need to find a record player."

Silas mumbled, opting for his kitchen and scooting off, but glanced at me. "Ms. Em, you'd best leave the past alone."

"I don't do that part well, Silas. I have to listen to this."

Windex shuffled to his washboard, strumming the board like he was caught in the past with his band.

In minutes, Renee, Cal, and I ended up around the corner and down the street at Jasper's Vinyl Revival, a narrow shop smelling of cardboard and nostalgia.

The owner, Jasper, looked like he'd been carved out of bourbon barrels and patience. His gray beard reached his collarbone, and his shirt read: Music Saves Lives—And Sometimes Lawyers.

He eyed the record like a surgeon studying an X-ray. "Ain't seen this label," he murmured. "You sure you wanna hear it? Some songs you can't un-hear."

"I'm sure."

Renee touched my shoulder. "Where's your brother?"

"I'm not sure. He was with us a minute ago." I glanced through the store's window. "He's out there, taking in the sounds. Cal's not too keen on finding out what our dad did or didn't do."

"I'll go talk to him," Renee said, as if she were in charge of the moment. Her friendly ways were nice, but continued dominance clashed with mine now that I've been here for a few months. She slipped outside, but quickly came back in, gluing herself to my side.

Jasper set the record carefully on the turntable. The needle hissed. Static filled the air. Then—

Piano.

Slow, delicate.

Then Celeste's voice, rich as smoke and light all at once: "I found my thrill... on Blueberry Hill..."

However, about two-thirds of the way through the song, the lyrics faltered. She laughed softly—a nervous, broken laugh—and another voice joined her.

My dad's.

"Don't stop singing, Celeste. Keep going." I whispered.

Celeste began, "Ben, some songs end before they're finished."

"Not if you believe in mercy."

"Mercy don't sell records." Celeste's voice cracked.

"Maybe it buys redemption. This is our chance for the record, let's make it a gem," Dad said.

The piano faded, replaced by a sound I couldn't place: a chair scraping, someone knocking on a door, or maybe, muffled voices.

Then Celeste whispered something so soft, the recording captured it, and I almost missed it: "He's coming,

Ben. If anything happens, promise me you'll keep The Blue Door safe and take care of my..."

The record scratched. A long, heavy silence. Then, faintly—the sound of water lapping.

Jasper lifted the needle. "That's all there is."

Renee exhaled. "That must have been a demo that she saved. It's hard to believe that's your daddy's voice. And Celeste's. How surreal."

"She trusted my dad. Trusted him," I said, my heart pounding. "Celeste asked my dad to protect someone, too."

Renee's eyes found mine. "It was her son. Kermit. Had to be."

I sighed. "Are you sure? What if she meant someone else?"

**

Back at The Blue Door Cafe, I replayed the recording in my mind. My dad's voice—gentle, tired—sounded like a man already asking forgiveness for something he hadn't done yet.

Renee told me Cal needed a good walk, and she said she'd planned to take a warm meal to Naomi and Miles, leaving me alone, again with the ghosts.

I texted Sergeant Laveau to tell her about the vinyl record. She immediately sent me a response: I'll come by and pick it up from you.

That's when I remembered something I'd missed before when listening to the record play. Near the end of the recording, beneath the static, another sound emerged.

Faint. Mechanical.

Like a camera shutter clicked.

Had someone taken a picture?

I giggled erratically; the stress was taking its toll, and history repeated itself: I was now the one hiding things in the cafe, thinking about the cassette with the flour sacks.

I texted Laveau: Could you send me a picture of the photo I gave you?

Her text came back: Sure. Then the photo flashed on my phone, and, glancing at it, I noticed, barely visible in the corner behind Remy and Celeste, a shadow—someone holding a camera.

And that someone was...

I zoomed in until the pixels blurred. The outline was clear: a tall, white-bearded man in a white suit and a familiar hat. And a cigar.

It was Gus Tiller. He was watching Remy, Celeste, and Kermit.

But who took this photo? Had my dad snapped this image?

A knock jolted me from my thoughts, and I opened the cafe door to find Naomi standing there, her face pale. "I think you should see this."

I glanced around. "Have you seen Renee? She was coming to see you." I asked, wondering where she was and what in the world had happened to my brother. "Did she have Cal with her?"

"You mean, Cal, as in your brother?" Naomi asked.

"Yes, he flew into town. But he's been missing or out of pocket for about two hours now." I said, ushering her inside.

"Haven't met him, but as for Renee. She doesn't come to see me. She avoids me. We're not really friends. We come from two different parts of town. Her part where shiny things live. And my part where life is real and often gray."

"Wait, but everyone loves Renee," I said, moving my hair behind my ears, which had slipped from the clasp holding my hair in a ponytail.

"Trust me. A wolf can hide in sheep's clothing and wear high heels and sundresses," Naomi said, glancing over her shoulder.

I cleared my throat, not sure what to make of Naomi's take on Renee. She handed me an envelope. "This was on my screen door, stuck in the mesh. No return address. Just my name, written in red ink."

Inside was a photograph—it appeared to have been printed from an old negative, with muted colors, a darker gray and green.

I stared, unable to focus, and said, "That's Celeste. She's standing on The Blue Door stage, eyes closed, microphone in hand. And standing beside her is Ben Vaughn. My dad."

Naomi pointed. "And behind them, half-shadowed, but unmistakable, stood Remy Duval." She pulled a note out of the envelope. "And read this, it says, 'Truth isn't mercy; choose wisely.'"

I sat down hard on the barstool, my legs shaking. Naomi poured me some water, her hand trembling too.

"Naomi, this is Remy Duval in the past, and now he's invading our present. I'm worried, he's making me feel like a fly trapped in the sticky honey from a honeycomb, and I can't get away from Gus Tiller, even though that man is in prison."

"I'm leaving town with Miles. We can't stay here. Kermit's past has slipped into my life too, and I've got to protect Miles. I have to go before anything happens to… to me, or heaven forbid, to my sweet boy." Her words cracked like splinters of wood breaking off from a tree rooted in crime, that was living in plain sight right on the streets of New Orleans.

I hugged her. "But you can't go. I've just met you. Miles is Kermit's son, and my… family. You are, too. We've got to help each other through this. The shadows can't win; they must fall."

Cal barged in, winded, his breath caught in his throat. "We've got to go now. We can't stay here. This isn't how I planned for my visit to New Orleans to go, not today, nor in life, nor for my future. We must pack our things and run."

I pulled my arm from Cal's grasp. "You've been gone for hours, and now, you run in here and tell me we're leaving. Why or what has you scared, Cal?"

I didn't let him answer and growled, "And then, you disappear and don't even listen to the tape! Don't come in here and tell me I'm leaving. I'm not. Not yet anyway!"

Cal argued, firm and without wavering. "It's not my fault. Honest. Something happened."

17

Something in the Water

MORNING CAME LATE, AND light crept through the shutters at the side of the curtain like it had a secret to tell. I sat on the edge of my bed, coffee gone cold, staring at my dad's journal, with the few pages left. And the words blurred and swam. And nothing made sense. Nothing fit. Everything was broken pieces of a story, buried with the past, trying to find its resurrection in my one act—to honor my dad with the cafe.

I'd been waiting for Calvin to call since sunrise after our conversation ended with me slamming a door at The Blue Door. I'd locked myself in the broom closet, arguing with my brother, and telling him to take the next flight to Wyoming. Renee had tried to negotiate our treaty, and Silas offered decaffeinated coffee. And Windex told Renee to mind her own business.

I finally convinced Cal to sleep on his request when I rushed past him to the hotel; that panic never makes a wise decision.

He'd texted after midnight, a short line that read: *We need to talk. In person. Not in this hotel.*

That kind of message from my brother usually meant one of two things—either he had some insight, not likely, or life had taken a left turn down the wrong alley.

Dressed, I tossed a fresh piece of gum into my mouth, put my hair behind my ears, pasted on a smile, and walked to The Blue Door around ten.

As for Cal answering my calls or texts, he has not responded once. And I didn't care. Okay, I cared, but I was fuming at him—one second, he's on my side, ready to help me see this through, then he's running home to avoid the problems that came with this trip. And he just got here.

I drank my second cup of coffee, thanks to Silas, and didn't touch the blueberry pancakes he'd placed in front of me.

"Ms. Em, a starving person somewhere, would love my pancakes." He said, pouring warm blueberry syrup over the stack.

"Then send these to them," I said, handing my plate to Silas. He mumbled, walked to the kitchen, and I caught a few words about "women with attitude" and "how honoring someone's dad doesn't come with such rudeness."

I didn't respond. I was too mad at Cal to fight with anyone else.

By eleven o'clock, Cal shuffled inside, looking like yesterday's storm had hit him twice. His shirt was wrinkled, his eyes red-rimmed, and his hands trembled when he shut the door behind him. He wasn't drunk—he didn't drink anymore—but something was off. He moved more slowly, his words delayed, like he was still catching up to himself.

Silas slipped into the room, poured Cal his coffee, "Morning, Mr. Vaughn. You doing, okay?"

"Not great. I've been better." Cal said, blowing on the hot coffee, taking a sip, his hand slipping, and he nearly dropped the mug.

"Hey," I said, using my grown-up voice, taking the cup from Cal's grasp. "You look like you tangled with the wrong end of a trumpet."

He tried to smile but didn't. "We need to figure out what's going on here. You got a minute?"

"Yes, but no more arguing. No more fights."

"And no running and hiding inside the closet."

"Okay, but I'm a wee bit edgy these days," I said.

Cal glanced around the cafe as if he didn't trust the walls, then motioned toward the stage. We sat on the edge where Celeste once sang, our feet brushing the old floorboards that still smelled of bourbon and mildew—like it was soaked into the grain.

He waited until Silas was out of sight and wrapped his fingers around the coffee cup. "Yes, the music out on the streets, at first, drew me in, and I planned to come back inside with you at the record store. Then Renee coaxed me with her sweet talk to wait outside, that she'd hold your hand while listening to the tape."

"Wait, she asked you to remain outside?" I asked.

"Pretty much. She talked about the romance of New Orleans and how she and I could have a drink, talk, get to know each other, and let me ease into the atmosphere."

Cal sighed.

I moaned. "She's a great tour guide," I said, tossing out sarcasm on each word.

Silas returned with the coffeepot, and I turned to him. "Not now, Silas. Thank you, though."

Cal ran his fingers through his tangled hair. "We landed at a place called The Coda, and Renee hung close, too close, I'd say."

I blinked. "The Coda? That's a bar at the next corner past Duval's Lounge, across the corner from his."

"Yeah," he said. "Renee said it was a little local spot, quiet, good for talking. She insisted we sit down and get to know each other."

I glanced outside; an orange cat sat on the hood of my green rental, curled up, and licked its paw. "She didn't mention any of that to me."

Cal rubbed the back of his neck. "She was friendly. Too friendly, maybe. She ordered me a Coke and said she doesn't drink either. I took one sip, Em." His voice cracked on that last word. "Just one. And I swear, it tasted strange."

I frowned. "Strange how?"

He hesitated. "Like medicine. Bitter. I thought maybe the syrup line was off or something, but I kept sipping. Dumb move. Because five minutes later, everything went fuzzy. I remember her talking, leaning close, saying something about Dad, how her parents had known him. Then... nothing."

A chill crawled up my spine. "You blacked out?"

He nodded. "Not exactly, but I wandered around the French Quarter, lost, the afternoon a blur, and couldn't find my way back. And Renee, like a fog that rolled in and blocked my view, then evaporated, just like that, gone."

"She set you up?" I asked.

"Appears so. The next thing I know, I'm coming to my senses and have to ask for directions on how to find my way back to the hotel. I couldn't remember anything."

I stormed to the edge of the stage, my hands on the top of the piano. "So, Renee knows you don't drink, but you were walking around like you were drunk. An officer could have arrested you or worse. Cal, that's—good grief—that's terrifying."

Cal marched up to me. "Sis, we need to get out while we're both alive."

I shook. "But Cal, this is my dream… for Dad."

"I know. But dreams change. Survival is better."

"Wait till I see, Renee. She's going to have a piece of my mind."

"But wait, I don't know that she put something in my glass. We can't assume she's in on that."

But something in my chest tightened, a knot forming just beneath my ribs. Renee's words from earlier in the week echoed: *'Duval's got people everywhere, baby. You just can't see them all.'*

I looked at my brother. "What was the last thing you remember Renee saying?"

Cal stared at the floor. "She said I looked like Dad. That my eyes were his, then she raised her glass and said, 'Here's to debts being repaid.' After that, everything's hazy."

I whispered, "Debts don't drown."

He looked up sharply. "What?"

"Nothing," I said too quickly. "Just something I found written on a note at the cemetery the day Renee took me there. The same day, she said she wanted me to let the past rest."

He leaned forward. "You think she's connected to Duval?"

"I don't want to," I said. "But she's got history she's not sharing. She knows him. She grew up here. And we barely know her. And now she's cozying up to you."

Cal's jaw flexed. "She didn't flirt, if that's what you mean."

"I didn't say she did," I said, though my heart didn't buy it. "But she's tangled in this, Cal. Every time I think I can trust her, another odd clue is tied to her behavior."

Cal and I moved back to the table by the window and sat down. He leaned on his elbows, staring at the cat on my car. "Whose cat? Yours?"

"No, just a stray. I think Silas feeds him out back."

Cal cleared his throat. "Maybe I'm wrong, Em. Maybe someone else slipped something into my drink, and she didn't notice. The place was crowded."

I wanted to believe that—oh, I *wanted* to—but the pit in my stomach said otherwise. "Did she act strangely?"

He thought about it. "She smiled a lot. But her eyes... they were sad. Like she was already sorry for something."

That line hit me square in the soul. Because I'd seen that same sadness flicker behind her laughter more than once.

"Cal," I said, "Surely, she didn't hope you would fall into the Mississippi River."

Cal took my hand across the table. "Stop it. Now you're making her sound like a killer. Our minds are toying with the unknown. But one thing I know. We should go home."

I cried, glancing around at the mirror behind the bar, the shiny glasses waiting for tea and lemonade, the stage with the lights, and hope of a new band playing in the future, and heard Silas humming, a pretty common occurrence in the Quarter.

"Cal, I have to open this place. I have to."

He pressed one of his hands to his forehead. "When I woke up around ten, I couldn't stop shaking. Not from fear, from whatever was still in my system. I felt sick. Weak. Like my blood wasn't mine."

"You're okay now. You're safe."

"Am I?" he asked quietly. "Because, Em, the way she looked at me—like she was torn in half. I don't know if she's our ally or the one loading the gun."

Outside, a trumpet tune drifted from somewhere down Chartres Street, a melody so soft it could've been Celeste's ghost practicing scales. The city never really slept—it just changed rhythms. And the orange cat jumped from my car and moved toward the music.

Cal watched me, eyes full of exhaustion. "You think she did it, don't you?"

I breathed in slowly. "I think she's hiding something. And Duval's still running his games so she might be a part of it—whether she wants to be or not."

Cal rubbed his temples. "I should've known better than to go with her. But wait…"

"What? Are you remembering something?"

"Yeah, she asked if Kermit, Windex, or Silas ever mentioned to you about a ledger that showed Remy Duval's past and wanted to know if you… knew about it."

"Wait, no way? That's way off from just getting to know you." I gulped hard, my throat aching with the obvious, my teeth clenched, and a headache was brewing behind my temples.

"Kermit and I never talked about such things," I said. "She has mentioned ledgers before, that her accounting came in handy for her dad's buddies. Maybe she found old records from long ago. Maybe Kermit knew too much, and now that's why Remy took him out."

"Yep, we need to go home." Cal insisted.

"Cal," I said, voice tight, "do you remember hearing anyone else's voice before you blacked out?"

He frowned. "Maybe. A man's voice. Deep, gravelly. Laughed at something she said. Could've been a musician. Could've been that Duval."

The air in the cafe felt thicker, heavy with the scent of dust and secrets.

"I'll talk to her," I said. "We can't accuse her yet. Not without proof."

He nodded reluctantly. "Just… be careful. Promise me, Em."

"I promise." I reached out and brushed his arm, then whispered, "We've survived worse."

"Barely," he muttered. "You still talk to Dad out loud?"

"Every day," I said. "Usually, when I'm sweeping or fixing something. Keeps me grounded. I've talked to Celeste, too."

"Then tell them to keep an eye on us," Cal said. "Seems we're dancing with devils again."

That line sat between us like a prophecy.

I whispered to Cal. "But we're not leaving just yet. This isn't over."

"I need some fresh air," Cal said, turning the doorknob and walking outside.

I rushed to the sidewalk. "Do you know your way around?"

Cal glanced back. "I'll be fine. Really."

I muttered under my breath, "Lord, if I'm walking through this storm, help me keep my eyes on You, not the waves. You've pulled me from deeper waters before. Don't let me drown in suspicion. If Renee's guilty, show me the truth. If she's innocent, protect her. And if I'm mistaken— if fear's making me blind—then give me clarity."

The prayer steadied me. Not much, but enough to breathe again. One second, I'm sure Remy's involved. Then I think it's Lucien. And then, I'm back to making a list about Renee. I must be sure before I react, or I might get caught in the bluster of my stupidity.

I dug in my pocket for some Spearmint, unwrapped it, tossed it into my mouth, smacked it for the flavor I loved most, and went back inside. I busied myself with rearranging the glasses by the mirror for the fifth time. Then, I counted out more daisies to put on the tables. And made sure the espresso machine was clean, too.

A soft thud startled me—the front door was easing open. I jumped, my heart beating outside my chest, and hit my ribcage on the bar as Cal stepped back in holding a paper bag.

"Late breakfast?" he said. "Beignets from down the street. I figured sugar might help."

Silas peeked from the kitchen. "I have pancakes I'm shipping to starving children, unless someone wants them."

I grinned. "Sorry, Silas. I've been rude to you. Forgive me."

"No forgiveness needed. Only need you to eat. You're getting too skinny." Silas said, holding a spatula.

"You're the best," I said.

"The Lord sent me here. I'm the cook for this kitchen." Silas said, assuring me with his grin.

Cal and I sat on stools at the bar, powdered sugar snowing over the counter. The sweetness almost masked the unease circling our cafe. Almost.

I moseyed to the window, peering out at the street. The air shimmered with heat, ordinary life pretending nothing was wrong. But every shadow looked too long, every stranger too curious.

And just as I turned, the front door flew open, and sunlight spilled in like an uninvited truth.

"Good afternoon, Blueberry Girl!" Renee's voice rang out, bright as brass, her orange sundress swirling around her like a summer breeze even though it's fast approaching winter. She carried a basket of muffins and a grin big enough to hide anything.

"Mercy, it smells like ghosts and coffee in here. Did y'all start without me?" she teased, her laugh lilting through the air like she hadn't just haunted our conversation.

Cal stiffened beside me, his third cup of coffee halfway to his lips. I felt him tense, his pulse visible in the hollow of his throat.

I forced a smile that didn't reach my lips. "Renee. You're a little late for breakfast."

She winked. "Honey, the city doesn't sleep, and neither do I. Breakfast can happen at any time. Figured we'd start fresh today—it's time to get those finishing touches in place for that grand opening. You ready?"

Cal set his cup down slowly. "Depends on who's mixing the drinks."

Her smile faltered for half a heartbeat—just long enough for me to see it. Then she laughed it off and walked behind the counter, unloading muffins like nothing was wrong.

"Don't you two look serious," she said lightly. "What'd I miss?"

I studied her face. No guilt. No fear. Just sunshine and sass. But her hands shook slightly when she reached for a napkin.

Maybe Cal was wrong. Perhaps she *had* been trying to warn us. Or the best liars know how to look like morning light.

I stepped forward, pretending to be calm. "Actually, Renee, you might clear something up."

She glanced up, eyes curious, voice smooth. "Oh? What's that, sugar?"

Cal looked at me—a silent agreement passing between us.

"Where were you yesterday afternoon?" I asked.

Her smile never wavered, but her knuckles whitened on the counter. "Why, Emory, that's a mighty strange question. Where else would I be? I went with Cal for a drink, sat down to chat, and introduced him to New Orleans. That's all."

"Wait, you told me you were taking a meal to Naomi," I said, my tone low, my firmness obvious.

"Did I? I guess that's today. Cal and I slipped off for a moment. You have the best brother…" her voice trailed, her cheery smile unfazed.

The clock ticked behind us. A saxophone cried from somewhere outside with a long and low note, the note stretching thin as a thread.

Renee clicked her heels and circled the bar. "Honey, why all the questions? I've heard you speak of your brother, and you love yours so much. I thought he and I could be close friends. After all, it's nice to meet a gracious and caring brother."

Cal wiggled at the end of the bar. "I'm not that gracious."

I gave Cal my ugly sister glance, and he raised his shoulders as if he was playing along.

Renee paced and glanced at her phone. "What was I thinking? I've realized I'm not ready for the group from Tennessee today. I'm shorthanded at the hotel. Seems a respiratory virus is loose in town, and my help is sick, and I'm needed there. See you two sweethearts after a while."

And she was out, skirting my questions, and flitting her wave in the air like I couldn't see what she was doing— avoiding me and walking away.

Cal took a sip of his now-cold coffee. "See, that's a weird woman if you ask me."

I rubbed my neck, the ache of that headache moving to my shoulders. "But Josie went to college with her in Denver. They're good friends."

Cal sighed. "Or so we've thought."

I joined him, and my wondering and wishing and worry mixed like batter in a blueberry muffin bowl—and I could not pick out the exact truth in my journey to rebuild the past so it could live in the present.

I let my mind race like I was flying too low over the traffic on a highway, like a pelican that migrated south, but crashed into more secrets.

The earlier discussion about leaving New Orleans flew out the window as a flight plan of resistance took hold, the kind that faces corruption head-on, as if God had given us wings to fly. The type that circles and lands and stays!

Chapter 18

Of Life and Death

I'D DISCOVERED KERMIT WAS MY cousin not many weeks back, and now, a funeral? How could this be? One second, I'm meeting him inside The Blue Door, ready to evict him for squatting upstairs in the old bar, only to embrace him as a family member. It's as if he never existed, not truly. A blur. A split second in my life. And now he's gone.

Kermit's steps were broken. But they were on the mend and highlighted by a past filled with crime and laced with prison time. But still, he loved, had a son, hoped for a better future, adored jazz, and now he's gone.

The river smelled like wet iron and old prayers. I stood on the riverbank with my hands shoved into my jacket pockets, almost as if keeping them confined meant I wouldn't reach for answers that weren't there.

The water moved too fast, the latest rains swelling the river beyond its banks, but it's like the Mississippi pretended it didn't swallow up lives. But I knew better.

As I wove through the bustling streets of the Quarter, snatches of music and conversation brushing past, I stopped momentarily to tie my shoe near a corner.

Across the street, a man leaned casually against the wall of a flower shop, fiddling with a small device in his hand. He seemed to take in the scene—watchful, but not in a way that drew attention. Just another face in the crowd.

Maybe he was going to Kermit's funeral, too.

He glanced up as I stood, offering a polite nod. His gaze held a flicker of recognition, though I couldn't quite place him. Perhaps he was one of the many patrons I'd glimpsed drifting in and out of Duval's Lounge.

"You headed to a funeral?" I asked, as if that was a normal thing to ask, but it was more to fill the air.

He smiled faintly, pocketing the device. "Not today. I heard there's a celebration for Kermit, though."

"Yeah, did you know him?" I tilted my head, trying to remember why I knew his face.

"I'd say, many of us did. Nice guy when you get to know him. Quirky. But then aren't we all?" He said, his voice carrying a hint of something unspoken, as if he'd love to tell me more, but held back.

I nodded and was about to move on when my shoe slipped on the cobblestone, unbalancing me. The man reached out instinctively, steadying my arm with a firm grip that contradicted his relaxed demeanor.

"Careful. Watch your step in the Quarter," he remarked, then released me with a courteous nod as I continued on my way.

As I walked, I couldn't shake the feeling that there was more to him—a story threading beneath the surface, waiting to unravel. But in a city that thrived on mysteries, perhaps it was just another layer of intrigue I'd have to piece together.

As I neared the view at the river, someone had left a coffee cup on the concrete edge—half full, gone cold. A police officer nudged it aside with his boot, and I wondered who'd planned to finish it. Kermit liked his coffee sweet. Too sweet. He said bitterness was already free in the world; no need to add more.

They pulled him out right down there, by the log, but the river hadn't let go of him entirely. It clung to the air, to the reeds, to my clothes.

I kept seeing Kermit's face the way it had looked when he smiled—half grin, half apology. Like he knew something was funny and tragic at the same time and didn't want to explain it. We shared blood, apparently. That felt like learning you'd been humming the same tune as someone your whole life without realizing it had words.

A woman from the neighborhood pressed a handkerchief into my palm. It smelled like lavender and cigarettes. "He played music for us," she said, as if that settled everything. Maybe it did.

Downriver, a trumpet started up—soft at first, testing the day. Someone answered it with a drumbeat that sounded like a heart remembering its job. I didn't see the musicians at first, just felt them. The sound rose and fell, sorrow carrying joy like a secret.

I closed my eyes and let it wash over me. Kermit had once told me music was how the city told the truth without getting arrested for it. I finally understood what he meant, and my eyes opened.

A boy stood near the water's edge holding a paper umbrella, blue with white dots. He spun it slowly, not dancing yet, just practicing. Waiting. That felt right. Grief always needs a warm-up.

When I looked out at the water, the river looked different. Still dangerous. Still beautiful. Still moving forward, whether I was ready or not, but moving ahead must happen—or I'll perish from the sorrow.

Naomi held her son's hand, and Miles wiggled, as if he didn't know how to say goodbye to his father—but the musicians played for them, a send-off for Kermit, with a song, "Just a Closer Walk with Thee."

The procession played, and the music shifted, and the joy of knowing I had a cousin sent tears down my cheeks. Handkerchiefs waved, feet shuffled, some slid to the right, others danced, and neighbors fell in behind the band, behind Naomi, Miles, and Windex—even behind me, and Cal.

I whispered a declaration, "You lived. Your music still walks these streets."

Some carried candles, others held flowers, and a hat with dollar bills tucked inside was passed to Naomi, and she wept.

At Naomi's apartment, gumbo was shared, stories grew taller, and someone said, "You remember when he…"

The entire afternoon was devoted to Kermit; his life had a rhythm, his kindness was not overlooked, his directness was a gift, and yet his song didn't end—it changed keys.

I whispered Kermit's name—not loud, not brave. Just enough for my heart to hold his memory. We were outside in front of Naomi's apartment, and the trumpets took over, and their notes climbed higher, and somewhere behind me, feet shuffled in time—a party for Kermit—his life mattered.

I barely knew how to be a cousin, and I didn't know how to carry his loss. But I knew this: Kermit wasn't leaving quietly. And neither was the love that had finally found its way to me.

Later, I walked near the river, alone, surrounded by tourists and locals, where notes faded over in Treme, but hope rose, too—in the beats of change I planned to bring to my street in honor of Kermit, his mother, Celeste, and my dad, Ben.

And off to the side, Renee lingered, holding a handkerchief, staring at the river. But wait, behind her, in the shadows, stood Remy Duval.

I stepped into the beam of the streetlight, ready to call her name, but when she noticed I saw her, she slipped away without a word.

And so did Mr. Duval.

Chapter 19

Christmas for Miles

A HOLIDAY BREAK TO HELP MILES and me enjoy Christmas became the next item on my list—or a moment to forget the threats lurking around corners and in dark alleys.

The quiet is so noisy; the ongoing music is a diversion, but I can't stand not having a mile-long list to check off. My mind doesn't know how to idle so that this shopping spree will bring a sense of normalcy to December.

The French Quarter dressed itself for the holiday the way it did everything else—loudly, lovingly, and with just enough contradiction to keep you honest.

I stepped out onto Royal Street with Miles at my side, the air alive with the smell of pralines and citrus peel, something sweet burning just under the sharpness of a wintry day. Most days, even now, are marked by humidity, showers, and early-morning fog.

December in New Orleans wasn't cold the way other places were, though. It didn't bite. It lingered. It pressed damp fingers against your skin and reminded you that winter, like truth, behaved differently here.

Miles tugged his knit cap down over his ears, trumpet case slung across his back. "Ms. Emory," he said, serious as a banker, "Mama says Christmas lights are prettier if you walk by them, slowly."

"I think your mother might be right," I replied. "She's right about most things."

We slowed, letting a mule-drawn carriage pass, the driver calling out holiday greetings like blessings. Garlands wrapped iron balconies overhead, twinkling lights stitched through history, as if someone had mended time rather than erased it.

A street band played "O Come, All Ye Faithful," but jazzed it up just enough to make the hymn sway. A saxophone slid into a blue note that made my chest ache.

Miles stopped walking. "That's the part Daddy Kermit liked," he said.

I didn't ask how he knew and just stood beside him, listening, holding his hand, and it was as if Miles propped me up, instead of the other way around.

The sound bounced off brick and memory, threaded its way through laughter and footsteps and old stone. When it ended, Miles nodded once, like he'd checked something off a list only he could see.

Miles pulled me along. "Okay," he said. "Now, can we shop?"

We wandered past windows glowing with handmade ornaments and beaded wreaths, Mardi Gras colors tangled with evergreen. A bookstore had stacked old jazz biographies next to children's picture books about angels who looked suspiciously like brass players. Another shop displayed vintage records in its window, each sleeve worn soft by hands that had once loved them.

Miles pressed his nose to the glass, and an orange cat nestled up to his legs, swirling in sweet meows. Miles petted the ball of fur, and I could have sworn the cat grinned at me.

"That one," he said, pointing. "The blue record."

I followed his finger. *Louis Armstrong Christmas.* I smiled. "Good choice." I paused. "But do you have a record player?"

"Mama does. Remember, Daddy had one in his room at The Blue Door."

I choked on his words. "That's right. I'd totally forgotten."

Inside, the shop smelled like dust and cinnamon. The owner, an older woman with silver curls and a sweater covered in bells, beamed at Miles.

"Are you shopping for someone special?" she asked.

"Yes, ma'am," Miles said. "My mama."

I felt my heart beating like a drum, the pounding harder than I'd expected, but every moment reminded me of losing Kermit. The ache. The pull. Naomi home alone.

We hadn't planned to stop by her place tonight—not yet—but the thought of her sitting alone with a half-lit tree and a silence too big for one woman tugged at my ribs.

We bought the record and stepped back into the street, where the lights seemed brighter now, like the city had noticed the flickering beams of color.

At a small boutique, Miles found a scarf he insisted Naomi would love, soft, deep green, with gold threading that caught the light.

At one gift shop, I nearly tripped; a wind chime of little Eastern bluebirds sang its own song, and a memory flashed back to when my mother, Rosemary, made wind chimes of different birds when I was a small girl.

"Emory, this one is for you. Since blue is your favorite color, the song of this bird will guide you home." Her words haunted me, a memory I'd tucked away and so needed right now.

I swallowed hard, knowing my mom had been mistaken. My color was still blue, but apparently, I should have a wind chime of pelicans, loud, with a big personality, and a wide wingspan. I coughed, the memory of her, one I'd totally forgotten about, like a newsflash from my childhood, one tossed with loss and too much crying.

Miles tugged on my arm, bringing me back to reality. "I love my mama's scarf. She's always saying she's cold, even when it's hot."

I laughed. "I'm always hot even when it's cold."

Miles giggled. "Thank you, Ms. Emory, for her record and for her scarf."

We moved on, stopping when a shopkeeper offered us hot chocolate in paper cups, steam rising like a prayer. The chocolate was thick and rich, dusted with cinnamon.

Miles took a sip and grinned, chocolate clinging to his lip. "Christmas tastes so good here," he said.

"It does," I agreed. "But don't tell anyone. Other cities get jealous."

As we walked, I felt it—the familiar prickle between my shoulder blades. And I glanced across the street.

A man leaned against the brick near a closed gallery, gray cap pulled low, hands tucked into his coat. Scar on his chin. Same brown skin. Like hot chocolate.

He wasn't hiding.

He wasn't watching me.

He was watching Miles.

Miles noticed him too—and lifted his hand.

He waved.

The man nodded once in return. Small. Almost nothing.

My steps slowed. "Do you know him?" I asked gently.

Miles shrugged. "He walks me home sometimes."

My heart kicked. "Walks you home?"

"Yeah," he said. "Mama says it's okay. He knows the way to the quiet streets. He knew my daddy."

I swallowed. "Do you know his name?"

Miles rubbed his ear. "Theo," he said. "Just Theo."

The name landed softly—but it landed.

I made a note to myself. A careful one.

We reached Naomi's apartment building just as the streetlights flickered on; the sky bruised purple and gold. She opened the door before we knocked, as if she was worried Miles might not return, and her eyes were tired but warm.

"Miles," she said, pulling him close. "You're back."

"I got you something," he announced, thrusting the packages at her.

"We should put them under the Christmas tree," she said, motioning to Miles.

He stopped and held them close. "But I want you to love them before Christmas."

Naomi glanced at me, and I shrugged, and she ran her fingers through Miles' hair. "Yes, let's open them now."

Mile smiled a grin bigger than the Mississippi River.

She opened them slowly. The scarf. The record.

"Oh," she breathed. "Oh, baby."

Her eyes filled, and she laughed at herself, wiping them with the back of her hand. "Stay for a bit, Emory," she said. "Please."

The apartment smelled like pine and sugar cookies. A small tree stood in the corner, its lights glowing softly and unevenly. Naomi poured cider and listened as Miles explained every detail of their shopping trip, every sound, every note.

I watched them from the rocker that squeaked by the doorway, my heart full, but weary, too.

This was what the city did: it ripped the hope from families when it took men like Kermit.

Naomi caught my eye as I sat on the edge of the chair.

"Stay," she said. "I have a gift for you."

"No, you didn't have to—" I protested, my hand up like a stop sign.

"It belonged to Kermit." She nudged Miles. "It's over there next to your big package."

Miles scooted across the floor in his sock feet, his shoes kicked off the moment we'd come inside. "I know what it is," he smiled, and handed it to me.

The paper, light blue with snowmen, fell from as I tore at the corner of the square and flat gift, revealing the Louis Armstrong record from Kermit's old room upstairs at the cafe. "No! This belonged to Kermit. You should keep it."

"I can't." She sighed, tears forming in her eyes.

"This is too personal. It's..." I argued.

"But Kermit knew you loved jazz, and you once told him it was your favorite album." Naomi insisted, her tone confident, as tears fell down her cheeks.

"But I don't even remember saying that to him. But it's true. This is the best gift ever!" I held the record close, knowing it was high time I bought a player for old vinyl records.

Naomi touched Miles on the nose with her finger. "And you get to open one tonight, too. Let's unwrap the one wrapped in gold paper with the trumpets on it."

Miles reached for a box, no bigger than a mug, and ripped the paper away like a mini hurricane. "Mama! I've been saving for a practice mute. Now I can play at night and not make the neighbors knock on the walls."

Naomi nodded. "The mute doesn't stop the music; it just teaches your notes how to whisper."

"Thank you, Mama." He ran to her, hugging Naomi as if he'd never let go.

Soon we were eating homemade sugar cookies, the taste from childhood rising like hope from the past.

Later, as Miles curled up on the couch with his trumpet mute in his hand, Naomi walked me to the door. "Thank you," she said. "Miles will remember this day forever."

"Thank you for trusting me with him," I replied, and stepped into the damp air, the fog rolling in like darkness dressed in gray. I clutched my album, a treasure I found by coming to New Orleans, and I, too, would never forget this day.

Outside, Theo stood near the curb. "Night, ma'am," he said, and walked along.

"Wait. Why are you following Miles?"

Theo tipped his cap. "Music needs protecting," he replied. "So do kids."

Miles opened the front door and yelled, "Thank you, Ms. Em. Merry Christmas."

I waved and stood there a moment longer, listening to the city breathe. A band played somewhere down the block, warm and searching, and for one night, the shadows stayed where they belonged—waiting.

I turned, and Theo was gone, but the orange cat that needed a home slipped in with my steps and walked with me to The Blue Door.

Chapter 20

Windex Tells Part of a Secret

MORNING SLID INTO THE FRENCH quarter like it was late for church. The sky was the color of brass, and the city smelled like rain and redemption—equal parts mud and grace.

Cal and I now had a room together with two queen beds, since he thought we should stay close.

Renee seemed to act like our rearranging of the sleeping quarters was normal, or she just pretended and went with the flow. I'm not sure. I'm just skeptical about everyone right now.

I hadn't slept again. My dreams were full of rivers and blue doors that wouldn't open. When I finally stumbled inside the cafe, Windex was already sitting at the bar, sipping coffee from a chipped mug that said *God Don't Like Ugly, But He'll Forgive It Anyway.*

"Morning," he said, nodding. "You look like the Lord's still working on your edges."

"He's got a lot of edges to sand down," I muttered.

Windex grinned. "Good. Means you're real. Smooth people never built anything worth keeping." He looked past me. "Where's your brother?"

"I'm not sure. We made a vow to stick with each other, but he wasn't in our room at the hotel when I got up. So, I'm not really sure."

My words slipped out like a confession. "I can't believe Kermit's gone. So much has happened, and it's so layered with pieces, I don't know who to trust," I said, moving to the counter.

Windex marched from the stage and picked up the saxophone. "What if we put Kermit's sax on this wall? We don't want to forget folks like him."

"I'm forgetting things all the time, it seems. I used to see my daddy's face, but the more time goes by, the harder it is."

He rubbed his chin, his gray whiskers a sign of his need for a shave. "Your daddy could play this piano like his fingers had soul. I remember that night."

I froze mid-step. "You what?"

Windex's eyes held secrets, too, apparently, and the past just slipped out from his lips.

"Wait, you knew my daddy? Seriously?"

"Yep. I was there, sugar. Playing washboard with the backup trio. I was a young man, and The Blue Door wasn't the fancy joint it became later. It was a heartbeat—sweaty, smoky, alive. Celeste sang like she was praying and singing in the same breath."

"You knew her, too." I spun around. "Why didn't you tell me?"

"I'm not sure. It never came up."

"You heard plenty of conversations where you could have shared this with me," I said, my tone rising.

He shrugged, his bony shoulders wiggling, and his eyes wide. "Sorry, Ms. Em. I get ahead of myself, then folks tell me to lighten up, to talk less. Meant no harm."

"But you knew them."

"I knew Celeste's pain or her wishing for a chance to change outcomes. She used to say she was two notes short of forgiveness."

My chest tightened. "And you never told me?"

"Didn't see the point till now," he said, setting the mug down. "You weren't ready to hear the song behind the story. You wouldn't have listened to me when we first met. I was…well, a lot drunker."

"Drunker? As in, you still drink?"

"I'm having less. Haven't washed my clothes in the fountain for a few months now." Windex nodded, grinning.

"Windex," I whispered. "What happened back then to Celeste?"

He stared at his hands for a long time. "Celeste was supposed to meet someone after the set. Said she was turning over the truth ledger, proof that Gus and Remy were laundering money through their clubs. Your daddy begged her to let it go. Said he'd take the ledger and deliver it himself.

But she wouldn't let him. She told Ben that if they hide sin, it becomes a family tradition."

My heart hammered. "A ledger."

He nodded. "Yeah, and somehow, I ended up with it. Not sure what happened, but I found it right here on this bar. But not until the morning after she died—so I hid it. And never told a soul—except for those ghosts when I drank too much."

I leaned on the bar. "So why didn't you turn it in?"

"Do you really have to ask that? Celeste was murdered over her questions and what she knew. I was a weak man most of my life. The bottle kept me alive. Not telling that secret, did too." Windex's eyes misted.

"You're braver than many," I said, touching his shoulder.

"No, you is brave, Ms. Em." Windex sighed. "The only person who saw her alive the night before she died was Remy. Or that's what the talk on the street said."

My throat tightened. "You think he killed her? But it was Gus, according to the evidence presented in court. He more or less confessed."

"Still circumstantial. I'm sure Gus Tiller was involved, too. He and Remy were buddies. It took two men to take her out. Not one."

"No way," I said, my heart about to explode.

"I think Remy don't like witnesses. And Kermit died for askin' the same questions you're askin' now."

I swallowed hard, the room tilting around me. "Then I have to see that ledger."

Windex nodded. "I figured you'd say that. Lucky for you, I know where it is."

He pulled out a crinkled paper floor plan of The Blue Door from his pocket and pointed to the sketch of the stage—a trapdoor marked in the far-left corner.

"Wait, where did you get that floor plan?"

"Found it in the trash can. Thought I'd save it," he said, shrugging his shoulders. "I helped build that stage," Windex said.

"So, I'm still not over the fact that we've known each other for nearly three months and you haven't, not once, brought this up."

Windex wiped his nose with the back of his hand. "When a man gets sober, his conscience works again. I regret my past. You didn't trust me at first."

"True, but…"

"Just let me tell you now."

"Fine, go on," I said, sitting on a stool by the bar.

"We added a hidden compartment to store cords, music sheets, and whiskey bottles. I ain't touched that ledger since. Might be what you could use for evidence."

I looked up at him. "Windex, why are you helping me?"

He smiled sadly. "Because grace helped me first. I used to drink with Gus and spent half my life wiping bar tops for devils like Remy, too, and calling it friendship. The Lord gave me rhythm to make music, and with you coming here, He's offered me mercy. It's time to clean up the past. I figure it's my turn to pass the cloth."

"Then we'll do it together," I said.

He tipped his head in agreement. "You grab a crowbar, I'll grab faith."

I rushed off and came back with a kitchen knife. "Will this work?"

The stage looked smaller in daylight. No matter how many times I've swept or mopped, the dirt collected in every corner, and the boards creaked beneath our weight. Windex knelt where his sketch showed and pried at a warped plank. It popped loose with a sharp crack.

"Hello, secrets," he murmured.

Beneath was a narrow compartment about the size of four shoeboxes. Inside lay a bundle wrapped in faded linen, tied with a blue ribbon.

My hands shook as I lifted it out. Inside, beneath layers of age and dust, was a leather-bound ledger. The name on the cover read: The Blue Door/Duval Lounge Accounts Number 1.

Windex exhaled. "Looks like you found the gospel according to Celeste."

We laid it open on the bar. The handwriting was neat, looping, and precise. Every page listed dates, amounts, and initials, money moving between Gus Tiller, Remy Duval, and several others. And then we reached the last entry. The date: April 11, 1998. The night Celeste died.

There was only one line.

R.D.–$5,000. For silence.

Windex whistled low. "That's murder money if I ever saw it."

But there was something else tucked between the pages, a photograph, brittle with age. Celeste, smiling widely, holding a baby.

Windex leaned closer. "That ain't Kermit."

I snatched the photo from his grasp. "No, this baby is white," I said softly.

The baby's blanket had a hospital tag—St. Joseph's Maternity, Baton Rouge. And written on the back, in what might have been Celeste's handwriting: Ben—keep your promise.

My world tilted again. "She and my father?"

Windex finished softly, "Wait, Ms. Em. You think they—had a child?"

"You said that as if it's a question. But the note tells me everything I need to know. Gosh, they were half-siblings. What was my dad thinking?"

"He was a lost soul when your mother died. Must've gotten lonely." Windex uttered, as if what he said made sense, but he said it with extra-long syllables. "But this isn't what you think."

I screamed, not asking Windex what he meant. "Dad, how could you?"

Windex held me. "Life falls hard when the past shows up in the present. But be careful, you might not have all the answers."

I pulled away. "The photo says it all."

Windex shook his head. "It says what you want it to say."

"Stop with the riddles."

"Yes, ma'am," Windex said. "I must confess. Back then, so much happened, and I came across the ledger, either left behind by Ben or Celeste. I don't know. I hid it there myself for the right time."

"Well, isn't this a little too convenient?" I asked, my mind racing.

"I wasn't sure how to include it in your story and if it would help. I'd kept it safe for all these years. Even forgot about it being there since I spent most of my time with a drink in my hand."

I gulped, clearing my throat. "But Windex, you are a part of this—we both are. And we didn't get a say on whether we wanted to walk this path."

"True, ma'am. I should have told you sooner."

"Yes, no doubt. But all I can think of now is that my dad had yet another child. I don't know who my dad was!"

I pressed a hand to my chest; the air gone from my lungs like a deflated balloon. "That means... my father had another son or a daughter."

Windex looked at me, his eyes gentle but steady. "Emory, you don't have the right answer."

"I don't?" I whispered.

Renee burst through the door just then, breathless, rain in her curls. "We've got company," she said.

My heart lurched. "Remy?"

"Worse. Two men with questions. Looks like the kind that won't believe our answers."

Windex set the ledger back inside the stage compartment and kicked the board over it, sealing it fast.

"Time to play dumb and holy," he said. "You handle the talking; I'll handle the praying."

Renee lunged toward the stage. "What was that?"

Windex blurted. "Just sheet music for our band."

"Really?" She said, her eyes cutting to me and back to Windex.

I straightened my shirt and turned toward the door as two men stepped inside and stuck the photo in my jeans pocket. Black suits, wet shoes, faces that looked allergic to compassion.

"Miss Vaughn," the taller one said. "We're here about your friend Kermit Delacroix. Mind if we come in?"

"I think you already did," I said.

The second one smiled thinly. "We hear you've been asking questions about an old case. Celeste Delacroix."

"Family curiosity," I said.

"Curiosity can be dangerous." The front man said.

Windex chuckled from behind the bar. "So can bad coffee, but we still drink it."

The tall one ignored him. "If you find anything that might interest us, call this number." He slid a card across the counter. "We work for people who prefer the past to stay quiet."

"Who do you work for?" I asked.

He smiled. "Let's just say we represent financial interests tied to Mr. Duval."

They turned to leave, rain dripping from their coats.

As the door shut behind them, Windex exhaled. "Lord, they even smell like trouble."

I locked the door behind them, leaving the key in the door. "They know we're close to finding out something. But I'm not so sure what I know at this point."

Renee hovered like a flag waiting for the right breeze. "Well, girl. That was strange."

I moved to Renee. "How did you know they were coming here?"

"Because they first came to find you at my hotel? So, I sent them to Jackson Square first and tried to beat them over here. So, I could warn you." Renee said, looking at her nails.

I swallowed and turned my attention to her again, with another question. "So, have you seen Cal today? I got up this morning, and he'd already left the hotel. He hasn't answered his phone or my text."

Renee clicked her heels. "I passed him in the lobby. He said he was going to visit Naomi so he could meet Miles. I gave him directions to her apartment."

"Okay, maybe he got tied up," I said, taking a deep breath. "Or lost, he's directionally impaired."

"Is that your way of saying he doesn't know north from south?"

I nodded. "Pretty much."

Renee's cell dinged, and she glanced at the phone, a name showing up for a second before she shoved her phone back into her purse. "I'll take that later."

"Wait? Did that say, Remy, on your phone?" I stepped back. "You're not friends with him, are you?"

"That wasn't Remy, girl. That was Randy, my assistant at the hotel." She skirted my question, but her tone left me wondering, if only for a second.

Windex leaned on the bar, eyes steady. "We're going to open this place on schedule. For Kermit. For Celeste. You were born for this, Blueberry Girl. Don't let the long way home end with fear, let it end with truth."

I looked toward the stage, where the ledger now slept beneath the floorboards.

"I'm not just finding the truth for Celeste anymore," I said with a crack in my voice. "I'm finding it for myself. For my dad. For every soul that ever got lost between sin and salvation."

Windex grinned, eyes crinkling. "Then let's make the devil nervous."

I nodded and walked to the door. "I'm going to find Cal. I need my brother, and I need him now." I unlocked the door, but before I could shut it, Windex said, "I'll keep watch. Watching is a good thing when you take notes with your eyes."

Renee countered. "I'll make sure our supplies are ordered and in place." And she flitted out the door.

I mumbled. "What is it with Renee, touching and overseeing and following me so closely? I'm ready to give her a piece of my mind, except I'm not sure what I'd say to her—that wouldn't make matters worse."

But no matter what, she can't know about the photograph in my pocket. Or the ledger inside the flooring of the stage. As for my dad, the idea of his having another child—unbelievable!

Chapter 21

Daddy's Kids

I FOUND CAL WHERE THE CITY liked to keep its confessions.

St. Louis Cemetery No. 1 stood open and quiet, the gates yawning like a held breath. Cal was sitting on the low stone wall near the entrance, elbows on his knees, staring at nothing in particular. He held what appeared to be a paper cup with a drink, and he looked smaller somehow, like the noise of the Quarter had finally stopped carrying him.

"Cal," I said.

He glanced up, startled, then relieved. "I thought you said you would be at the cafe."

"I was," I said, crossing the street and stopping short of him. "I needed to find you."

"That sounds ominous," he said lightly, but his eyes were already scanning my face, reading the worry I hadn't hidden.

He glanced at his cup. "This isn't what you think?"

"What do I think?" I asked, leaning in, the aroma of beer fresh from the tap touching my nose.

"I bought this. Wanted it. Everyone here is having such a great time. I thought, maybe, one drink wouldn't hurt."

"And?" I didn't sit. If I sat, I might not get the words out. "What did you learn?"

"I didn't take a sip. I wanted it. So much. But I can't go back. I can't be that person. I won't. But the temptation is everywhere here." Cal said, and the red in his eyes was a sign of his struggle to remain sober.

"I know it's difficult. But this is how you can make Dad proud, by not becoming Uncle Harlan, who drank away his life." I said, taking the paper cup from Cal and pouring the beer out on the grass.

"You ever notice," I said instead, "how cemeteries make the truth feel louder?"

He snorted softly. "That's because nobody's arguing back."

I swallowed. "Cal… I have to tell you. I have found something."

That did it. He stood, brushing dust from his jeans. "Okay. Now you're scaring me."

I pulled him a few steps away, out of earshot of the tourists drifting in and out, and lowered my voice. "I think… I think Dad had another child."

The words landed between us like a dropped plate.

Cal stared at me, unblinking. "That's not funny. That could make me drink." He glanced at the grass near us.

"I'm not joking." My hands shook, and I shoved them into my pockets. "There was a ledger—a photograph. Celeste holding a baby. And a note on the back of the photograph, written to Dad. About a promise."

His face drained slowly, like someone turning down a dimmer switch. "You're saying… Dad and Aunt Celeste?"

"I don't know what I'm saying," I snapped, then immediately softened. "I just know what it looks like."

Cal dragged a hand down his face. "Emory. They shared the same father. Celeste married right after high school, and it didn't work out, remember? She was a Vaughn."

"Okay, that's right." My voice cracked. "That's why I feel sick."

For a long moment, neither of us spoke. Somewhere behind us, a guide launched into a rehearsed monologue about above-ground tombs and yellow fever. And about life, continuing after so many deaths.

Cal finally shook his head. "Dad loved rules."

"That doesn't mean he didn't break them," I said.

"No," Cal agreed quietly. "It doesn't."

I took a breath and pushed on. "The baby was born in Baton Rouge. At St. Joseph's. There was a hospital tag."

Cal closed his eyes. "Do we know… what happened?"

"No," I said. "I don't even know if the child lived."

That was the moment his composure cracked, too.

Cal turned away, pressing his palm to the stone wall as if he needed something solid. "We've already lost Dad," he said hoarsely. "Now you're telling me we may have lost… someone else?"

"I didn't say lost," I blurted. "That was so long ago. They could still be alive. And would be about twenty-six."

He laughed once, sharp and broken. "You always do that. Look for life when the evidence says otherwise."

I stepped closer. "And you always assume the worst, so you don't get blindsided."

He looked at me then, eyes red. "We're not built for this, Emory. This family. Secrets stacked on secrets."

"I didn't ask for this," I whispered. "I just found it."

Cal nodded slowly. "Okay. Then we don't panic. Not yet. We verify."

"Verify what?" I asked. "Another sibling? A lie big enough to swallow us?"

"We verify the *story*," he said firmly. "Because someone always benefits from the version we're handed."

That stopped me.

He took a breath, steadier now. "Who showed you this?"

"Windex."

Cal blinked. "The washboard philosopher?"

"Yes."

He sighed. "Of course."

I hesitated, then said the part that mattered. "Cal... what if Dad wasn't who we thought he was?"

Cal's shoulders slumped. "Then he was human. And deeply flawed. Same as the rest of us."

I nodded, tears finally slipping free. "I don't know how to hold all of this."

He pulled me into a firm, grounding hug. "You don't have to hold it alone."

I pressed my forehead into my brother's shoulder, the cemetery humming softly around us. "Whatever this is," I said, "it's not over."

"No," Cal agreed. "But before we accuse the dead, we make sure the living aren't lying."

We stood there a moment longer, the city breathing around us, both of us unaware that the truth we were bracing for wasn't waiting in the past at all—but buried just a few feet away, under a stage that had already given up one secret and wasn't done yet.

Cal didn't let go of me right away.

He held on like he was anchoring something that might float off if he loosened his grip—me, the truth, our childhood, maybe all three.

I pressed my face into his shoulder and breathed in soap, dust, the faint smell of coffee—everyday things. "I need normal," I spoke.

"Repeat the story, slower this time," he said. "Slowly."

I pulled back just enough to look at him. "There was a photo. Old. Worn as if it had been handled too many times. Celeste holding a baby. A hospital bracelet on the blanket. And a note to Dad. Written in her handwriting."

"What did the note say?" he asked.

I hesitated. "For Ben—and something about a promise."

Cal closed his eyes again. "That's... not nothing."

"No," I said. "It's everything."

I pulled the photograph from my pocket, and we gazed at it as if a funeral procession might show up with its band.

We stood there, the cemetery stretching behind us like a city made of pauses. A breeze moved through, rustling magnolia leaves, carrying the faint scent of flowers that didn't belong to anyone specific anymore.

"Did Windex say how old the baby was?" Cal asked.

"No, not in so many words. Just that the ledger ended the night Celeste died. And the photo was tucked inside."

Cal rubbed the back of his neck. "Emory... people stash things together that don't belong together all the time. It doesn't mean—"

"I know," I cut in. "I know. I keep telling myself that. That grief tangles memories. That people lie. That stories get... reshaped."

"But?" he prompted.

"But," I said, my voice dropping, "The hospital tag was real. And Celeste's handwriting—"

He winced. "Okay. So worst-case scenario?"

I laughed weakly. "That Dad crossed a line so unforgivable I don't know how I would have looked at him anymore."

"And best case?"

"That there's another explanation I haven't earned yet?"

Cal nodded slowly. "I like the second one better."

"Me too," I admitted. "But I'm scared that liking it doesn't make it true."

We fell quiet again. Somewhere inside the cemetery, a gate squealed, metal on metal. A reminder that even resting places weren't immune to noise.

Cal cleared his throat. "You said Baton Rouge. St. Joseph's. That narrows things."

"You're already thinking like an investigator," I said.

"I have to," he replied. "Because if you're right—and I'm not saying you are, but *if*—then this isn't just family business. This is history someone tried to erase."

"And people don't erase things without a reason," I said.

"Exactly," Cal said, sighing.

I hugged myself, suddenly cold despite the rising sun. "What if I'm wrong, Cal? What if I'm reading sin where there was sacrifice? What if Dad was protecting someone, not betraying us?"

He studied me carefully. "Then you forgive him for what he couldn't tell you."

"And if I'm right?"

"Then you forgive him anyway," Cal said gently. "Just... slower."

That made my throat burn.

"I don't want to know," I whispered suddenly. "I mean, I do—but I don't. I liked believing our family story was messy but decent. Complicated, but not... this."

Cal's voice softened. "Truth doesn't ask what version we prefer."

"No," I said. "It just shows up and demands a chair."

He smiled sadly. "You always hated uninvited guests."

I huffed out a breath that almost counted as a laugh. "Only when they rearrange the furniture."

Cal reached for my hand again. "Listen to me. Whatever that baby represents—life, loss, sin, love—it doesn't undo who Dad was to us. It adds to him. That's different."

I squeezed his hand. "I wish he were here."

"Me too," Cal said. "But since he's not, we do this the hard way. Together."

I nodded, though my stomach still twisted. "I haven't told Renee."

His brows lifted. "Good."

"You don't trust her?" I asked.

"I don't trust *anyone* who arrives cheerful when everyone else is bleeding," he replied quietly.

That settled deeper than I wanted it to.

We stood there a moment longer, the city beginning to wake in earnest. Somewhere, a horn warmed up—soft, searching notes drifting over the stones.

"Come on," Cal said finally. "Let's get you back to the cafe before you convince yourself this was all a dream."

I glanced once more at the rows of tombs. "If it were a dream, it wouldn't feel like it's still watching me."

Cal didn't argue.

And as we walked away, neither of us noticed how close we were to the truth—only that whatever waited beneath it was already shifting, preparing to surface.

Cal walked closely at my side, his shoulder brushing mine like he was afraid the city might steal me if he didn't keep contact.

"I didn't find Naomi's apartment. Got turned around, and then you found me at the cemetery. With a beer. I'm afraid one day, I'm going to fail."

"And if you do, I'll be there to remind you who you are," I said, bumping his shoulder with mine.

Cal looked over his shoulder. "I hate that I've not been able to meet Miles yet. At first, I didn't want to, but now, I do. This whole thing with his dad is not his fault. He's just a boy. I'm ready to see him before we leave New Orleans."

"We'll go see Naomi together and take muffins for Miles. But let's go tomorrow. This is too pressing." I said, shuffling along, my body like noodles drenched in too much sauce, covered in worry and too many questions.

We hurried, and the lone cloud hovering above us offered its downpour.

I hollered at the sky. "Seriously, New Orleans is the wettest city."

Cal whispered, "It's snowing in Wyoming."

"Somehow, that doesn't make me feel much better."

And we ran the rest of the way to The Blue Door.

Chapter 22

Where There's Smoke

BY NOON, THE RAIN HAD BURNED off, and the heat came down like a decision. I've gotten used to keeping another set of clothes at the cafe, although Cal was still dripping wet, trying to dry off with a hand towel from Silas's kitchen.

And The Blue Door smelled like old wood, no matter how many times I've cleaned.

On the windowsill, outside, basking in the sun, the orange cat sat, licking his paw as if someone had provided him a meal.

I muttered beneath my breath. "Maybe I need a pet to calm my nerves."

"A cat. That's your answer?" Cal laughed.

"He needs a home, apparently."

I took to working inside the cafe because busy hands help me talk slower and not overreact. Windex was out front on the sidewalk noodling a rhythm on his washboard for two tourists and the stray cat that refused to tip.

Renee arrived with a bag of po'boys and a look that meant she could use a nap. "You eat, or you fall," she said, handing me a sandwich like a sermon. "And what's that in your hands?"

I marched to the counter, holding the ledger after having just retrieved it right before Renee bounced inside.

"It's a ledger, and I'll eat after I open this." I held up the ledger, not sure why I didn't shove it beneath the bar, as I genuinely didn't want Renee to see it. Or did I?

She cocked a brow. "What did you find?"

"I told you. It's a ledger." I ran my fingers over the leather again. It had a thickness to it, a wrongness, as if another book were hiding inside the cover. There was a slight bump on one end.

"Knife," I said.

Renee didn't ask why. She pulled a little paring knife from her purse, because, of course, she carried one. New Orleans women carry what life requires.

I slid the blade along the edge of the spine. The leather lifted with a tired sigh. Under the lining, something hard shifted, thin and rectangular. I eased it out.

A microcassette. Small little thing. Two inches at best.

Windex slid into the cafe and joined us. "What you got there, Blueberry Girl?" Then he cut his eyes at Renee, then back at me.

"I'm not sure. A ledger that needs opening. And a tiny recording from who knows when." My breath stuck, and I whispered, "Oh, Daddy."

Cal moved closer. "What in the world?"

Windex moved to the stage, digging through his satchel on the piano, and held up an Olympus dictation recorder. "I use this when new songs bust out."

Cal raised an eyebrow. "And that thing still works. That must be—"

Windex finished his sentence. "—Oh, about 30 years old. I've gotten my money's worth."

He brought it over like an offering and set it on the bar. The little machine hummed to life after I placed the cassette in it and pressed play. Static, a breath, the faint shuffle of a creaking chair. Then my father's voice, tired and tender.

His voice sounded steadier than grief alone. "If you found this, I'm most likely gone where the Lord makes cowards right. This is Ben Vaughn. Celeste, if it's you, forgive me for not being stronger. If it's Emory or Calvin, I'm sorry you're hearing me like this."

I grabbed the edge of the bar. Renee put a hand on my back, steadying me.

Windex touched my hand. "It's time. I've got to come clean." He stopped the tape from playing, pressing the off button.

My head felt like it was going in circles. "What are you talking about?"

Windex reached for his washboard, holding it close like a security blanket. "At the end of her pregnancy, Celeste asked me to keep her safe from Remy—he didn't want her to have the baby. I brought her to St. Joseph's in Baton Rouge, and I signed the papers for her because she couldn't stop crying long enough to hold a pen. She said adoption was mercy. I said mercy would come later. But I was wrong."

The room tipped sideways.

Cal moved to my side, and I nearly collapsed. "Wait, so whose baby did Celeste give birth to?"

Windex squirmed, his fingers hitting a note on the washboard. He licked his lips, sighed, and said, "Remy Duval."

Windex went on. "The family who took her named her—" he glanced across to Renee and stopped talking.

I nudged him from across the bar. "Named her?"

He gulped and made a long, crackling, possibly overdue swallow, and cleared his throat. "The couple who adopted her named the baby Renee Yvette Baptiste. Good people. Church people. Hotel people. Accounting people. They promised to stay in New Orleans, so Celeste could see her baby girl grow up, even if it was from a distance."

Renee jumped up, knocking over a chair at one table nearby, and she tripped out of her heels, almost falling. "What are you saying? This is ridiculous. Absolutely bizarre and not true. This would make Kermit my older brother. No way!"

Windex inched to one end of the bar. "Secrets come in all colors. Remy didn't want a baby. Celeste wanted to have you. But Ben thought he could help by paying off Remy to silence Gus, too, but that didn't happen. Celeste knew too much about Remy Duval's dealings with Gus Tiller."

Renee planted her feet back in her shoes, brushing her hands over her dress as if doing so wiped away what Windex had just said. "That's outrageous!" she screamed, marching to the cafe window to stare outside. "Outrageous!"

Windex moved to her side. "With Emory and Cal stirring up the past, and with Kermit becoming a casualty, it was a truth needing telling," Windex said, his eyes big, and he glanced at me, and he put his arm around Renee—but she pushed him away.

Silas joined us from the kitchen. "What do we have in here? Church? Or a funeral? Or did someone give birth?"

Cal shook his head and hushed Silas. "Not now, Silas. Not now."

I waved my hand to hush Windex, too, to stop him, and pushed play on the recorder instead. "Wait, we need to hear the rest of this."

In the next few minutes, the second-hand clock on every Timex in Louisiana, still in existence, most likely stopped working when the earth tilted as my daddy's voice dripped from the player and repeated almost word for word what Windex told us.

As the player rolled, Renee paced, muttering, and Windex moaned under his breath, and Cal kept me from falling over. And Silas never left the room but sighed constantly.

The tape ended with, "If anyone who isn't blood listens to this, take care of Renee for Celeste. If it's you, Emory, and Cal, that means she's your cousin. Don't let the sins of her birth drown her. Don't let Remy know his daughter lives. Remy never knew Celeste had given birth, hiding the pregnancy. And if he learned the truth, Renee wouldn't have survived."

The tape clicked softly, like it had to catch its breath. My breathing was shallow, and I ripped open two pieces of Spearmint gum and chewed like a cow smacking its cud.

Renee's fingers, which had been anchored steady at my back during the last part of the recording, slid away like they were looking for gravity.

"Renee," I whispered, turning.

Her eyes had gone far away and then slammed back to me, full of shock and something I could only call grief-shaped relief. She pressed her palm to her mouth.

A sound emerged, a laugh and a sob.

"I—" she said, then had to start again. "My mama used to tell me I was a city child. That the city named me, she said, I was God's kindness after a long hurricane. She said I was a twin. But I'm not. And Remy's my..." she couldn't say the word.

I whispered, "...your father."

I marched to her side and held her hand; it trembled for the first time since I'd met her—and Renee Baptiste never trembles.

Cal pressed play on the player, as if checking for more words, and the tape kept going, my father's voice refusing to give us breathing room.

"Renee, if you ever hear this, Celeste loved you. I was a coward and should have helped her keep you. Forgive me for letting men with money scare me out of becoming your uncle. If I could have brought you home without breaking you, I would have. I'd already broken Emory and Calvin. And if I could bring Celeste back, I'd trade my breath."

A long inhale ended the tape.

Windex commented. "Ben must have put this tape inside the ledger to hide the truth."

Silas said from across the room. "Truth makes us face who we are."

No one spoke.

The dad I trusted with my whole soul sounded like he'd been carrying a brick in his chest all of his life, and to his own grave, and I can't even scream at him. Or hug him. Or ask him the questions pressing inside my chest.

The tape had stopped, but my head swam with waves crashing inside as if I'd exploded from all the secrets that had lived all these years silently.

Then my dad spoke one last time, a whisper broken and holy. "Debts don't drown. Neither does mercy. Choose mercy, Em and Cal. You, too. Renee."

Click.

Silence landed like a verdict.

Renee leaned both hands on the bar as if her knees didn't trust her. "I... I manage a hotel two blocks away from here. I grew up five streets over. I went to college. And I've been trying to mother this city with hand towels and room upgrades because I didn't know where to put my ache. All this time..." She swallowed hard. "God was circling me back to my own *blue door*."

I was already crying. "Cousin Renee," I said.

She pulled me in, and we stood there shaking, holding each other as if we might never get to again.

Cal didn't move. Didn't speak.

Renee rushed from my arms, and she held her hands palms up, as if offering them for judgment.

"Before you say anything," she began, her voice taut, withheld, by possibly lost emotions, "I need you to know— I didn't mean to set Cal up to get hurt. That wasn't the plan, but Remy's man put something in your drink. I saw him. But then, I ran. Remy forced me to comply, or else. No one's safe from drowning in the river."

Cal and I stiffened, and his eyes narrowed as remnants of their afternoon encounter must have rippled through his thoughts. He nodded, urging her silently to continue.

Renee folded her hands in front of her. "But when it happened, I didn't know how to change or fix what Remy inflicted on you, all at my expense. I can't move one step without him texting, calling, or following me. I'm so afraid."

Cal's jaw clenched, his fists tightening subtly by his sides. "You thought drugging me was protecting us?" he snapped, his voice rough with betrayal.

"It was a mistake. Many I've made these last few years," Renee confessed, tears simmering beneath her lashes. "I was scared. I know how far Remy's reach extended, and he..." her voice faltered, "He uses people until they break."

I placed a hand gently on Cal's arm, muting my anger enough to seek the truth beyond Renee's choices. "Why are you telling us? Why now?"

"Because you deserve honesty," Renee swallowed. "And because we need to stand together if we're going to survive this. I've allowed Remy to use me, too. My own biological father. He's not worthy of being called my father, either. And… I'm tired of living afraid."

Renee's confession hung between us, a fragile truth waiting for the weight of our forgiveness or condemnation.

Cal moved to the bar, and I stood next to him, and no one said a word.

Windex pretended to search for something in his satchel. "Well, the Lord keeps a better rhythm for introductions and confessions than any band I've ever played with."

I wiped my face and gathered myself. "We have to hide this tape and this *truth* ledger. If Remy suspects this—"

"—he'll burn it all down," Renee finished.

As if the devil had been waiting for his cue, the building popped like it had swallowed a spark. We turned in unison. A thread of smoke curled up from the baseboard near the back hall.

"Windex—" I started. "Silas, is that smoke?"

Windex responded with, "I see it." He grabbed the fire extinguisher. And Renee was already calling 911, crisp and calm in a way that made me proud but also worried about how fast her personality switched between advocate and victim.

Smoke thickened. Windex blasted foam into the wall cavity. It hissed and spat like a snake unwilling to let go.

"The back wall!" Renee shouted. "It's much hotter there; somebody lit it from outside."

I screamed, "Of course! Next comes fire, the note had said."

"We have to split up," I said, coughing. "If they want what we have, they can have my decoy."

Windex didn't ask, just nodded, eyes damp. "You run," he said. "I'll play usher."

I stuffed the microcassette and the photo into my bag. And Silas provided a flour sack, and I slid the ledger into it and handed it to Windex.

"If I don't come back, give that to a pastor with teeth," I said.

Cal, already moving in circles, said, "I'll go with Windex." He grabbed the extinguisher from him, spraying a spot Windex missed, and vanished into the smoke, moving fast and steady as if he'd already decided who wins this battle today.

Silas announced, "Every good pastor has teeth."

Sirens wailed in the distance, the city's other brass section and the smoke alarm above the door woke up and started screaming.

Renee and I slipped out through the kitchen door that no one uses, but Silas, and the delivery trucks, and we ran into the thin alley that ran between the buildings. Heat chased us like a jealous family member.

At the mouth of the alley, beyond the trinket store, a figure peeled off the brick and fell into step beside us.

Scar on the chin. Gray cap. The man from Jackson Square. It was Theo. Watching, simply being there, and standing. He was old enough to be my father, something I'd not noticed until now.

"Keep walking," he said without moving. "You've got eyes on you from Duval's corner."

"You with Remy?" Renee asked, voice like steel inside velvet.

"I ain't with anybody who thinks women are easy targets."

"Why help us?" I asked.

"Because Kermit taught my boy to play the sax, and now, he's in the high school band and making good grades. And because Celeste gave my wife a sandwich when the saints didn't, and she was just a young girl herself. Because Remy Duval and Gus Tiller threaten people, they end up in the river. Ain't his puppet." He tipped his hat. "You didn't hear this from me."

Theo vanished down the alley as if he'd never been there. And we hurried away from Duval's Lounge, running like the Mississippi River rapids were tailing us.

We ducked around the block and into Renee's hotel through the employee entrance. Air conditioning hit like grace. Renee flashed her smile, and the security guard looked away on purpose. Every city has gatekeepers. The French Quarter prefers them with soft hearts.

In her office, she closed the blinds and locked the door. "Sit," she said, already clearing a space on her desk. "We'll make copies of the ledger and the tape. We'll give one to the DA, one to someone whose job it is to be loud, a reporter who won't turn suddenly quiet after a phone call. And we keep one where the devil can't find it."

"The church?" I asked.

"The church," she said. "Old stone and stubborn deacons. And Miss Loretta, who reads the bulletin like it's the Constitution."

I almost smiled. Then my chest pinched tight. "Kermit."

Cal turned to Renee. "So, you know a reporter we can trust with this?"

"Yes, he's the friend you hope for, tire of, and long to have on your side," she said, sighing.

I nearly asked if we could trust her—but the way she offered herself in this moment spoke of truth. "What's his name?" I asked, my curiosity growing, but then a knock came on the door, and Renee let a man inside, the man I'd met at Duval's Louge weeks ago.

I pushed back with more words. "No, this man drinks at Remy's all the time. He can't be with us."

The man, slender, in a pullover shirt, said, "I'm Marcus LeBlanc, a reporter who reports but does so at a cost."

"Wait, you're doing a story on Duval?" I asked, my hands still on my hips.

"Yes, and this ledger will be just what I need to make headlines."

I squinted. "But wait, who called you?"

"Oh, Renee sent me a text, and I'm always within a block of Duval's place. It's time to expose the truth." LeBlanc said as he let out a sigh.

Renee reached across the desk and squeezed my hand. "We take The Blue Door back for Kermit, Emory. And for you. And for my mother… Celeste," she said lowly.

Sirens fell away to a weary hush, and my cell lit up with a text from Windex: Fire out. Wall scorched. Ledger safe. Men gone. God louder.

"God louder," Renee repeated, relief slipping out as a breath as she read the text over my shoulder.

I stood, the decision forming in my bones like new architecture. "We're not tiptoeing anymore. We'll put the last nail in Remy's coffin. And we take care of Naomi and Miles when the ground under them shifts."

"You're thinking money," she said, reading me as a cousin does, even when the word is brand-new.

"I'm thinking of Daddy's inheritance. His life insurance and property investments left Cal and me enough money for several lifetimes, so it's time to do brave things for my dad. When this is over, Naomi and Miles won't have to worry about how rent gets paid."

Renee's eyes softened. "You are one of the kindest people I've met, big heart, big mouth, and lots of faces to fit your moods."

"Yeah, I've been told that," I said, not sure how I might react when the reality of having yet another relative hits me.

A knock at the office door made us both jump. Two soft taps. A pause. One more tap — the rhythm Windex uses when he doesn't want to scare anybody.

Renee cracked it. Windex slipped in, smelling faintly of smoke and salvation. He set the flour sack down and unrolled it halfway to show the ledger's corner.

And Cal hurried in like a shadow that detached itself from a body, and he hugged me. "Not much damage. Really."

"Are you sure? I've made so many improvements." I cried, my exhaustion and senses heightened beyond their limits, and I crumbled to the floor.

Cal helped me to a chair. "We'll fix this. I promise."

I wept; the thought that I could ever make a go of the cafe eluded me amid the continuous threats. "Cal, I can't do this by myself."

"I'm not going anywhere. I promise."

I glanced up. "No turning back," I said. "We've got to make some noise and let the trumpet of truth sound off."

LeBlanc said, "Let's make the people listen and let's drive out the snakes."

Windex reached for my chin. "Blueberry Girl. You are changing history."

And with that, Cal glanced at Renee, not with hatred, but also not with trust or love.

The city answered with distant brass, as if a band somewhere practiced, "When the Saints Go Marching In" just for us. New Orleans has a way of underscoring your life at the exact right moment.

Renee picked up her purse and her courage. "Let's go wake up the ghosts."

We stepped out into the hallway, a group of people bound by blood, music, a microcassette tape, a ledger, a news story, and a musician with a washboard who survived Remy Duval and Gus Tiller.

So far. Now, if we survive this day.

Chapter 23

The Shape of a Lie

THE FRENCH QUARTER HAS A way of pretending nothing bad ever happened, like Renee Baptiste.

Windex and Cal spent most of the morning with a fire inspector who said, "Whoever lit the fire in the alley was simply sending a message. This dampness and the rainwater pooling put the fire out almost before it started."

I circled Cal and the inspector. "But if I thought Remy Duval did this, wouldn't he be worried about burning down his bar?"

"This was a message. And these buildings have fire walls, and he knows that." He turned to me. "You got any hard proof Duval is involved?"

I chuckled. "Doesn't he have his hand in everything in the town?"

The inspector took his notes and left, and Cal shook his hand.

By early afternoon, the street outside The Blue Door looked scrubbed clean—rain-washed brick, fresh flowers wired to iron balconies, a trumpet somewhere practicing scales like yesterday never existed. Tourists walked past the building's invisible haunted past without knowing it had been a part of my family's life for years.

I knew better now.

I sat at the cafe's front table with the ledger after I'd made copies at the library and distributed them to many people—LeBlanc, Sergeant Lavaeu, a lawyer Silas knew, and a crime podcaster, Windex, connected me to. And several extra copies, if needed, were tucked away.

Beside it lay my notebook. Claire Landry's name was written at the top of a clean page. I couldn't forget her life was a part of this story, too.

I didn't write *victim*. I wrote *witness*.

Three months had passed since Claire died. Lucien Baptiste had been arrested shortly after, released on bail, and quietly disappeared back in the Quarter like guilt with a short memory.

People love a simple story. Man loses temper. A woman dies. Case closed. And Sergeant Laveau is not happy with that idea of such an ending for Claire's life, nor am I.

Kermit's death was different in some ways. Fresher, but only because he was my cousin. And nothing about his death wanted to stay buried either.

But lies, I'd learned, always had a shape. And if you studied the edges long enough, they told you where the truth had been cut away.

The bell above the cafe door chimed, a recent addition since I wanted to know whenever someone came inside.

Lucien stepped through the open door, his fingers twitching, his eyes searching the cafe's room. He looked thinner than I remembered. Not sick—just hollowed out. Like grief had taken a permanent lease inside his bones. His hand shook when he reached for the chair across from me.

"I didn't think you'd agree to see me," he said.

"I didn't say I trusted you," I replied. "I need answers. And apparently you do, too."

He nodded. "You're smarter than people think."

"I'm tired of being underestimated," I said, and slid the notebook closer. "Start from the beginning. Not your beginning. *Hers.*"

Lucien's eyes flicked to Claire's name. Then away.

"She came into my shop angry," he said, his words sliding together too fast. "Not screaming. Focused. That was worse."

"When?" I asked.

"A day before she was found by your car."

I pulled the pad closer and wrote it down.

"She kept telling me Remy was lying to me, that I was a placeholder. A buffer. Someone he kept close, so he didn't have to get his hands dirty." Lucien said, swallowing.

"Was she right?" I asked.

Lucien swallowed again. "You got any water?"

"Sure," I said, and before I could ask, Silas marched into the room, placing the water in front of Lucien.

"Thank you, Silas. You're a good one to have around."

"I can be. I look out for those the Lord places in my path."

Lucien watched Silas until he disappeared into the cafe's kitchen. "He's your cook?"

"Yes, he's highly recommended." I brought Lucien back to my questions. "So, tell me what Claire was worried about."

"She figured Remy had gotten to me. And she was right. I owed him money. Gambling troubles. She thought he was dangerous."

"Was she right?" I pressed.

"Well, Claire died for asking and pushing Remy too hard."

"Too hard?"

"Yes, she was caught in his schemes, too. Could pay her debt either."

The words *pay her debt* landed clean. No hedging. No excuses.

Lucien sipped the water. "She said she'd found proof. That money was moving again. Old accounts. Old names." His jaw tightened. "I told her to stop. Told her Remy didn't forgive curiosity."

"But she didn't," I said.

"No, she hoped to find something to hold over him, so her debts would go away." Lucien glanced out the window.

"And you? How do you fit into this? They have you on camera slapping her." I said, almost wishing I hadn't.

"Yes, I slapped her. She was out of control." A broken sound slipped out of him. "She loved me. That was her mistake. I was as trapped as she was."

I didn't ask another question. I let the silence do its work. And Lucien went on, "She said she'd make Remy pay. But no one has successfully done that."

I looked up. "Claire wasn't blackmailing Remy?"

Lucien met my eyes. "She was bargaining for her life."

The room felt smaller.

"Why didn't you go to the police?" I asked.

He laughed, once. "Because where do you go when the rot owns the floorboards and a lot of its people?"

I wrote again. *Rot owns floorboards.*

"Did she tell you where the proof was?" I asked.

"No," he said. "She said if anything happened to her, I'd know it wasn't an accident."

My pen paused.

"What happened the night she died?" I asked. "And don't clean it up."

Lucien closed his eyes.

"She met me out front on the sidewalk, in the open. Said Remy had agreed to talk. I told her it was a trap. She told me I was a coward."

"And then?"

"And then I slapped her." His voice cracked. "Once. I've hated myself every day since."

I didn't flinch. I didn't excuse it either.

"She fell," he continued. "More like a stumble. And she stood back up. I pulled her inside my store to talk, and she ended up leaving out the back door."

I leaned forward. "Did you kill her?"

"No," he said immediately. "But I didn't save her either."

That answer mattered.

"What time did she leave?" I asked.

"Just after midnight."

"And when was Claire pronounced dead?" I asked.

"The next day, when you drove into the ditch on the highway."

I sat back.

"The sergeant told me Claire was injured more seriously than your slap," I said slowly. "She had bruising consistent with a blow to her head and bruising on her arms. Laveau said the autopsy showed a blunt force instrument caused her death."

Lucien stared at me. "They told me—"

"They told you what closed the case," I said. "Not what solved it."

He leaned forward, urgent now. "I loved her."

The tension in The Blue Door increased, and I felt the weight of every choice, every lead still hanging.

My phone rang, and I saw the sergeant's name, so I picked up. "Hello."

"Emory, it's Laveau," the voice came through. "Listen, I can't say much, but we're learning more about Remy's moves. I sense some pieces falling into place. You must watch your surroundings."

"I will. I am," I assured her, not taking the time to tell her I was interviewing Lucien at that exact moment.

Laveau's guidance was the continued push I needed to make truth a priority for Kermit and for Claire—her insistence on seeking answers drove me forward.

"Thank you, Sergeant," I said, my resolve hardening. "I won't quit asking questions."

"I know, but keep watch," Laveau replied. "Sometimes, truth needs a little nudge, but it's risky."

"I agree," I said softly. "That's why Claire died. She was after the truth, and so was Kermit."

I said goodbye to the sergeant and sighed.

Lucien shook his head. "Remy wouldn't—"

"Remy doesn't kill people by himself," I cut in. "He creates situations where people don't survive."

That shut Lucien up.

"Claire threatened the wrong man at the wrong time," I continued. "And then she spoke to the wrong witness."

Lucien frowned. "Who?"

"Kermit Delacroix."

The color drained from his face.

"Claire met with him twice," I said. "Once before she died. Once the day before."

"She trusted him," Lucien whispered. "But how do you know this?"

"It seems a man with a comma-shaped scar on his chin followed Kermit a lot. And learned a lot."

"What? You serious?"

"Yes," I said.

Lucien pushed back from the table, standing abruptly. "I didn't know."

"I believe you," I said. "And that's why I need you alive."

He froze.

"Remy thought Claire was the problem," I continued. "Then Kermit kept asking questions. And then I showed up."

Lucien sank back into the chair.

"So, you're next?" he asked.

"Not if I can help it," I replied.

Outside, a drum broke into a clean, continuous heartbeat of sound, and a trumpet let out a rich, haunting, hopeful tone. The sound threaded through the cafe like a memory refusing to stay buried.

Lucien wiped his face. "What do you want from me?"

"The truth," I said. "And your cooperation."

"With whom?"

"With me," I replied. "Because the case is three steps behind and Remy is five ahead."

He stared at me for a long moment. "You're not just fixing a cafe."

"No," I said. "I'm finishing a dream someone hopes I don't finish."

Lucien nodded slowly. "Claire told me something else."

I waited.

"She said if anything happened to her, the proof wouldn't be where people were looking. That she sent part of it somewhere safe."

"Where?" I asked.

Lucien exhaled. "Savannah."

The word settled into place like it had been waiting.

"Why Savannah?" I asked.

"She said money moves like water," he replied. "And it always pools where the ground already knows how to hide it."

I closed the notebook.

"Lucien," I said, standing. "Claire died trying to save you."

He nodded.

"However, Kermit died because he refused to let the truth disappear," I added.

Lucien's shoulders shook.

"And Remy," I finished, "he's on my list."

As Lucien left, I wrote in my notebook Kermit's name beneath Claire's. Witnesses.

Both of them.

And beneath that, I wrote one more line—quiet, steady, unafraid.

Remy Duval gets his hands dirty and pays for the silence.

The lie finally had a shape.

And now I knew exactly where to cut next.

But would I need even more help in using the proverbial knife to cut out the horror of the past, to bring healing, to let sin be exposed?

**

Late evening light filtered through the cafe's windows, casting soft patterns on the floor. I noticed Miles sitting in his usual spot at the corner, cradling his trumpet as though it were a fragile, precious thing. Cal hesitated beside me, watching the boy with an unreadable expression.

It was in this moment that something shifted in Cal. He stepped away from my side, left The Blue Door without a word, and approached Miles, his movements deliberate and steady. I hovered nearby, having stepped with him like a shadow, ready to eavesdrop.

"Hey, Miles. I'm Calvin Vaugh, Emory's brother," Cal said gently, his voice carrying between a delay in notes.

Miles looked up with wide eyes and a bright smile. "Hi, Mr. Cal! Want to hear my new song?"

There was a warmth in Cal's smile that I hadn't seen in a long time. "I'd love that."

The street filled with the beautiful, lilting sound of Miles' trumpet, and Cal nodded along, as if imprinting each note onto his heart. When Miles finished, Cal clapped, the pride evident in his gaze. "That was amazing, Miles. You've got a real gift."

I saw Miles' face light up at the compliment, his admiration for Cal showing in his smile. And then, Cal did something that surprised me. He crouched down, bringing himself closer to Miles' level.

"You know, it sounds like your dad taught you a lot. And I just wanted to say, if you ever need someone to talk to—I'm here for you. Like a... big brother, or a friend. Maybe even like family."

I held my breath, watching as Miles took in Cal's offer. "Thanks, Mr. Cal. I miss him a lot, but playing helps. Mama said he's in heaven playing his sax for Jesus."

"She's probably right," Cal said, glancing at the woman who tossed some bills into Mile's bag on the sidewalk.

Cal placed a hand on Miles' shoulder—firm, reassuring. "Your music keeps his spirit alive. Remember, you're never alone. You've got your mom, Emory, and me. We're all part of this big, messy family."

Miles' eyes shone with something that was more than gratitude; it was hope. "You mean it?"

"Of course," Cal replied, ruffling the boy's hair. "Family sticks together, no matter how far apart we started, no matter what."

As I watched them, something warmed inside me. Cal had found a piece of himself here—a connection to a child who needed guidance, love, and the promise of family. And in reaching out, Miles had given Cal something rare: the chance to be the kind of leader and protector our dad never was.

The moment had been unexpected, yet it felt like a gift—to Miles, to me, and I'm sure, especially to Cal.

My heart skipped a beat. The thought of Kermit's last breath at the hands of the past made me ill if I thought about it too much.

But keeping quiet wasn't something I planned to do—someone must pay for this—no boy should grow up without his father.

Chapter 24

When the Truth Hits Daylight

THE FRENCH QUARTER DIDN'T whisper when the truth broke. It shouted. Often. And every day.

By noon the next day, The Blue Door had a crowd outside that didn't care about coffee or jazz. Cameras stacked shoulder to shoulder. Microphones bloomed like steel flowers. Someone chalked *WHO KILLED CLAIRE LANDRY?* on the sidewalk, and someone else circled it twice as if punctuation mattered.

I stood behind the cafe's front windows, watching strangers argue about life.

"Don't go out there," Cal said, already placing himself between me and the door like gravity pulled him there. "They don't want answers. They want a face."

"I am the face," I said.

"That's exactly the problem." I sighed. "I've leaked enough pieces of this puzzle to the newspaper and two different news outlets. It's high time someone made some noise."

Windex leaned on the bar, tapping his washboard once, twice—nervous rhythm. "City's hungry," he muttered. "Once it smells blood, it forgets how to chew."

Outside, through one of my open windows, a reporter's voice rose above the rest. "...sources confirm documents tied to long-dormant financial crimes in the French Quarter have surfaced—"

I turned toward the counter, where the *real* ledger lay open. The copies were enough to wake up the city without feeding it everything.

"Cal," I said quietly. "If I don't go out there, Remy controls the story."

My brother exhaled through his teeth. "And if you do, he controls the consequences."

"I've lived with consequences my whole life," I said. "I'm done living with lies."

He held my gaze for a long second—brother to sister, protector to equal—and then nodded once.

"Five minutes," he said. "I stand to your left. Windex stays to your right. If anything feels wrong, we leave."

"When does anything ever feel right?" I asked.

He didn't answer that.

Silas came in through the kitchen door. He always did.

He paused when he saw the crowd at the front windows, his jaw tightening just a notch. Silas wasn't a man who startled easily, but he knew trouble when it gathered weight. "They've been here since sunrise," he said. "Two vans. One plain sedan that never turns off. That's more than curiosity."

Cal looked at him. "You sure?"

Silas nodded once. "I've been unloading deliveries for kitchens in this part of the city for fifteen years. The same faces don't appear unless someone sends them. You've got Remy's guys watching the reporters."

The noise outside hit instantly before I responded to Silas, and I marched to the sidewalk with Cal and Windex by my side, carrying the ledger.

"Miss Vaughn! Is it true your family was involved?"

"Do you believe Remy Duval ordered the murder?"

"What about Kermit Delacroix? Why now?"

Cal stepped forward, palm raised. "One at a time."

I didn't wait for permission.

"My name is Emory Vaughn," I said, voice steady, louder than my normal pitch. "I own The Blue Door. I first came to New Orleans to reopen a cafe to honor my dad, Benjamin Vaughn. But once I arrived, it was clear, I came because something here couldn't stay buried."

That got their attention.

"Three months ago, Claire Landry died," I continued. "The city called it simple. It wasn't. Claire wasn't a victim of passion. She was a witness."

Murmurs rippled.

"She knew money was moving through this block again—old routes, old names. When she tried to protect someone she loved, she became expendable."

A reporter shouted, "Are you accusing Remy Duval?"

"I'm accusing silence," I said. "I'm accusing a system that profits when women disappear quietly."

Someone tried to interrupt. I didn't let them.

"As for Kermit Delacroix, he didn't die because he was careless; he died because he, too, asked the wrong questions in a city that punishes curiosity."

The moment landed hard and clicks from cameras and notes were being taken.

"Kermit was a father," I said. "A musician. A man who believed truth was worth the risk."

I lifted the ledger—not high, just enough.

"This document is the proof that someone tried to hide the money that silences people."

"Are you turning this over to the police?" A man with a pad yelled.

"I've made copies for several who need it and given it to people who won't lose it."

A camera zoomed in. Flash. Flash.

"Is Remy Duval responsible?" A voice pressed.

I looked straight ahead.

"Remy Duval didn't pull a trigger or push anyone into a river," I said. "He just paid for the silence."

That line would run all day.

Cal's hand tightened on my arm. "Time."

I nodded.

"One more thing," I said, raising my voice. "Claire Landry deserves to be remembered as brave. Kermit Delacroix deserves justice. And this city deserves better than pretending a good memory is optional."

I stepped back.

Cal moved immediately, guiding me inside as questions erupted behind us like broken glass. And Windex tried to block the door.

Inside, Silas had already moved the tables. Not dramatically. Just enough. Creating a way to block the reporters from outside, as if he'd done it a hundred times before.

"Media stays outside," he muttered. "Delivery door stays locked. If anyone says my name, I don't exist."

One reporter tried to push past him. Silas didn't raise his voice. He didn't touch him. He stepped into the man's space and said, "Kitchen's closed. So is the cafe."

The reporter stopped and turned back.

Windex stood at the counter, eyes wet but proud. "Blueberry Girl, you just made the devil nervous," he said.

"Good," I replied. "He's been too comfortable."

My phone buzzed. Then buzzed again. Unknown numbers. Voicemails with threats wrapped in politeness.

Cal checked the door, making sure it locked. "We need to find Renee."

I nodded. "I haven't seen her."

"She's probably worried with all the media coverage," he said.

"I've got to check on her. This is messy for her, too." I said, and marched upstairs, went down the hallway, and slipped down the alley staircase as Silas conveniently created a diversion with a delivery truck.

And behind me, my brother followed.

"Hurry, Ms. Em. Go quickly. Keep her safe, Mr. Calvin," Silas said.

**

We found Renee at St. Louis Cemetery No. 2. She sat on the stone steps, dress wrinkled, hair unpinned, hands clenched in her lap as if she were holding something invisible together.

She didn't look up when we approached.

"They know," she said flatly. "Don't they?"

"You mean about your Remy being your father?" I asked.

"Yes, my life is ruined. It's all been a lie."

"The truth about Remy's relationship to you isn't out yet, but you can control how this ends. The city knows something," I said gently. "The truth's halfway out."

Renee laughed, a sound too sharp to be joy. "Halfway is the most dangerous part."

She finally looked at me. Her eyes were red, hollowed, stripped of polish, and a faint scar on her cheek revealed the worry on her face.

"I built my life on order," she said. "Clean books. Clean rooms. Clean stories. Top grades. Honors. Awards. A degree. I told myself that if I kept everything neat enough, my deliberate choices would stay in line. But I never expected to fight with Claire in the alley. Not ever!"

"Renee, you fought with Claire?" I asked, pressing her a little.

"Yes, I promise. She'd scratched me and pushed me away, but she was very much alive!" She gestured at the tombs. "Turns out grief doesn't respect spreadsheets or Mr. Duval."

I sat beside her.

Cal stayed back, respectful, watchful.

"I saw the newsbreaks on my cell," she continued. "Your face. My block. My town. It's like my name was hovering just outside the frame like a threat."

"You're safe," I said automatically, knowing that her safety wasn't something I even had control over.

She shook her head. "No. I'm exposed."

Her voice broke then—not loud—and she said, "I met Lucien the night he hit Claire in the alley because he was so agitated and he'd texted me, asking for $10,000," she whispered. "I knew what would happen if Claire didn't stop asking. Or if Lucien gave Remy the money. It would never end. Lucien went back into his store, infuriated with me, and I grabbed Claire's arm, telling her to leave things alone."

The words landed between us, heavy and undeniable.

"I told myself Remy wouldn't go that far," she said. "I told myself Kermit would back down. But he's been pushing for a way to expose Remy since he got out of prison. And I told myself if I stayed useful, helpful, organized, and smiling, nobody would bleed."

She pressed her palms into her eyes. "I was wrong."

I swallowed hard. "Renee—"

"I helped him," she said. "Not with my hands. With my silence. With my smile. With my compliance."

She looked at me then—really looked.

"You trusted me," Renee said. "That's the part I can't forgive. Remy showed up when I cornered Claire in the alley, and he made me leave and pulled her to his bar."

She whimpered, "I just let him take her. It's my fault."

I didn't flinch.

But I gulped as if sin choked me. "I trusted you because you were Josie's friend. Because you stood beside me. Because you believed in redemption. It's not too late to do the right thing."

She laughed bitterly. "Redemption costs more than I thought."

"It always does," I said.

Cal stepped closer. "The city's brewing," he said with confidence and resolve. "Remy's losing control of the narrative."

Renee wiped her face and stood slowly. "Good."

She squared her shoulders—not polished, not composed, but real.

"I'll testify," she said. "I'll give them everything. Names. Accounts. Routes. I won't hide anymore. I'm fully aware of Remy's connections. I've got access to the old ledgers my dad kept, too, but I looked the other way."

I studied her. "This doesn't absolve you. You knew things and let it sink deep like the past didn't matter."

"I know," she said. "It just ends the lie. And I'm not over the fact that Remy was… is my biological father."

As we left the cemetery, my phone buzzed again with a text.

A single message. No number. Just a text: Savannah knows your name.

I closed my eyes once.

The city had spoken.

And now, so had the past.

"Cal," I said, steady. "We're not done here. But Savannah's next."

He nodded. "We'll talk about that."

Behind us, Renee stood between the tombs, finally crying where no one could watch.

Ahead of us, the truth kept moving—like water, like a river that will meet the ocean, where waves mix salt with fresh, where surviving is the way to truly living.

And I wanted to follow it.

Chapter 25

What the Dead Never Said

CLAIRE LANDRY NEVER HAD THE chance to speak to me. She never warned me. Never begged. Never left behind a neat sentence that could be underlined and solved. She didn't hand me the truth; she asked me to carry it forward.

But everyone else wanted her voice. Wanted a quote. Wanted a final message that made the ending feel earned, or justified, or clean. People preferred a version where Claire explained herself, where her words softened what happened or sharpened it into something simple.

But Claire Landry died without telling her story.

Which meant if I wanted the truth, I had to gather information on where she'd been seen before she died.

I sat at my office desk upstairs in Kermit's old room at The Blue Door, the late afternoon light slanting in through the window, turning dust into something almost holy.

Windex had politely moved his belongings into the room next to Silas, giving me my special spot to remember my cousin.

The cafe had been open a week now—officially open, anyway. The blueberry pancakes were already earning their keep, thanks to Silas's insistence on real butter and Windex's refusal to let the band play anything halfhearted.

People kept coming.

Not because they were hungry.

Because of the story.

Curiosity traffic. The crime halo. Folks eating where something terrible had happened, to prove the world hadn't stopped.

And I let them.

I chewed more spearmint gum than ever, my jaws aching with overload of worry.

A copy of the ledger pages sat in front of me because Sergeant Laveau confiscated the real one after I held it up for the reporters to see. She had allowed me plenty of leniency, but I'd crossed the line with that move.

But thankfully, I'd kept a few copies for myself, two hidden in the stage floor, and this one on my desk, and now my notebook lay open beside it. Claire Landry's name was written at the top of the page, with Kermit's.

Silas came in, no knock, just a giant of a man with scruples, and he slipped inside like someone who preferred not to announce himself, carrying a thin accordion folder tucked under his arm. He didn't sit right away in the chair beside my desk. He glanced out the second-story window first. Then back to the door leading to the hallway.

Only then did he take the chair beside me.

"I pulled everything I could," he said. "Legally. Questionably. A favor or two I'll pretend not to remember."

"That's my favorite kind of help," I said.

He slid the folder across the table.

Inside were photographs. Grainy. Time-stamped. Printed from security systems that belonged to places no one ever thought of as important—corner stores, dive bars, a dry cleaner with a crooked camera that caught more sidewalk than doorway.

Claire, in pieces.

Not her body.

Her movement.

"She didn't drift," Silas said. "She tracked."

I picked up the first photo.

Claire outside Remy Duval's lounge. Daytime. Sunglasses on. Her posture straight, not hesitant. Remy stood half-turned toward her, one hand lifted like he was calming her—or warning her. The timestamp was three days before her death.

"She went to him for answers?" I asked.

"Most likely, ma'am." Silas nodded. "Public. Daylight. That tells me she wasn't threatening. She was negotiating."

The next photo showed her two blocks away, outside a cafe that served nothing but bad coffee and better secrets. Renee stood with her this time. Close. Too close. Claire's shoulders were tense. Renee's hand was raised, fingers spread, nails unmistakable even in the low resolution.

Red.

I felt my jaw lock.

"She didn't stumble into Renee," I said.

"No," Silas replied. "Renee must have found her."

Another photo. A dive bar near the river. Claire again. Alone. Sitting at the bar with a man I didn't recognize—but the reflection in the mirror behind them showed Remy in the doorway, watching without entering.

"He didn't talk to her there," Silas said. "He let her see him watching."

I set the photo down carefully. "That's not just intimidation. That's conditioning. And control."

Silas's mouth twitched. "You've done this before."

"At a young age, I learned patterns in my family and made mental notes. To breathe." I inhaled. "I also cried a lot growing up."

Silas touched me on the nose. "Girl, you don't need to cry. God brought you here to save a building and those who will follow behind you."

I wiped a tear and took a deep breath, hoping that was true.

The next set of images showed Claire moving differently. More open spaces. Sidewalks. Corners with cameras. Getting coffee and sitting at a table by the river, glancing around, and she watched others.

I noticed her brown hair was wavy. Her freckles. Her pointy chin. Her dimples. That's something you don't see when you roll up to a body in your care, and that person is dead.

Silas pointed. "It seemed she stopped going inside anywhere that didn't have at least two exits."

"She was afraid," I said. "But she wasn't panicking."

"Exactly," Silas said. "Panic is messy. This was controlled."

I wrote: Claire Landry didn't confront Remy Duval. She repositioned herself around him.

"She thought if she stayed visible, she'd stay alive," I said.

Silas didn't argue.

The last photo was taken the night she died.

Claire walking in the alley. Alone. Her shoulders squared. Not drunk. Not stumbling. A streetlight caught her face just enough to show determination, not fear.

"She knew someone was waiting," I said.

Silas nodded once. "And she went anyway."

That was the part that hurt.

"She believed someone would stop it," I said quietly.

Silas didn't say Renee's name. He didn't have to.

Cal appeared in the doorway a few minutes later, coffee in hand, eyes already scanning the room. He took in the photos. "You found some threads," he said.

"I found traces of her last steps," I replied. "Claire left behind her movement."

Cal rested a hand on the back of my chair. Protective. Present. "Hey, look," he said, pointing to the ivy in the window, distracted by the onslaught of green vines. "It's growing. It's taking over the place."

"I know. Poor thing was dead, now it's thriving. I had it downstairs for weeks, and nothing. But once I put it up here, it's growing again." I smiled, happy to see the green, even if the old clunker I still drove was a horrible color.

Cal smiled. "A little light does good for plants and for us, too." He paused, "So what do your photos say?"

"That she underestimated how badly Remy wanted control. And that Renee stepped in when Remy needed a cleaner solution."

Cal exhaled slowly. "And Kermit?"

I slid one last photo forward. Kermit outside the club, talking to Claire two nights before her death. His posture angled toward her. Listening.

"Kermit must have recognized fear that didn't belong to a lover's fight," I said. "And once he saw it, he couldn't unsee it."

Silas closed the folder. "Witnesses don't last long in Remy's world."

"No," I said. "They get out-waited. I never expected my presence could cost someone their life."

Later, after Silas left and the cafe settled into the evening, I went downstairs, carrying the folder, and Miles showed up with his trumpet case. He didn't ask questions. He never did anymore. He just sat on a step near the stage and polished the brass as if it mattered.

"Daddy Kermit liked for my trumpet to shine," he said.

"I know," I replied, and I dropped the folder holding the photographs.

He glanced at the pictures on the floor. "Is that why people keep coming in and asking so many questions?" he asked. "Because something bad happened here?"

"Yes," I said. "And because something good is still here."

He nodded, satisfied. Then he lifted the trumpet and played—soft, steady, a tune Kermit used to hum when he thought no one was listening.

Cal sat by a table in the front, and as the sun set, Miles lowered the trumpet and slid it back into its case like he was putting something fragile to sleep.

I moved the window. "It's pretty dark out there, and it's not safe."

"I can walk home," he said, matter-of-factly.

I blinked. "Miles—"

"It's okay," he added quickly. "I got a security guard now."

Cal straightened. "You what?"

Miles pointed with his chin toward the doorway.

Theo stood just outside the cafe window, hands folded in front of him, hat low, posture easy but watchful. Not lurking. Waiting.

He caught my eye and gave a slight nod.

"That's Theo," Miles said. "Remember, he walks me home when Mama's working late. And sometimes, to school."

Theo. A name that had learned how to disappear when it needed to. But showed up when a small boy needed protection.

My chest eased a notch.

"He waits by the corner," Miles went on. "So, Mama doesn't worry. Says he's part of the neighborhood watch."

Theo stepped just inside the door, respectful of the space. "Theodore Delaney," he said firmly with a nod. "And I give you my word, Miles won't take a step alone."

Cal studied him, the way he does when deciding whether a man is worth trusting. "You law enforcement?"

Theo shook his head once. "No, sir. Just someone who learned the hard way what happens when nobody walks a kid home."

That did it.

Miles slung the trumpet case over his shoulder. "I'll text when I get there," he said, already halfway to the door.

I caught myself. "Wait, you have a phone now?"

"Yeah, Mama got me one. Put your number in there for emergencies. She told me we have to watch out for each other." Miles said, his matter-of-fact tone like a jazz note on a trumpet, and he tapped the back pocket of his jeans.

I knelt in front of him. "You listen to Theo. And don't take shortcuts."

"Yes, ma'am," he said, solemn as a vow.

Theo opened the door for him, one hand resting lightly at Miles's back, not steering, not pushing. Just present.

At the threshold, he paused and looked at me. "Ms. Vaughn," he said. "You're doing right by that boy. Giving him a space to play and remember his pa."

"I'm trying," I replied.

He nodded once. "So is his mama."

They stepped out together, Miles talking nonstop now, trumpet case bumping his knee with every step. Theo matched his pace exactly, slow enough for a child, steady enough for the street.

I watched them until they turned the corner and vanished into the Quarter.

Cal let out a breath he'd been holding. "You trust him?"

"Yes, I trust the way he stands," I said.

Cal sighed and squeezed my hand.

That's when I grabbed my phone, ready to send a long-overdue text to Josie to clear the air, or at least, let my truth be present in her world.

I typed the text that kept auto-correcting my word choice: Josie, I've been doing some thinking. Was it Renee's idea for me to come to New Orleans? Or were you trying to get me out of Wyoming? Somehow, it makes sense now, after Claire, Kermit, and all that's happened, that Renee reached out to you. Even so, I need to understand why.

I glanced at my phone, but there was no response.

Nothing.

Outside, the city kept moving.

And for the first time in weeks, something inside me settled.

Claire never had the chance to speak publicly.

Kermit tried to add his voice to the city, too.

Someone had been watching.

And silenced them.

But still, Miles lived and Windex aged with a seasonal purpose. And truth rushed in like a spring rain in late January. And Silas kept our fortress safe.

Sometimes, truth also showed up in protection. Or in the care of a brother. Or in the words held safe from the past. And yes, it showed up as a security guard for a ten-year-old boy, too.

Chapter 26

When the Music Stops

RENEE DIDN'T CRY WHEN THE latest news broke. That should have been my first clue.

The French Quarter was already awake—too awake—for what was about to land. Cameras crowded the sidewalk outside The Blue Door once again, cords snaking over cracked pavement like the city itself was wired for confession.

Someone had tipped them off early.

Someone always did.

Cal stood beside me, close enough that I could feel the heat off his arm, the silent signal he used when things were about to turn sideways.

Windex hovered just inside the door, hands folded, eyes tracking exits like he was counting heartbeats instead of people.

Renee came down the street fast, heels in hand, hair pulled back in a way that meant she hadn't planned on being seen and came inside.

"What's happening?" she asked.

Not *is this true?* Not *who said what?* But *what's happening?*

I turned my laptop toward her.

The headline was already everywhere.

DUVAL EMPIRE EXPOSED: YEARS OF RECORDED CONFESSIONS LINK BAR OWNER TO MONEY LAUNDERING, INTIMIDATION, AND MULTIPLE COVER-UPS.

Below it, a video. Remy Duval, half-lit, drink in hand, leaned too close to a bartender who had learned the hard way when to keep the tap running and his mouth shut.

Renee stared.

The city roared around us, reporters calling names, microphones rising like weapons.

"That's not—" she began.

The video auto-played.

Remy's voice filled the air, careless and cruel. "You boys think money disappears on its own? I make problems go away. That's the job."

Another clip. Another night. Another bar.

"Claire talked too much. That kind of woman always does."

Renee's knees buckled.

Cal caught her before she hit the floor.

The reporter's name appeared at the bottom of the screen: MARCUS LEBLANC, QUARTER WATCH.

Renee said, "I know him. Dated him a few times."

I summarized what I'd read, or some of it. "Well, it seems Marcus LeBlanc had been drinking at Duval's place for years. Not sloppy drinking. Mostly listening. The kind of customer bartenders trusted because he tipped well, laughed softly, and never asked questions that sounded like questions."

He'd recorded everything. And I noted the headshot of LeBlanc at the bottom of the screen, the man who moved over that day I barged into, when I tied my shoe and yelled at Duval, and the day in Renee's office.

It seemed LeBlanc caught every shift-change and confession. Every brag. Every threat disguised as a joke.

He kept records until now.

He'd waited.

For patterns.

For corroboration.

For confessions behind closed doors.

For names like Claire Landry and Kermit Delacroix to stop being rumors and start being repetitions.

I scrolled up and down the page on my laptop, and my eyes caught on a sidebar feature. It highlighted Remy Duval as a generous benefactor to the city, with his name prominently displayed across banners at former charity events, on a youth jazz scholarship, and at cultural heritage festivals.

The article noted Duval has been a pillar of the community, his generous contributions supporting the very soul of New Orleans.

The irony sickened me: here was a man cloaked in the guise of good deeds, orchestrating the shadows that haunted the very people he claimed to help.

My shallow breaths made me dizzy, the revelation darker than I'd ever expected.

Renee pulled away from Cal and stood up on her own.

"No," she said quietly. "No, no, no."

She pushed past me and walked straight toward the cameras outside.

"Renee—" I called.

Too late.

"I want to say something," she said, voice shaking but loud enough to cut through the noise. "I want to say something *now*."

Every microphone surged.

"Remy Duval does not speak for New Orleans. He does not own us. And he does not get to decide who disappears."

Her breath hitched. "I didn't know he was capable of murder, but I suspected," she said. "And that lie has been killing me for years."

The silence that followed wasn't polite. It was stunned.

"My name is Renee Ivette Baptiste," she continued. "And Claire Landry was not reckless. She was brave. Kermit Delacroix was not careless. He was faithful. And if you think this city survives by swallowing its dead, you don't understand her."

Someone shouted a question.

Another voice yelled, "Did you help Duval?"

Renee closed her eyes. "I helped him in ways that made things or people disappear," she said. "By believing silence was safer than truth."

That was when the second explosion hit.

Not metaphorical.

Literal.

Duval's Lounge went dark.

Power cut mid-block, music snapping off like a severed nerve.

Sirens followed fast, police already moving because Marcus LeBlanc hadn't just dropped a story. He'd handed the DA hard drives.

Names.

Dates.

Audio timestamps.

Including the night Claire died.

Including the week Kermit was killed.

Including Remy's voice saying, clear as daylight, "Witnesses don't last long in this town."

Cal grabbed my arm. "Em."

"I know," I said.

Renee looked at me then—really looked.

And for the first time, she understood something I hadn't known how to say.

This wasn't about guilt anymore.

This was about survival.

And they took Remy at sunset.

Not in cuffs.

In silence.

No shouting.

No grand exit.

Just a man walking out of his kingdom while the city watched without clapping.

And the music didn't follow him.

Later, after the cameras cleared and the street settled back into its pretending, Renee sat alone at my lemonade and tea bar.

She didn't speak.

She didn't drink.

She just stared at the mirror like she was waiting for someone else to answer for her.

"I didn't mean for it to be this way," she said finally.

"No one ever does," I replied.

She nodded. "I don't know who I am without my past telling me where to go."

"You'll learn," I said. "Sergeant Laveau texted me. She's coming for you herself. Said you have a lot to explain."

"I thought the police would have come for me sooner," Renee said, exhaling, a long breath with a huge sigh.

Cal stepped in, hand resting lightly on my back, and turned to Renee. "You won't be alone. You've done so much to help Emory that it can't be ignored."

She nodded. "My helping was to keep me in the loop with her plans, for Remy. I wanted to change that, but I'd been threatened, too. The rope he's had on my life didn't come without a struggle. I so wanted a genuine friend—it almost felt real."

I sighed. "Friendship is the dash between the dates on our tombstones. We have to do better."

Cal muttered, "Dash?"

"Yeah, we are born. We live. We die. What we do today is that important." I said, gulping hard.

I let out the longest breath ever, choosing not to tell Renee that Josie had texted me about their online chat back in September, when Josie told her I might come to New Orleans, and yes, a little break from my drama was necessary for Josie's sanity. But she meant no harm.

Laveau pulled up outside and came in alone. "I can't thank you enough, Emory Vaughn, for your insight and continued push for truth. We've cut the head off the snake, but there are still plenty of eggs in the nest. We've got leads in Savannah, Georgia. Remy's brother lives there, and those connections are quickly bringing more arrests. This is a start, not an ending." And with that, she escorted Renee Baptiste to the patrol car.

Outside, a trumpet played—not a performance—a practice note. A beginning sound of someone learning to play their instrument, and with this latest revelation from the sergeant, I wasn't heading to Savannah any time soon.

As the cafe buzzed with the aftermath of Remy Duval's arrest, the ambient sounds of a jazz band tuning their instruments mixed with the chatter of promises and anticipation.

Life will continue at The Blue Door despite the turmoil. Music will play. Jazz will stay. The blueberry recipes Silas has mastered will add flavor to the present, and the leadership of Windex, an untapped commodity, will keep everyone in tune.

Hopefully.

I packed that night.

Not in a rush.

Not in fear.

Some truths don't travel light—and some cities aren't meant to be carried, but they are filled with jazz, blueberry muffins, pancakes, and a great assortment of people who love truth and living with purpose.

With Cal's insistence, after a two-hour drilling session of my brother reasoning with me, I finally changed my mind. Silas and Windex would run The Blue Door Cafe together. But I agreed only if Silas kept his appointment to get new hearing aids so that he could keep tabs on Windex.

So now, I'm running into my future. I'll follow the truth to see where it will go next. And let two brothers finish their music on stage and in the kitchen at The Blue Door.

**

As the first wave of morning light kissed the French Quarter two days later, I drove up in my new, shiny blue car, another 4-door Honda Civic.

The Blue Door Cafe had opened its doors to embrace a new beginning, and before I left Louisiana, I was behind the counter, arranging freshly baked blueberry muffins on a tiered stand when Cal's laughter rang out near the tables by the windows. "Come look at this," he yelled.

I peered through the window, eyes widening at the sight that met me.

There, right in front of the cafe, stood a pelican, on the sidewalk, its wings folded neatly, watching a passerby with a peculiar calm. It was an odd sight—this majestic bird, seemingly misplaced amongst the bricks and cobblestones of New Orleans on Chartres Street.

But there he was, and the pelican remained statuesque, as if guarding the entrance to a newly reclaimed oasis.

Cal stepped outside, his smile broadening with each stride. "Looks like we have a new doorman," he joked, nodding towards the bird.

I joined him, wiping my hands on my apron, unable to suppress a grin.

The pelican cocked its head, unblinking. It was one of those curious encounters that hover on the line between nature's joke and a miracle. The air seemed to hum with an unspoken understanding, bridging the unexpected appearance with the cafe's fresh start.

"Well," I said, folding my arms with a theatrical sigh, "At least it's not sitting in the backseat of my car this time."

Cal laughed again. "I wonder if he's interested in our blueberry pancakes or the muffins."

The twenty or so patrons waiting for a table moved up as Windex showed a man and woman to a recently cleared spot by a window. This apparently spooked the pelican, and it flapped, honked, and flew away.

The jazz band played softly, its music spilling into the street, wrapping around my heart like the scent of blueberries and the promise of a new day. And since it's Saturday, Miles played his trumpet like a pro with the band.

The Blue Door was now in tune with the rhythm of hope, where the south remembered jazz and truth won.

Cal touched my arm. "You ready to go?"

"Yes, but where are... are we going?" I asked, unsure if leaving now was the right time.

Cal tugged on my arm. "Well, we could always go to Arkansas. Our mom was from a small town, and we don't know much about her. And since I'm with you. Let's take the long way home and drive there.

I smiled. "Arkansas sounds peaceful. Let's do it."

I took off my apron, hugged Silan and Windex for the umpteen time, and smiled.

"Yeah. The Blue Door is in good hands. And Naomi and Miles will be set financially, too."

Cal nodded. "I made sure the trust is set up for Miles' college, too."

We stepped to the sidewalk and across the street; a tip of the hat from Theo assured me I was standing on solid ground again. I'll never forget that the South is where jazz remembered the truth!

Windex rushed outside, carrying something. "I almost forgot. I have something for you."

I held up a blue shirt with cracked white lettering: *I survived New Orleans, and all I got was this T-shirt.*

South isn't a place...

...it's where jazz remembered the truth.

Books by Pam Kumpe

<u>Annie Grace Kree Chronicles Series</u>
1 Untied Shoelace
2 Unknown Soul
3 Rescue of Undaunted Spirit
4 Unwanted Sidekick
5 Unwavering Hope
6 Unshackled Courage

<u>Other Novels</u>
Rescue at Three Sisters Springs
Looking for Daddy's Girl
Summertime Sprinkler

<u>The Long Way Home Trilogy</u>
Where Horses Run Secrets Hide (book one)
Where Jazz Plays Shadows Fall (book two)

<u>Devotional</u>
Looking for Daddy's Girl Devotional
See You in the Funny Papers
A Scoop of Inspiration
You Are Not a Typo
A 25-Day Countdown to Christmas
14 Reasons to Roll Your Eyes at Valentine's Day

<u>Bible Study</u>
Think Outside the Pit Devotional
Think Outside the Pit Workbook

<u>Children</u>
In the Lick of Time
A Goat with a Tote
Hattie Holmes Holds Her Breath
Hattie and Mattie! Oh, They Love the Bunny!
Cranky Camel and the Candy Cane Caper
Cranky the Camel and Max Go to School
Cranky the Camel and Barnyard's Got Talent
Spike's Glow
Lil'Foot and the Big Search

<u>Rehab Ministry Devotionals</u>
Things I Learned in Jail
From Court to Christ

<u>Homeless Ministry</u>
My View from the Bridge
My View from the Street
My View of the Heart

<u>You Are Lost Series</u>
Book One: The Mystery of Sneaky Pants
Book Two: The Mystery of Sneaky Paws
Book Three: The Mystery of the Sneaky Parrots
Parrots, Pranks, and Prayers Devotional
The Mystery of Dill Pickens

www.pamkumpe.com

Questions and Discussion

1. **Character Development:** How do Emory and Cal's characters evolve throughout the story? Discuss pivotal moments that contribute to their growth and self-discovery. How does Emory balance her determination with vulnerability? Or does she?

2. **Family Dynamics:** The Vaughn family has its share of secrets and tension. Discuss how past betrayals and hidden truths impact Emory and Cal's relationship with their family and each other. How do these dynamics redefine their concept of family?

3. **Themes of Healing and Forgiveness:** How are themes of healing and forgiveness explored in the story? In what ways do the characters find closure and forgiveness, both with themselves and with others?

4. **Setting's Impact:** Examine how the settings of Wyoming and New Orleans enhance the narrative. In what ways do these locations contribute to the story's themes, mood, and character development?

5. **Symbolism of Pelicans:** Discuss the symbolism of the pelican mentioned in the story. How does it relate to Emory's journey and her search for freedom and authenticity?

6. **Role of the Journal:** Emory's father's journal plays a significant role in uncovering the past. As does The Blue Door. How does the past function as a narrative tool, and what revelations does it bring to the surface about family secrets?

7. **Morality and Choices:** The characters in the story face difficult moral choices. Discuss the complexities of their decisions, particularly regarding Kermit, Windex, Renee, and Remy Duval. Do you believe these choices were justified?

8. **Resolution of Mysteries:** Were you satisfied with how the mysteries surrounding Celeste, Claire, and Kermit were resolved? Discuss the effectiveness of the revelation and how it ties the narrative together.

9. **Subplots and Secondary Characters:** How do subplots and secondary characters like Renee, Windex, and Miles enrich the main narrative? Are there any character arcs you found engaging or surprising? What about Silas?

10. **Impact of the Past:** Explore how the past continues to impact the characters in the present. In what ways do they attempt to break free from its hold and forge new paths for themselves?

"But let justice roll down like waters, and righteousness like an ever-flowing stream."
Amos 5:24 (ESV)

MILES' PECAN PIE

• *MUSIC TO YOUR MOUTH PER KERMIT DELACROIX*

INGREDIENTS	BAKING DIRECTIONS
1 stick of margarine, melted	Peheat over to 400 degrees
½ cup Karo syrup	Combine all ingredients in
½ cup of Maple syrup	a mixing bowl, except pecans.
3 eggs (slightly beaten)	Beat with an electric mixer until well mixed.
⅓ cup milk	Remove mixer.
½ cup sugar	Add chopped pecans. Stir.
1 TBSP corn starch	Pour into the pie shell and bake for 15 minutes.
Pinch of salt	Reduce the heat to 350 degrees,
1 tsp vanilla	and bake 30-35 minutes longer.
½ cup chopped pecans	Outer edges of filling should be set,
1 unbaked pie shell	center only slightly soft.

PELICAN APPROVED